Lady Helen

FINDS HER SONG

Lady Helen FINDS HER SONG

Covenant Communications, Inc.

Cover images: *Woman* © Lee Avison / Trevillion Images, and *Jaswant Thada Rajah Memorial in Jodhpur* © Sira Anamwong

Cover design copyright © 2016 by Covenant Communications, Inc.

Published by Covenant Communications, Inc.
American Fork, Utah

Printed in the United States of America
First Printing: April 2016

25 24 23 22 21 20 19 18 17 16   10 9 8 7 6 5 4 3 2 1

ISBN 978-1-68047-893-8

For my sister Mandy.
Because she loves India.
And I love her.

Acknowledgments

How can I ever begin to acknowledge all of the wonderful people who make my life easier so I can do what I love?

Thank you to Frank and my boys for all the support you give, the interest you show, and for making me feel like I've won the amazing-family lottery every day.

Thanks, Mandy Kimball, Kerri and Alan Erickson, Dan Schwebach, and Chris Miller for showing me pictures and video from your time in India and for answering so many questions. That's the best kind of research.

So much thanks to Jen Ward, Margot Hovley, Mandy Kimball, and Kerri Erickson for reading my rough draft and helping me smooth out the roughest parts.

Nancy Allen and Josi Kilpack, your help, as always, makes my stories the best they can be. And Carla Kelly, thank you for answering random research questions that I can't quite figure out. I don't know what I'd ever do without you.

And thank you to Stacey Turner and the team at Covenant for catching so many embarrassing errors, polishing, designing, marketing, and turning this story into a beautiful book that I am so proud of. So many people are involved in creating the final product, and I could not be more grateful for your faith in me.

Chapter 1

LADY HELEN POULTER STOOD ON the deck of the ship, her gloved fingers tapping on the railing, playing invisible keys in a melody that only she could hear. The vessel made slow progress up the sandy-banked Hooghly River. During the three days since the ship had left behind the blue waters of the Bay of Bengal on its course toward Calcutta, Helen had watched as the river gradually narrowed and the muddy banks covered with scrubby plants gave way to green fields. Trees with smooth, twisted trunks spread their branches over the riverbanks, their long vines trailing in the water, and occasionally Helen caught sight of a village through the thick vegetation. The Hooghly was more than twice as wide as the Thames and much longer—they'd been riding it for three days.

She watched the river come to life in the early morning. Women in brightly colored apparel chatted together as they washed clothing and bathed brown-skinned children. Water buffalo were driven along the shores by men in loose-fitting trousers. A flock of green-and-red parrots burst from the trees, rising in a chaos of shrieks and flutters.

Helen could not believe she was the only passenger on deck while such spectacular sights occurred. How could the others bear to remain inside their cramped quarters? Every sight around her was new and fascinating.

The shallow river with its gentle waves was a welcome change from the endless tossing of the sea. For nearly four months, she and the other passengers had braced themselves against the violent storms of the south Atlantic, then shivered in the bitter cold of the Cape of Good Hope, and finally sweltered in the hot sun of the Indian Ocean.

From the first days when she'd lain in her berth, overcome by seasickness, Helen had spent the entire voyage questioning her decision to accompany her mother and her mother's new husband, Brigadier-General Jim Stackhouse, to his latest military assignment in India. She missed her friends and siblings. She missed her home in Somerset, and she missed her pianoforte. But in spite of her homesickness, she felt a rush of excitement as she contemplated what awaited her in India. Aside from London and one summer in Bath, she'd never traveled anywhere; she had been elated—and a bit surprised—when her mother had allowed her to come along.

She turned her eyes from the colorful birds and walked along the rail, admiring the view ahead, with the rising sun reflecting pink and yellow on the swells and dips of the water. A flurry of movement on the far bank caught her eye, and she crossed the deck, nodding at the sailors who tipped their hats or bowed their heads in greeting. When she reached the starboard side of the ship and peered across the water, she saw that the activity was actually some sort of procession. In the center of the bustling crowd was an elephant. The animal's skin was painted in bright colors, and between its eyes hung an elaborate metal headpiece. Ornate silks covered its back, and atop them rode a man in a white turban.

Helen pressed her fingers against her lips to stifle a gasp. She had seen an elephant once before in the Prince Regent's menagerie at the Tower, but she never would have imagined a sight like this. The colorful elephant looked as if it were dancing. It raised and lowered its head, swinging its trunk as it marched. The man rocked from side to side in his seat as the people surrounding him cheered and sang. Even from this distance, she could sense the group's excitement.

"I should have known you would already be on deck," said a voice behind her.

Helen turned and curtseyed quickly to her new stepfather. "Good morning, sir." She smiled as she thought how, only a few months earlier, she would have shied away nervously at finding herself alone with Jim Stackhouse. But she had grown accustomed to his curt manner and found that, beneath his gruff exterior, he was thoughtful and kind—although she did not think he would welcome that observation. Jim used his scowl and stern temperament as a tool to keep soldiers in line and to repel people who irritated him. He had asked her numerous times to call him Jim, but Helen wasn't quite comfortable enough to address him so familiarly. She waved her hand toward the elephant. "What do you think is happening?"

He inclined his head in greeting; then his gaze moved past her to the commotion on the bank. "A wedding party. That man is journeying to the home of the woman his parents and matchmakers have chosen. Until they are married, he will never have met his bride or even seen her face. She will have been chosen because of her caste and her family's status in society."

"Marrying a person one has never seen? It sounds like a terrible idea," Helen said.

Jim turned his attention fully to her, pulling his brows together and tipping his head to the side. "Why is that?"

What if he is not handsome? she thought but did not say it aloud. The patch over Jim's eye and the jagged scar that cut through his face deterred her. He might take offense to such a statement. "What if they do not like each other?" she answered instead. "I would not wish to marry someone without the chance to determine whether either of us feels any affection. It is a strange custom."

"The custom is not so very different in England, is it?" The manner in which he asked the question and then turned, clasping his hands behind his back to watch the bridegroom's entourage indicated that Jim did not expect a reply; although Helen knew he would welcome it if she chose to answer.

Helen would have normally felt uncomfortable speaking about the delicate topic of matrimony with a man, but over the long voyage as she had come to know Jim, she had found that her stepfather listened closely to what she said and considered her opinions, never acting as if her thoughts were unimportant even when he did not agree. As the youngest child, she had become accustomed to being ignored or being treated as though her words were of little consequence, and Jim's interest made her feel special.

She stood next to him, watching the activity on shore and considering what he had said. Was marriage truly the same in England? She thought back to her London Season last spring and realized she had seen firsthand the truth in his statement. Her friends and acquaintances had painstakingly measured the qualities of each and every eligible bachelor, discussing for hours which would make the best husband based on his rank in society as well as the value of his family holdings. Even her own brother's and sisters' marriages, she thought, were decidedly a jointure of convenience with the purpose of furthering the family's interest through growing their holdings and producing well-bred heirs. Marriage in England was certainly similar to the arrangement in India, but Jim, of all people, should know it wasn't the same.

She glanced around the rim of her bonnet at the man who stood beside her. Jim and her mother's marriage was different. She had been initially distressed at the idea of her mother being remarried. Helen had a special relationship with Lady Patricia and didn't like the idea of a new person coming between them. But over time, she had gotten used to the idea and thought more about the relationship she had seen between her parents. As a child, she had assumed her mother and late father got on well enough, but looking back with a more mature eye, she realized that aside from events they were both expected to attend, they rarely spent time in each other's company. And she had never seen any hint affection between the two. *Tolerated* was the word she would use to describe her parents' interactions.

Once she had seen her mother with Jim, Helen realized the difference. Although most people were frightened or repulsed by Jim Stackhouse's appearance and manner, Lady Patricia glowed in his presence. Helen noticed that the two sought each other's company, even changing plans in order to spend time together. They drifted toward each other when they were together in a room, and though she knew they didn't intend for anyone to see, Helen had observed hands clasped beneath a table and soft looks exchanged. Jim never spoke in a condescending tone to his wife, nor did he act irritated at the milliner's shop while she deliberated between bonnets. Helen had only seen the public face of married couples, and now she was able to examine the more intimate side of a relationship.

Lady Patricia adored Jim and had married him without hesitation even though the *ton* had thought it ridiculous for a woman with grown children to behave like a lovestruck girl. Jim was untitled, unconnected, horribly scarred, and in most people's opinion, a bit frightening. But her mother gazed at him as if he were capable of capturing the moon and presenting it to her if she would but ask. And the way he looked at his wife in return, Helen suspected that Jim would indeed try if it would please her.

Helen wished someone would look at her in such a manner. She imagined being deeply in love with a gentleman who gazed at her with such adoration that there was no doubt he would move mountains if only to make her smile.

She often dreamed of the man she would fall in love with. He would be handsome, dashing, strong. The moment their eyes met, they would both know that their hearts were meant to love only each other.

Helen sighed and leaned a hand on the rail. Only then did she realize that Jim had spoken and was awaiting a reply. "I am sorry, sir. I was woolgathering. What did you say?"

Jim pointed to a sandbar that jutted out into the river. "The James and Mary Shoal," he said. "Named for a ship that ran aground nearly 120 years ago. We'll see Calcutta soon." They both looked to the left, toward the land beyond the ship's bow, but saw only thick trees.

"It will be a relief to get off this boat," Jim muttered. "Blasted unnatural way to travel."

Helen rubbed her arms, suddenly nervous. She glanced back at the elephant procession. It was one thing to talk about India and look at beautiful drawings or even watch the green land from the safety of the ship, but actually making this strange country her home sent an uneasy prickle over her skin. Tales of crocodiles, tigers, cobras, tropical fevers, quicksand, and native uprisings no longer sounded like faraway stories. In spite of the heat, she shivered and gripped the rail. How would she fit in as a member of the Raj? "And will someone meet us at the docks, sir?" Helen hoped to sound as if she were simply interested in their travel plans and wished her voice did not tremble.

He darted a look at her and turned back to look over the water, patting her hand where it rested on the rail. "I expect someone will be sent for us." He blew out a breath. "Last time I arrived in India was nearly twenty-five years ago. A lieutenant with a new commission and a fresh uniform. I never imagined I'd return. And I never imagined I'd bring a family with me." Jim cleared his throat and rubbed the back of his neck, looking decidedly uncomfortable. "I admit I rather enjoy—"

Jim's words halted abruptly as he looked past Helen. Somehow his expression managed to appear at the same time relieved and annoyed when Fanny Cavendish joined them. "Miss Cavendish." Jim clicked his heels together and inclined his head sharply.

Fanny curtseyed. "General."

"If you ladies will excuse me." He walked away quickly.

Helen was not surprised by Jim's rudeness. She had learned, as had the other passengers on the ship, that her stepfather had little patience for flirting or gossip. Fanny, on the other hand, had little patience for anything else.

Fanny's bottom lip dipped into a perfect pout, and a line formed between her delicate eyebrows. "How do you withstand this dreadful heat, Helen? Really, I cannot imagine why you would venture out on the deck today—and without a parasol."

"Oh, yes . . . I did not . . . it was cool earlier, and I thought, with my parasol . . ." She fumbled for her words, as usual feeling unsophisticated around Fanny even though Helen was a full year older—nearly twenty—and a noblewoman to boot. "Did you see the elephant? My stepfather told me it is part of a wedding party. The man in the white turban is to be married." She waved her hand toward the far bank.

Fanny crossed her arms and curled her lip. She turned to Helen with an expression that showed utter repulsion. "Heathens! Look how they dance and carry on. Have they no decency? A wedding. You would think even pagans would have been taught to behave properly at such an event." She pushed out a huff of air through her nose.

Helen looked back at the procession that was starting to disappear behind the sandbar. She'd thought the wedding party with its pageantry was beautiful and romantic. Of course, it *was* peculiar when compared to a formal church wedding in England, but it had seemed so extraordinary. She glanced back at her companion.

Fanny raised an eyebrow. "Certainly you agree their deportment is completely vulgar."

Helen hesitated and looked down. She felt her cheeks redden. She hoped Fanny wouldn't think her naive for being charmed by the sight of a painted elephant and a parade. She really was behaving like a child.

Helen was spared from having to answer when two officers approached. She imagined they must be dreadfully hot in their woolen regimental jackets. The two men bowed, and the ladies curtseyed in return.

Fanny blinked her eyes with a flutter of lashes and then opened them wide as she lifted her shoulders and tipped her head in the most charming manner.

Helen wished she could imitate the action. She'd tried again and again in front of the mirror in her cabin, but she could never get it exactly right. She certainly couldn't make her movement look as natural as Fanny's.

"A fair day for an end to our journey, is it not, Lady Helen, Miss Cavendish?" Ensign Porter looked forward to the ship's bow. "Captain says we've less than an hour until we reach Calcutta."

"I will certainly miss your company, Miss Cavendish," Sergeant Jacks shifted, turning his shoulders to subtly block Ensign Porter from the ladies' direct view. "It has been a pleasure to make the voyage with such gracious company. And I particularly enjoyed partnering with you in whist last evening."

Fanny lowered her lashes, and an enchanting blush pinkened her cheeks. "Oh, Jacks, you know I have no mind for cards."

"Quite the contrary, miss. I daresay—"

Ensign Porter pushed his way around the other soldier, and Helen was forced to step back against the rail to avoid being knocked aside.

"I think we made a fine couple in the minuet, Miss Cavendish."

"And I enjoyed dancing with you as well, Lady Helen," Sergeant Jacks added, turning so that he faced Helen.

"As did I, my lady," Ensign Porter said.

Helen lowered her gaze, mumbling her thanks, wishing she knew how to giggle and flirt and blush the way Fanny did. It seemed that any time a gentleman was near, she suddenly didn't know how to act and instead did her best to disappear into the background. Her worry that she would say something foolish prevented her from saying anything at all. Her friend Meg, from America, had told Helen to speak of things that were interesting to her, but Helen could not imagine that any gentleman could possibly be interested in the colorful birds or the way the sun sparkled on the river. She had made a big enough fool of herself pointing out the elephant to Fanny.

Fanny sighed loudly, recapturing the men's attention, and her pout returned. "Oh, it is so hot today. I don't know how I shall endure India. Perhaps I should have remained in England."

Both men protested loudly, reassuring Fanny that they were infinitely glad for her company and that the voyage would have been dull without her. She would get used to the heat.

Fanny maintained her pout, fluttering her lashes as the officers continued their protests, and at last she permitted a smile to pull at her delicate lips.

"Come, Miss Cavendish, allow me to accompany you to the dining room." Ensign Porter offered his arm.

"Lady Helen, will you join us?" Sergeant Jacks asked.

"Thank you, no." Helen shook her head. "I should like to remain here."

Fanny waved her fingers as she and the gentlemen took their leave.

As Helen watched them walk across the deck, she felt both relieved they were gone and frustrated that she had been too shy to accompany them. She wished she didn't turn into such a goose whenever the situation called for her to make conversation with gentlemen.

She turned back, scanning the shoreline in anticipation of a glimpse of the city that would be her new home. Boats of various sizes became more numerous, filling the river, and Helen saw small dwellings with thatched roofs clustered together on the banks.

As the ship continued up the river, more passengers filled the deck, lining the rails as they awaited the first sight of their destination. Helen attempted to recapture her earlier excitement but found she was unable to due to Fanny's disapproval and her own growing nervousness.

Finally, the delicate white spires of a building Helen assumed was a temple broke through the forest. Soon after, one large mansion with elegant lawns and gardens appeared on the banks, and then another came into view. When the ship rounded a bend, the green jungle gave way, and Calcutta, the capital of British India, emerged in all her glory.

From what she could see, the city was much larger than she had expected. Through the greenery, she could make out the rooflines of modern European buildings interspersed between exotic Eastern-style towers with pointed roofs.

Helen's mouth went dry. Could this unknown place ever feel like home? What awaited her in India? She left the rail and searched the crowded deck for Jim and her mother, locating them near the entrance to the companionway below.

From the expression on her mother's face, Helen could see Lady Patricia did not harbor the same worries about their new life. She was the type of woman who approached every challenge with an even temperament. She was practical and organized. And Helen was grateful for her steadiness.

"Good morning, Mamá." Helen linked arms with her mother.

"There you are, my dear." Her mother looked around briskly. "And are you ready to leave this boat behind and begin our adventure?"

Helen nodded and attempted to smile although she felt as far from ready as possible.

Lady Patricia patted her arm.

In a matter of moments, the anchor was dropped and the sailors set about unloading passengers and cargo. Instead of disembarking into a waiting dinghy or walking down a gangway to a pier, crew members helped Helen and her mother over the gunwale to climb down a rope ladder onto a shallow-bottomed boat that was nearer to a raft than a dinghy.

Helen stood uncertainly on the wet boards until the bobbing of the vessel made her grab on to a small bench and sit next to her mother before she tipped overboard. Other passengers joined them, and after a moment the boat began to move away from the larger ship. She looked to the rear of the ferry and saw a man pushing a giant pole against the bottom of the river to propel them forward. He wore nothing more than a turban on his head and a strip of fabric around his hips. Helen's face burned, and she whipped her head around. She had never seen a man so sparsely dressed, and she kept her eyes on the shore for the remainder of the distance.

Arms pulled Helen out of the boat, and she stumbled ashore, finding herself surrounded by chaos. Passengers, crates, barrels, and luggage—all were discharged on the shore in an unorganized fashion. Clipped chattering syllables of words she couldn't understand pounded at her from every side. Bright colors moved around her as women with glossy black braids pushed past in silken saris. Soldiers in red coats and helmets moved purposefully through the masses. Bullock carts creaked, dogs barked, birds squawked, and children dodged in and out of the disorder like scampering mice. Large cattle moved among the crowd, untended. Above it all was the heat and the smell of humanity combined with animal odors and pungent foreign spices. Helen found her mother's arm and clung to it, worried about becoming separated as they were jostled by the crowd. Her head felt light, and a combination of panic and faintness washed over her.

Lady Patricia led her through the crowded dock area and stopped beneath a canopy.

Helen was grateful for the shade. They stood next to barrels and stacks of crates and piles of rope as she caught her breath.

"Jim will see to the luggage and come for us." Lady Patricia took a few steps away, scanning the crowd as she looked for the general. "I will walk a bit closer to the corner so he will be sure to find us."

Helen couldn't believe her mother was capable of maintaining her composure in the midst of such confusion. She leaned against a barrel and let out a sigh. From the corner of her eye, she saw movement and started, jerking back at the sight of a small black face surrounded by a mane of white hair. Once her heart calmed, she saw it was a monkey sitting atop the barrel, holding its hand out toward her. Helen scooted away, her breath coming in short gasps.

"Don't be afraid. Badmash can't resist greeting a pretty lady."

She looked away from the monkey's dark eyes and saw the speaker step out of the shadows where he'd been leaning against the wall. Although Helen did not have enough experience with the army to determine the man's status, she could tell from the golden stripes on his red sleeves that he was fairly high ranking. He took a few steps closer, and she noticed he walked stiffly, as if he were marching. The soldier's jaw was square, his eyes gray, and his hair a dark auburn. For some reason, Helen felt immediately calmed by his presence. *It must be because he is an English soldier, a familiar sight, a relief in all this turmoil.*

"The monkey has a name?" Helen asked.

"Badmash. In Hindustani it means *rascal*."

At the sound of his name, the animal turned his head.

"And is he your pet?"

"He is more like a friend." A smile pulled at the man's mouth, and Helen could not help but smile back. "A friend who believes himself to be human."

Helen studied Badmash for a moment. He had a black stripe from the top of his head down his back, but aside from his face, hands, and feet, the rest of him was covered in thick dirty-white fur.

The animal still held his hand toward her, waiting patiently.

The officer stepped closer. "Do not be afraid; he'll not hurt you."

She glanced at the soldier then slowly offered her hand to the monkey.

He clasped her fingers in his small grip and bent his head to touch his mouth on her glove. His actions were the very epitome of a gentleman. And a flirt.

Helen giggled and dipped in a curtsy. "Pleased to meet you, Mr. Badmash."

"Oh, do not call him *mister*." The soldier folded his arms and rolled his eyes to the heavens, shaking his head from side to side. "It will go straight to his head, and he will be impossible to live with."

"I shall remember that." Helen's smile grew. She looked at the soldier again and saw that he was watching her closely. "I am not certain it is smart to make conversation with a person who befriends wild animals. One might wonder if you are right in the head."

He burst into a laugh.

The sound delighted Helen and made her feel like laughing herself.

He wagged his finger in a teasing manner. "I assure you, the complete opposite is true. People with animals for friends are infinitely more sane than those without."

Helen opened her mouth to reply, but the sound of a man clearing his throat stopped her.

The soldier snapped to attention, clicked his heels together, and saluted Jim, who had joined them, along with Helen's mother.

"General Stackhouse, I presume?" All traces of teasing were gone, and Helen found herself looking at a solemn-faced soldier.

"Yes."

"Captain Michael Rhodes, sir. I served as adjutant—an intelligence adviser to General Spencer."

Jim nodded as he studied Captain Michael Rhodes. "At ease," he muttered.

The captain lowered his salute but still stood at attention.

"I've heard good things about you, Captain. And your reports show you've a sharp mind for strategy and understanding the local customs and native way of thinking. You speak Hindustani like a native, I hear. As well as Bengali and Punjabi."

"Yes, sir. I was born in Bombay. My father was a bookkeeper for the John Company."

"Educated in England?"

"Yes, sir. Sandhurst."

Jim took a step back and looked down at Captain Rhodes's boots. "Impressive that you remained . . . in your circumstances."

Helen glanced at her mother, but Lady Patricia lifted a shoulder in a barely perceptible shrug, indicating she did not know what circumstances Jim was talking about.

"India is my home, sir, and the army my family."

Jim nodded. "If you are amiable to continuing in your present position, I'd welcome your expertise on my staff."

"It would be an honor, sir."

"Well, that's settled, then." Jim took a step back and spread his hand to the side. "Allow me to introduce my wife, Lady Patricia, and her daughter, Lady Helen."

"A pleasure." Captain Rhodes took each woman's hand in turn and performed a military-style bow.

When he lifted his head, still holding Helen's hand, the side of his mouth quirked in a small smile, and she saw a twinkle in his eye.

She felt the same tug on her mouth and struggled to keep her smile from turning into an enormous and highly improper grin. She thought how pleasant it would be to have Captain Rhodes here in Calcutta. His cheerful smile and easy manner would make it much more comfortable to be in this place where everything was unfamiliar.

"Ladies, if you will allow me to show you to the *ghari*." When he saw Helen and her mother exchange a questioning glance, he added, "A *ghari* is a carriage."

Lady Patricia took her husband's arm, and Captain Rhodes offered his arm to Helen.

She took a step toward him but stopped when her gaze was drawn to a soldier riding through the crowd. From his position atop his prancing horse, he blocked the sun, causing a glow around his head, highlighting his dark curls. Though she could not see his face, his silhouette showed broad shoulders, a straight nose, and pronounced cheekbones. He reached the group and dismounted with a flourish, saluting Jim. "Lieutenant Arthur Bancroft, sir."

The men spoke, but Helen did not hear anything further, aside from the pounding of her heart. The world slowed down as Lieutenant Bancroft turned toward her, sweeping her hand into his. A slow smile exposed his straight teeth and a perfect dimple. When their eyes met, Helen's skin felt both heated and cold as ice.

"Lady Helen, it appears India has found its brightest diamond." His voice was low, and the sound of it shot a jolt through her heart. Helen gasped for breath, knowing without a doubt she would never be the same.

Chapter 2

MICHAEL LEFT HIS HORSE TO the care of his *syce* and followed the path to his bungalow. Step, *thud*. Step, *thud*. His limp was more pronounced when he was tired, and it had been a long day. After delivering the general's family to their new home in Chowringhee, he'd accompanied General Stackhouse to purchase a horse and tour Fort William, his new command, then Michael introduced the general at the Raj Bhavan—the government house—to Lord Minto, the Governor-General of India. Michael had spent a few hours on paperwork and then taken his horse, Ei-Zarka, for a late-night ride along the strand beside the Hooghly. He'd hoped to keep his mind occupied and to tire his body to the point that his thoughts wouldn't continually return to Lady Helen.

And there were numerous reasons why they should not. First and foremost being that even a simpleton could see she was too young for him. She could not be older than twenty, which made her more than ten years his junior. She was also the daughter of his commanding officer—although he did not think such a thing would deter many men. It had not seemed to matter to Lieutenant Bancroft, that delicate-faced young buck who managed to charm every woman—young and old—with whom he came in contact. Lady Helen certainly had not seemed bothered by his attention.

In his mind appeared the image of Lady Helen blushing at something the lieutenant had said. Michael's heart felt as though its steady rhythm paused and heat spread from it. Merely the memory of the woman was enough to cause such a reaction. The heat continued to spread, making his chest feel light when he thought of the easy way he and Lady Helen had teased one another and her delightful laugh at

Badmash's actions. But what had captured him was her eyes. He had never seen such a vivid blue—the color of a rare jewel in a *maharaja's* crown, he thought. Her mother's eyes were nearly the same shade, but Lady Helen's sparkle and youth made the effect of her gaze so striking that he'd felt a physical reaction when she looked at him—a burst of energy that had rendered him nearly breathless.

Her dark brows arched playfully; her pink lips were small and ever so slightly pouted. She was petite and slender, and everything about her seemed delicate. But he also sensed a strength inside her.

He pushed the thoughts away. His age was not the only reason to rein in his thoughts about Lady Helen. She was a vibrant young woman with endless possibilities ahead of her. And he, well, his options were terminated abruptly two years earlier with a Maratha's explosive on the banks of the Narmada.

At the doorway to his bungalow, Michael's servant, Basu Ram, squatted down on his heels in the Oriental manner awaiting his master's return. Basu Ram was from the Punjab and had served the Rhodes family since before Michael was born. He wore a blue turban, identifying himself as a Mohammedan.

Basu Ram stood slowly, his elderly bones stiff, and placed his palms together, touching the sides of his thumbs to his forehead in a greeting. "Rhodes-Sahib, you are tired."

Michael nodded. "And hungry." He sniffed the air, and his stomach rumbled at the smell of rice and stewed goat floating from the small kitchen building behind his bungalow. He stepped toward the door, but Basu Ram moved in front of him.

He studied Michael's face closely. His eyes squinted, and the thick white mustache with its curled ends twitched. "Something has happened to you this day, Sahib. You are a different man."

Michael looked away, not liking the scrutiny. He schooled his expression, wondering if his thoughts about Lady Helen showed on his face. "The new general arrived today from Belait. General Stackhouse."

Basu Ram's eyes remained narrowed. "No, there is more."

"*Kāfī.* Enough." Michael shook his head and turned to walk past. "I am hungry and tired. And you worry like a nursemaid."

Badrash stood on one of the wooden chairs at the table. When he saw Michael, he jabbered and screeched angrily until Basu Ram shooed him away. The monkey climbed onto the windowsill and continued his tirade.

Michael felt the beginnings of a headache prickling at his temples. He rubbed his eyes. "I shall have to remember to notify my servants and animals of my schedule," he grumbled.

The door at the rear of the bungalow opened, and Naveen, the cook, entered with a tray of food. Naveen did not speak often. He was young and very strong. Michael thought that in another society, the young man would be a soldier, but Naveens's caste did not give him that option. He was Shudra—born into a caste of servants and unable to change that for the rest of his entire life. Michael knew that Naveen hoped to be born again into a higher caste; perhaps in the next life he would be Kshatriya, a warrior.

"It smells wonderful," Michael said in Hindustani as he sank into his chair.

Naveen bowed his head in thanks and poured cool mango *lassi* into Michael's cup. Badmash returned to his chair, and Naveen set one plate in front of the captain and one in front of the monkey; the pair ate together in silence.

Once Naveen and Basu Ram were assured that their Sahib did not require anything further for his supper or his comfort, they left him, and a few moments later, Michael heard the low murmur of voices and smelled the fruity tobacco smoke of the hookah drifting in through the windows.

He smiled as he thought about his peculiar household. He stabbed the last piece of goat meat with his fork and bit down, glad that Naveen did not serve fish tonight, as was the usual fare.

Basu Ram did not eat pork because he believed it to be unclean. Naveen refused to eat beef because the animal was considered holy, so their meals typically consisted of fish and vegetables. After his years in England, Michael had to admit that sometimes a man just needed a plate of meat and potatoes with gravy covering the lot.

When Michael's mother died, his father had sent him to England, the place Indians called Belait, when he was nine. He'd been frightened and lonely in the closed-windowed school with its narrow passageways and strange food. He had endured the cold and constant fog by throwing himself into his studies with the goal of finishing his schooling as quickly as possible, accepting his father's funding of a commission, and training to be an officer at Sandhurst. Once he graduated, he applied immediately for an assignment in India and arrived fourteen years earlier, just in time to fight the Tipu of Mysore at the Siege of Seringapatam.

Michael had climbed the ranks of the army through a combination of luck and skill as he led his men in one battle after another. He was well on his way to the highest military offices in the country when—

He reined in his thoughts, refusing to allow them to travel that path again.

The sound of laughter outside drew his gaze to the window, but he knew it was only his servants. Basu Ram had met him at the docks the day he returned from England, arguing with Naveen, a young Hindi servant assigned to Michael by the army. The men both pled their cases to Michael, and what could he do but retain both of them? Although they came from different parts of the country, were decades apart in age, spoke different languages, and practiced different religions, Michael had seen the two servants become friends. He thought the remainder of the world could learn a thing or two from the men's examples.

He glanced at the animal eating beside him—taking small bites of fruit in a manner than seemed almost human—and thought how strange life could be. If it weren't for this little companion finding him at his lowest time and befriending him, Michael did not know if he would have survived the months after his injury. Though Basu Ram acted irritated with Badmash, the man would never send him away. He had been there through the dark times too. Michael thought he probably owed his life—if not his sanity—to the furry little nuisance. And it is why he ate his supper in his quiet bungalow with the monkey for company.

Michael could have taken his meals with the officers at the Bengal Club, but he didn't want to endure the other men's inquiries after his health—or worse, their pity. *Perhaps I am just getting old and set in my ways.* He grimaced and shook his head. Thirty-two was hardly old. His men respected him, and the other officers were friendly enough, but he was not like them. He did not consider his time in India merely as an assignment to be endured. He'd told General Stackhouse the truth. India was his home. And since the death of his parents, the army was the only family he had left.

The feeling of loneliness returned. Basu Ram and Naveen cared for him, especially Basu Ram. Michael knew the old man loved him like a son, but it did not matter how dear they were to each other; the Indians would never accept him as one of their own. They would never sit at his table and share his food. If he joined them, they would not eat in his presence. And if he ate from their plates, they would break the dishes afterward to prevent anyone else from eating on them and becoming unclean. As low as servants were in the Indian caste system, Michael was *ferengi*, a foreigner, an outcaste, and as such he was even lower.

He had grown up with the cultural divisions and never questioned them until he returned from England and began to see how very different this world was from a British perspective. But even though he was a sahib, his attachment to the Indian people and way of life often made it difficult for him to see the British point of view. Sometimes he felt as if he did not fit into either role. Perhaps that was why he shared his meal with a monkey and afterward spent the evenings with two Indian servants, hunkering down on the ground outside to discuss religion or politics or gossip from the bazaar.

With 180 native languages, fourteen major tongues, and seven hundred minor dialects in India, Michael's fluency in Hindustani, Bengali, and Punjabi was a small drop in the bucket, but it was the reason General Spencer had offered him the adjutant position. His ability to speak with the natives and to understand their ways is what had kept him from being sent home to early retirement on half pay.

And where was "home" anyway?

Against his will, his mind returned to Lady Helen. Was she happy in her new home? The mansion assigned to the general in Chowringhee was one of the more beautiful residences in the city, but as a lady, the daughter of an earl or marquess, she had likely grown up in an English manor house or even a castle. Surely it was an adjustment, and India could be frightening to British miss-sahibs who found themselves surrounded with insects and heat and a culture that was so very foreign. Although the British threw dinner parties and picnics and tried to maintain as "English" a routine as possible, India was not England. As he'd watched Lady Helen make her way through the crowded docks, he'd seen nervousness in her eyes, but there had also been interest and an excitement that he'd not seen in any of the British women. He hoped she found the country beautiful and fascinating the way he did.

But he told himself it was too much to hope for. Not one young British woman of his acquaintance had ever enjoyed her time in India. They had complained of everything from the heat to the smells to the insects, and most returned with their children to India long before their husbands' military service was completed. He'd thought there was something different in Lady Helen. The way she'd played with Badmash for example—he could not imagine many ladies allowing the monkey to kiss their hand without recoiling. Michael smiled again as he thought of the incident, and he hoped he could hear her laugh again. That was a sound he did not think he would ever tire of.

Between working closely with her stepfather and Michael's position in society as an officer, he would undoubtedly spend a fair amount of time in Lady Helen's presence. His heart constricted as he found himself looking forward to seeing her again and at the same time dreading another meeting. His interest would all come to naught, and he did not know how he could smile and make polite conversation with the woman when he knew she would never— It was impossible.

Michael rose from the table but did not go outside. He didn't want to make excuses for the change that Basu Ram had seen in him. He knew he could not hide the truth from one who knew him so well. Even with all of his training and discipline, he feared he could not prevent himself from losing his heart to Lady Helen.

Chapter 3

HELEN LOOKED DOWN AT HER plate, pushing around the bits of spicy chicken and rice with her fork. The food tasted strange, but it was not unpleasant. She set down her fork and lifted her hand to cover a yawn. Although her body was exhausted, her mind buzzed with all the newness surrounding her.

She and her mother had spent the majority of the day in the sitting room, speaking with the head servant—a man in white clothing and a multilayered turban, whose name neither of them could pronounce—and the housekeeper, or *hamal*, as they learned she preferred to be called.

Although her mother had said Helen's presence during matters of business was unnecessary, Helen insisted on remaining. Not only did she want to aid her mother in sorting through the household organization, but she also found the entire Indian system of labor and the rules that governed it to be fascinating.

Both Helen and Lady Patricia had been utterly overwhelmed by the amount of people in their new home. The number of servants was well over fifty, and the pair had gone over lists for hours, learning which people bore which responsibilities. It seemed as though there were multiple people for each duty, but the hamal had explained in her careful English that because of their castes, the servants were confined in the labor they were able to perform. For example, two servants were required for each horse—one to groom the animal and the other to prepare its food. Another was responsible for cleaning the stables. The water carrier brought water to the door, but another person was required to deliver the large jars to the kitchen.

Helen wondered about the castes. Was it the same as class division in England? She didn't find it strange that certain people performed particular duties, but the idea that they were forbidden to perform other, seemingly similar tasks confused her. She wished there was someone she could ask about it. Perhaps Jim could explain it to her.

As a servant cleared the plates, the room was quiet save for the creaking of the *punkah*—a large wooden frame covered in fabric that hung from the high ceiling of the room—swinging back and forth to stir the air. Apparently the household employed a servant, a *punkawallah*, whose entire job consisted of pulling the cord that ran down the wall in order to keep the contraption moving. She glanced at her stepfather at the head of the table and thought it was the perfect opportunity to ask him.

"Helen, dear."

When she heard her mother's voice, Helen turned her gaze to Lady Patricia. "Yes, Mamá?"

"Would you mind making me a cup of tea? I am feeling a bit under the weather."

Helen looked closer and saw that her mother's face was pale. The travel and long day must have taken their toll on her. "Of course, Mamá."

Jim studied his wife with his one eye squinting. "Patricia?" He could not hide the worry in his voice.

"Pishposh, I am just fine." She waved her hand at her husband then turned to Helen. "My herbs are in the sitting room next to my bedchamber in their usual box. If you don't mind, I think peppermint and chamomile, dear."

Helen hurried from the table and into the sitting room for the ingredients. Based on her mother's request, Helen knew Lady Patricia must need to calm her stomach. When her mother was using tea for a medicinal purpose, she preferred for herself or her daughter to prepare it.

Helen found the herbs directly and brought them down the stairs but realized she had no idea where to find the kitchen. The servants had brought the food from the doorway that led to the drawing room, so she began her search in that direction. Once her mother had tea, Helen was eager to explore the rest of the house.

After walking through a few different rooms, she thought she must have gone too far. The kitchen must be closer to the dining room. She turned around and decided to inquire of the servants that had brought the meal. The evening light shining through the windows was fading. Helen's footsteps sounded on the bare floors and echoed off the high ceiling. She spotted a servant who was wiping a cloth over the furniture in the drawing room, and Helen waved a hand. "If you please?"

The servant turned, put her palms together, and bowed while Helen approached.

Helen tried to remember if she had come across this woman earlier. She didn't think so. She would no doubt have recognized the dramatic pattern of the blue-and-green silk wrapped around her. The sari was beautiful, and Helen found it rather surprising that the servants wore such vividly colored clothing. "Would you please fetch me a teapot? Or tell me where I might find one?"

The woman raised her head and said something Helen did not understand. The servant motioned with her hand in the direction from which Helen had just come.

Helen glanced over her shoulder then back to the woman. She shook her head. "I'm sorry. I do not understand. Is that the direction to the kitchen?" She held up the bag of herbs and with her other hand pinched her fingers together and lifted them to her mouth in a charade of drinking from a teacup. She felt a bit foolish and hoped the servant would realize what she needed.

The woman spoke again, nodding and beckoning for her to follow. Helen followed her to a door beside a window, but the servant reached for the door handle.

"No, I do not want to go outside." Helen nearly groaned in frustration. She had been searching for the kitchen for nearly twenty minutes. A simple thing. Is this how it would be every time she tried to communicate with the staff? "I simply need a teapot."

The woman opened the door and stood aside. Helen let out her breath in an irritated puff that reminded her a bit too much of Fanny Cavendish. She humored the servant and stepped outside, meaning to turn directly back around and find another person to help her. But she stopped when she saw, in the dim light, a small wooden building behind the main house. She inhaled the aroma of spices and realized she had found the kitchen. Outside the building, a fire burned inside a small box of bricks that she decided must be an oven. A man sat on the ground next to it, wearing only a turban and a cloth around his hips. He was mixing some sort of dough in a bowl he held between his bare feet.

She looked back at the woman, who nodded toward the building and said more strange-sounding words, lifting her hand and pointing.

Helen crossed the space toward the open door and looked inside, expecting to see tables and ovens and shelves containing pots and dishes—perhaps even a cooling box for meat. So she was surprised to see people squatted down on the floor, washing out pots and using knives to chop things on boards between their feet. The only table was a small one upon which sat a bowl of fruit.

For a moment, Helen stared as she fought to swallow the sour tang that rose in her throat. The meal she had just eaten had been prepared by partially naked people on the floor of this small room. She wondered if her mother had any idea what the kitchen looked like and thought perhaps it would be best not to mention it.

A woman who seemed to be in charge hurried over, bowing her head.

She must be the head cook. Helen schooled her face, hoping for a pleasant expression as she attempted to keep her nose from wrinkling at the spicy smells in the air. "I need to boil some water, please."

The servant who had accompanied her from the house spoke briefly. The cook glanced to the parcel in Helen's hand and stepped toward a cupboard, opening the wooden door and lifting out a silver tea set.

"Yes," Helen said, smiling in relief. "Thank you." She thought she should probably learn the words the woman had used to ask for the teapot and avoid any confusion in the future.

Next, the cook pulled a brass kettle from the cupboard and called to a boy who brought a jar, carefully filled the kettle with water, then carried it to the fire outside.

Helen did not want to stand next to the practically bare man mixing the dough so remained in the kitchen doorway, watching the people.

She realized that there was a definite system to what they were doing. A feel of orderliness pervaded the room. In the few minutes that she watched, she saw each person tend to their duties unhurriedly, ensuring that they'd done a thorough job but not feeling as if they must rush. It was a characteristic she'd noticed about the various servants she'd met, a calmness that set her at ease.

The boy approached, bowing, and said something as he motioned toward the kettle. She followed him, thanking him as he poured the hot water into the silver pot and thinking again how much simpler it would be to communicate if she understood just a few words of their language. Perhaps Captain Rhodes could teach her. Did he not say he spoke the native languages?

Darkness had come quickly, and she was glad to return inside. But by the time she entered the dining room with the tea tray, she found only Jim.

"Your mother has already retired to her room." Jim took the tray. "I will deliver the tea, and that woman's knowledge and use of herbs should have her feeling well in no time."

"Thank you, sir." Helen wondered if she should go to her mother as well but decided against it. Lady Patricia was undoubtedly worn out from a long day of trying to organize a colonial Indian household, and sleep would do her well.

She bid Jim good night, but Helen was not ready for sleep herself. There was still so much of the house she hadn't seen, and now that most of the servants were gone, she took the opportunity to explore the mansion. She recognized the rooms and what they were used for, but the arrangement was unlike that of an English home. Though the upper floor rooms branched off a hallway, she found it strange that the rooms on the main floor opened into one another. The ceilings were high and the beams bare. When she'd inquired about it, Jim had told her plastered ceilings were a hiding place for rats and snakes, and the earlier colonists had done away with them completely, adopting the Indian style.

Helen walked from room to room, holding a candle high to see the details of her new home. She stepped on thick, colorful rugs that spread over the wooden floors. Palm trees and flowering plants grew from large pots around the whitewashed walls. With the high ceilings and large rooms, the house seemed wide open, and in the darkness it was a bit unnerving. It definitely lacked the warmth and coziness she was accustomed to in an English house.

She studied the pictures and perused the shelves of books in the library. The majority of the furniture was bare and stark, and she noticed that many of the small windows did not have glass but carved screens that allowed light and air to flow in but kept large things out. The screens were not completely effective—moths and flying insects clustered around the small flames on the wall sconces. The fluttering was surprisingly noisy, and the movement cast strange shadows around the large room.

Helen felt a chill as the darkness seemed to change just outside her vision. She heard a noise that sounded like something scuttling along the wooden floor, and cringed. Perhaps she ought to retire and explore the house in the light of day.

Turning quickly to leave the room, she rounded the large desk and walked directly into the path of an enormous tiger!

Helen screamed and stumbled back, hitting her arm against the desk as she fell. She looked over her shoulder at the tiger as she scrambled to her feet.

It stood unmoving in the corner of the room, staring at her with black eyes flickering in the candlelight, its teeth bared in a snarl.

A surge of terror shot through her so strongly it hurt her fingers. How had it gotten in the house with nobody noticing?

The realization came suddenly that the animal hadn't moved. It had not made a noise. Embarrassment replaced her panic. The tiger was stuffed.

In an instant, the room was filled with servants. Jim bounded into the library in his robe and slippers, brandishing a pistol, his eye patch askew. He looked around the room frantically, and when he spotted her, he ran toward her. "Helen, what is it?"

"The tiger, sir." Her voice shook. "It startled me. I did not realize . . ." Whether a product of embarrassment, abating fear, or the exhaustion from her long day, her voice cracked and tears welled in her eyes. She put her hand over her mouth and looked away from the confused faces of the servants. The entire household seemed to be in the library.

Jim ordered everyone to return to their duties and then helped Helen to a sofa. He sat next to her and patted her shoulder until she stopped shaking.

Though she felt foolish for her display, Jim's presence soothed her.

"I am sorry, sir," she said once she had control over her voice. "I feel completely ridiculous."

"There is no need to apologize. You did exactly the right thing should you ever find yourself in danger. Did you see how quickly the household came to your rescue? You are safe here, Helen."

She nodded, wiping her fingers over her cheeks.

"Now, are you injured?"

"I hit the desk but not badly." She craned her neck to the side and rubbed her arm. "I think it is only my pride that is injured."

Jim peered closely to inspect the reddening mark. "You may well have a bruise tomorrow, but I do not think it is serious." He stood, offering his arm, and Helen slid her hand into the crease of his elbow.

Jim led her from the library, through the entry hall, then up the staircase. "I came face-to-face with a tiger in the jungle outside Nagpur, and I do not believe a moment in my life has ever come close to frightening me that badly since." Jim cleared his throat. "Until tonight."

Helen stopped walking and looked up at Jim. "Tonight, sir?"

"When I thought you were in danger—" He cleared his throat again, brushing his loose hair back from his face. "Helen, you and your mother . . . I've never had a family, and, well, I am glad you are all right," he finished.

She squeezed his arm and laid her head on his shoulder as he accompanied her to the door of her bedchamber.

When her door opened, Jim stepped back, rubbing his neck. He told Sita, her *ayah*, to check Helen's arm, and then he hurried away.

Once she had climbed in bed, she considered the events of her day, until her thoughts became images, and images became impressions slipping through her mind—a sharp-toothed tiger, a father's concern, a handsome lieutenant on a horse, a monkey who flirted, the kind smile of Captain Rhodes. They all wrapped around her like a warm blanket, and she drifted to sleep.

Chapter 4

HELEN WAS JERKED AWAKE BY the sound of chanting—or singing. She did not recognize the voice or know from whence it came. Laying in the darkness, she wondered briefly why her cabin was so still.

In an instant, unfamiliar smells and sounds invaded her consciousness, and the reality of her new home flooded over her. She was in India. Memories of the evening before filled her mind and put her nerves on edge. Creeping from her bed to the window, she held aside the curtains and looked out across the wide gardens in the direction of the voice, but she saw only shadows against the lightening purple sky.

A light behind her caused her to twist quickly around.

Sita had entered the room carrying a candle. "Miss-Sahib is well?"

Helen was not used to people entering her bedchamber without knocking. "Yes, I am well. Thank you." She spoke more sharply than she intended, but between this woman she had only met yesterday taking such liberties and the haunting voice outside, she felt decidedly on edge.

Sita set the candlestick on the bedside table and pressed her palms together, touching her thumbs to her bowed forehead. She knelt on the floor and sat calmly, as if waiting for Helen's command.

Helen did not like the feeling of standing over a woman who humbly waited to be ordered about. She stepped across the room and sat at a round table. "Sita, if you please, what is that noise?" She motioned with her hand toward the window.

"*Azān*," Sita said. "Call to prayer for the Mohammedans."

"Oh." Helen glanced to the window. She realized the voice was coming from the other side of Chowringhee, from the direction of the building Jim had told her was a mosque. Now that she knew what it was, she sat back to listen. It was so very lovely. She wished she understood the words. The melody was in a minor key with sliding notes that reminded Helen of the ornaments used by Baroque composers to make their music complex and elaborate. But in the Azān, the effect was a feeling of yearning and gave a spirituality to the music that went straight to her heart. Helen swallowed over the lump growing in her throat. "Does he sing every morning?"

Sita nodded. "Five times each day."

Helen wondered why she had not heard the singing the day before. She supposed the noises of the city would have covered it. In the early morning, it was quiet. "What do the words mean?"

Sita shook her head, her long braid swishing across her back. "I do not know. I am Hindu, Miss-Sahib."

Helen leaned her head back to listen, taking the opportunity to study her ayah in the growing dawn. She thought Sita was probably close to her mother's age. A few gray hairs wove down into her black braid. Her face was smooth, her skin the color of amber, and her eyes dark brown. Helen had noticed last night as her ayah helped her dress for bed that Sita had the longest eyelashes she'd ever seen on a person. Red paint dotted her forehead and was spread along the part in her hair. Helen wanted to ask her about the markings but did not want to seem rude.

She grimaced as she thought of the embarrassing spectacle she had made the night before, but her expression softened into a smile when she thought of Jim and how safe she'd felt with him. The feeling reminded her of the soldier, Captain Rhodes, from the dock yesterday. His friendly manner and laughter felt reassuring in the midst of the chaos of the dock. And Badmash. She smiled as she remembered the silly monkey and the way he'd kissed her hand.

Helen sat up straight. Her heart jumped as she remembered Lieutenant Bancroft. How could she have forgotten?

Did gentlemen make morning calls as they did in England?

The music stopped as the sky grew light. Helen did not think she had ever risen before dawn. She stretched and yawned. "I am going back to sleep, Sita. But please do not allow me to sleep for too long."

She wanted to be certain she was dressed and ready should a particular lieutenant call on her.

Her ayah bowed and left the room.

Hours later, Helen woke to the bright sunlight shining over her bed.

She dressed and hurried downstairs, certain there would be at the very least a calling card from her lieutenant, but when she reached the entry hall and looked on the table, she saw only cards sent by ladies and a few large envelopes that must be invitations.

Lieutenant Bancroft must be very busy and would undoubtedly call later. He had, after all, paid particular attention to her at the docks for the few moments they'd been in each other's company. And surely he'd felt the same jolt when he'd held her hand and their eyes met. How could it be otherwise?

As she walked toward the dining room, Helen heard voices in the library and stepped into the doorway to see Jim speaking with a man in uniform whose back was to her. Her eyes darted to the stuffed tiger in the corner.

Jim stood when he saw her.

The other officer's words cut off abruptly, and he stood, turning to face the doorway.

The sight of Captain Rhodes brought a smile to her face. "Good morning, sir. And Captain Rhodes. How nice to see you again." She dipped in a curtsy.

Both men bent forward and bid her good morning.

Captain Rhodes returned her smile, raising his brow the slightest tick.

Helen nearly giggled at his teasing expression and looked instead at Jim. "I am sorry to disturb your meeting. I only thought to ask after my mother. Have you seen her this morning?"

"She is sleeping late. I imagine she will feel much improved when she awakens."

Helen noticed Jim's mouth was tight. She wondered if he were more worried than he let on. "Very well. I shall give her a few hours then."

Jim nodded his head.

"Gentlemen." She curtsied once again and left them to their discussion. After a quick breakfast of toast and eggs, she thought she would venture out into the gardens before her mother awoke and before it became too hot. Lady Patricia would be interested in finding a suitable location for an herb garden.

Helen was tying her bonnet when she heard Jim's and Captain Rhodes's voices nearing the entrance hall.

Captain Rhodes was speaking. "General Spencer did not see the importance of maintaining the relationship either, but what he did not understand is that to a man like Shah Ahsan Ali, the neglect of such courtesies can be perceived as hostility."

"And is he powerful enough to pose a threat?" Jim asked.

"In my opinion, yes." Captain Rhodes ran his fingers through his hair. "I recommend maintaining a relationship of trust with—" He stopped speaking when he saw Helen.

"Very well." Jim glanced up the stairs. "I will attend to my wife, and we can continue our discussion when we meet with Lord Minto tomorrow."

"Yes, sir," Captain Rhodes said.

Jim nodded to Helen and began to climb the stairs, but after a few steps he stopped and turned back to Captain Rhodes. "And the other matter?"

"Tomorrow afternoon, definitely."

Jim glanced to Helen, and a small smile lifted the corner of his mouth before he continued up the stairway.

"And where are you off to, Lady Helen?" Captain Rhodes stepped next to her as she pulled on her gloves.

She noticed how straight he stood. A military man for certain. "I thought to tour the gardens for a bit this morning. Would you care to accompany me, Captain?" She thought his eyes widened the slightest bit. But he did not seem irritated and maintained his pleasant countenance.

"I certainly would." Captain Rhodes stood aside, indicating for Helen to precede him.

Before she stepped outside, the turbaned butler hurried into the entry hall and cleared his throat.

When Helen looked at him, he held an envelope toward her. "This was delivered for Miss-Sahib moments ago."

"Thank you." Helen took the envelope and looked at her name written on it. She glanced to Captain Rhodes. "Do you mind, sir?"

"Of course not." He took a step back to give her privacy.

Helen tore the envelope and slid out a sheet of paper.

Lady Helen Poulter,

On such a beautiful day as this, I should be disappointed not to spend time with you. My friend and I should love to pay you a call. Shall we say this afternoon at four? I shall count the hours until I am once again in the presence of the loveliest young lady in all of India.

Very truly yours,

Lieutenant Arthur Edwin Bancroft

Helen's heart pounded furiously when she saw the signature. She felt her cheeks flush and pressed the letter to her chest, closing her eyes and breathing out a sigh. *Lieutenant Bancroft.* She glanced up, only now remembering that Captain Rhodes was waiting for her. "Please, if you will excuse me for just one more moment, I must speak to my lady's maid—I mean ayah. I promise, just one moment, Captain."

She hurried up the stairs to her bedchamber and found Sita straightening the bedding. Helen opened the large wardrobe, smiling at the new gowns her mother had purchased before their voyage. She had received warning from a few officers' wives that finding decent dressmakers in India was nearly impossible, so both she and her mother had brought trunks full of clothing with them. "If you please, Sita. I should like to wear my lavender dress this afternoon. Please press and air it out." Helen tugged on the skirt to indicate which gown she meant and, seeing Sita's acknowledgment, hurriedly wrote a note, accepting the lieutenant's invitation. She instructed it to be delivered then hastened down the staircase to meet Captain Rhodes.

Chapter 5

MICHAEL KNEW HER CORRESPONDENCE WAS none of his business, but he could not help but glance at the note Lady Helen had left on the entry hall table. His stomach tightened when he saw Lieutenant Arthur Bancroft's name. It tightened further when he read the flowery phrases. And it turned sour when he thought of Lady Helen's reaction to the note—her smile and enchanting sigh. He sighed himself and pushed away the image of Lady Helen laughing and blushing in her drawing room at something the charmer said. He had no right to his resentful feelings. He'd only met the woman yesterday. Why did she occupy the majority of his thoughts?

At the sound of her slippers on the stairs, he stepped back, waiting next to the door. Lady Helen's face was slightly flushed, which only served to brighten her already bright eyes, which only served to accelerate the pace of Michael's already accelerated heartbeat. Would he ever get used to the sight of her extraordinary blue eyes?

"Thank you for waiting," she said. The butler opened the door, and Helen stepped out into the sunlight. "I am so glad you—"

"My lady," he interrupted, stepping closer. The sun shone brightly, illuminating an ugly purple bruise on her fair skin. The sight drew Michael's heart into his throat. Had the general—no, he could not believe the man to be capable of striking a woman. "Did someone hurt you?" He lifted her arm, looking closer at the bruise. He should not have acted so boldly, touching her in this way, but seeing such an injury on her delicate skin made him grind his teeth. His thoughts immediately moved to how he would punish the person who had harmed her.

Helen gently pulled her arm from his grip. "No, it was an accident. You see, this mark is the result of a tiger attack." She began walking down the pathway.

Michael stepped quickly to catch up with her and studied her face, not sure exactly how to react to her statement. She glanced at him, and her eyes seemed to be teasing, which lessened his anxiety considerably. "A tiger attack?"

"Do not look so worried, Captain. I did not perish, and as it turns out, I was never in any actual danger."

Michael's worry turned to relief and then to curiosity. "And will you tell me the story?" He matched his steps to hers, clasping his hands behind his back.

"Yes, but you mustn't laugh. Not yet anyway. The entire episode is still too recent, and it is a bit embarrassing."

He laid his palm against his chest. "I promise."

"You do not have to promise. I fear it is a pledge that might be difficult to keep once you hear the tale." Lady Helen sighed. "Please keep in mind that I am still new to this place, and it *was* rather late in the evening." She rolled her eyes sheepishly, and Michael already found it difficult to keep his promise. "You no doubt noticed the horrible stuffed tiger in the general's library?"

"It attacked you?" Michael's lips quivered, and he pressed them together.

"I'll have you know, in the candlelight, that horrid decoration can look quite alive, especially if one is not expecting to see it. Well, it can be terrifying."

"And you . . . turned quickly away and bumped your arm?"

She raised her brows, shaking her head from side to side and blowing out a breath. "If only I had managed to act so dignified."

Michael noticed a pink flush creeping over her cheeks.

"Imagine the most humiliating reaction and you will be close."

Helen's expression was a combination of sheer embarrassment and mirth, and Michael struggled to keep a straight face.

"Suffice it to say, there was screaming," Helen said with an even expression that did not hide the laughter in her eyes.

"Screaming?"

"*Dreadful* screaming." She nodded, blew out a breath, and then turned to continue walking. "And falling."

"Falling?"

"Extremely graceless falling."

"It is a relief that you are not hurt."

"I do not think the servants had any idea what to do about a woman going completely to pieces over a stuffed tiger."

A laugh burst from Michael's mouth. He hurried to disguise it as a cough. "My lady, I am sorry you endured such a frightening evening."

"Well, we can certainly be assured that in the case of a real tiger attack, I will be of little use to anyone except for pure comedic relief." Helen turned toward him and rolled her eyes to the heavens dramatically.

He coughed again as he imagined Helen's reaction to the stuffed tiger. She must have been completely terrified, but here she was, a few hours later, making jokes at her own expense.

A smile grew on her face. "Oh, Captain Rhodes, thank you for trying to protect my feelings, but you are going to make yourself ill if you keep your laughter bottled up." Helen laughed, and Michael did not think a Sultan's trained *jetti* strongman could have prevented him from joining her. He could not remember the last time he had felt so completely happy. Certainly not in the past two years.

"Have you seen a tiger, Captain? An actual living tiger, I mean?" Her expression had lost its levity and sparked with interest.

"Yes." He didn't want to tell her how often he'd encountered the fierce cats. How often he'd dispatched a company to protect a village threatened by a tiger that had developed a taste for humans. How often he'd seen men he knew pounced on and killed with just a swipe of claws and a flash of teeth before any of their companions could react. Calcutta itself was formerly a tiger-infested jungle, mostly cleared over time but not entirely free from the threat. It was only a few years earlier that the tiger in the general's library was killed not even a mile away from the city. Michael decided on a story that did not represent the true ferocity of the beasts. "Once, as a child, I was walking along a path near my home when I came upon a tiger walking in the other direction."

Lady Helen's hand pressed at the base of her throat, and she sucked in a gasp. "Oh, my. What happened?"

Michael shrugged. "Luckily, I was too afraid to run or the cat might have chased me out of instinct. The tiger was apparently not hungry, and we simply stared at each other for a moment, and then it turned away and walked back into the jungle."

Helen's eyes were wide. "Your parents must have been terrified."

"I did not tell them. If I had, they would not have allowed me out of their sight alone."

"I would not blame them. Just the idea of their little son . . ." Helen moved her hand to her arm and shivered then raised her eyes to his. All trace of teasing was gone. "Now my reaction last night seems even more ridiculous. Even as a child, you were much braver than I, Captain Rhodes."

They walked in silence for a moment then turned down a path lined by poinsettia trees and onto a small bridge that spanned a brook. Out of habit, he glanced down beneath the bridge to the shade at the water's edge, looking for the telltale yellow-and-black pattern of a cobra. Did Lady Helen know to watch for these things? Did she know to check her shoes for scorpions and her water basins for the deadly blue krait? She seemed so fragile, and he felt a strong impulse to protect her.

They continued to follow the path, which led around a pond toward a white gazebo with a pointed, pagoda-shaped roof nestled among the trees.

"And it is such a horrible decoration, don't you think? I cannot believe anyone would think a dead animal is suitable decor for a library."

It took Michael a moment to bring his thoughts back and realize that Helen was still speaking about the stuffed tiger. "Truly. But I'm sorry to say I've seen worse. A friend of my father's in Bombay had an umbrella stand beside his front door made from an elephant's foot."

Helen wrinkled her nose and winced. "How very barbaric." She looked at Michael and pressed her lips together, seeming to hesitate for a moment. "As we neared Calcutta yesterday, I saw an elephant on the bank of the river. It was painted in bright colors and surrounded by people in a procession. My stepfather told me the man riding the elephant was journeying to the home of his future bride." She stopped speaking and turned her gaze down to the pink-and-white lotus blossoms floating on the water. "I thought the entire display was splendid." She looked up at him shyly as if waiting to see how he would respond to her declaration.

"I completely agree. I have often seen similar sights, and I find I never tire of the pageantry of Indian traditions."

Helen's expression relaxed, and she smiled. Michael felt as though he had passed some sort of test, and he wondered why she had worried about speaking of a wedding procession with him.

"The elephant seemed so happy, as if it knew how beautifully it was adorned and felt honored to perform an important duty. I should love to see a painted elephant again."

"My lady, there are likely very few places on this earth where that wish might be fulfilled. Luckily, India is one."

"And do you think my hope childish, Captain?"

Her eyes squinted the smallest bit, and the look of uncertainty returned. Michael wondered if she had been made to feel foolish in the past and hoped his agreement would reassure her. "Of course not. I hope to see a painted elephant myself. A delight such as that should not be taken for granted."

The *chee-chee-chee* call of a kite bird filled the pause, and Helen looked toward the sound, turning to follow the path of the black-and-white bird with its split tail. As she turned, the sight of her purple bruise made him cringe again, and Michael lightly touched the backs of his fingers to the mark on her arm. "If you like, I am acquainted with a native doctor—a *hakim*. He is skilled with herbs and would prepare a remedy or poultice to ease your pain and help your bruise to heal."

Helen glanced at her arm then lifted her gaze to his. "Thank you, but my mother will know the very thing. She herself is quite an expert in herbal medicine. I fear that two hundred years ago people would have thought her a witch, but so many of our friends have depended on her to help with ailments. In fact, that is how she met Jim. He attended a house party in Southampton shortly after his injury, and she mixed a salve to lessen the scarring and ease his discomfort."

Michael thought the man must have been quite charmed by Lady Patricia to accept her help. He did not seem like the type of man to readily agree to being nurtured or fussed over.

"My mother has little patience for traditional doctors," Helen continued. "Butchers, she calls them. Their use of leeches, blood-letting, tranquilizing, cutting and limb removal—"

Michael felt his stomach rise into his throat and knew his face went pale.

"She prefers natural homeopathic—" Helen looked up at his face and stopped speaking. "But I am sorry; you look unwell. Did I say something to upset you, Captain Rhodes?"

"No. I am not unwell." He swallowed over his dry throat, frustrated with himself for the wave of nausea that had flowed over him.

Helen's gaze moved from his face, and he knew he had not been able to disguise his distress. "But I have talked too much. It is your turn, Captain. I am so very curious, how did you meet your simian companion?" She spoke in a light voice and might have thought she was changing the subject from one that had disconcerted him, but in actuality her question approached the same topic from another direction. He studied her for a moment then turned and continued walking around the pond. "It is a rather long story, and I fear I would not do it justice if I only told a small part."

She glanced toward the gazebo. "Shall we sit, then? And I do not mind a long story in the least. I am quite enjoying the company and the setting, and I have been told I'm a good listener."

When she looked at Michael, her brows were raised and pinched slightly together. He wondered if she was still worried that she had made him uncomfortable. He gave her a reassuring smile, and they moved to the stone gazebo. The structure was whitewashed with lime, and the style of the richly carved columns and arched doorways reminded him of a Hindu temple.

Out of habit, he glanced quickly into the shady spots beneath the bench to ensure no serpents were hiding from the sun, and then he took up a place next to Helen.

She looked at him expectantly, giving a small smile that he took as an invitation to begin.

"In order for you to understand why that flea-bitten vagabond is such a welcome companion, I should give a little background." He smiled affectionately. "Two years ago, the company under my command was marching near Jabalpur to meet up with the rest of our regiment. There were rumors of unrest with the Marathas, who you know we have fought nearly constantly for decades." He glanced at Helen to ensure that she was still interested and, seeing her nod, continued.

"I led a small group ahead to scout the best means of crossing the Narmada River. In that part of the country, the river flows through a rocky canyon. As we rode along the top of a cliff, we stumbled upon a group of enemy soldiers. My men put up a good fight, but we were outnumbered and the enemy had explosive rockets."

Michael swallowed, his mouth dry, as the memories poured back. He hadn't allowed himself to think of that day and, after making his formal report to his colonel, hadn't spoken of it to anyone. The faces of men he'd thought of as brothers again floated into his mind. He clenched his hands into fists on his knees, hoping she could not see them shaking.

"My horse was hit by a rocket and killed. He fell on top of me, crushing my"—he cleared his throat—"my leg." He shook his head, willing away the swell of emotions associated with the memory. "The enemy thought us all dead and left us for our companions to find hours later. I remember the moment the soldiers removed the horse; the pain was so intense it rendered me unconscious. I awoke the next day in a hospital tent and—"

He could not tell her the whole of it. Helen's eyes were wide and full of such sorrow that he felt a stab of guilt for being the cause of any distress to her. How would she look at him if she knew the extent of his injury? Glancing down, he saw that she had placed her hand on one of his fists. How had he possibly failed to notice that? Her soft touch sent a warmth through him that immediately calmed the strain he felt at reliving the dreadful memory. "My lady, I am upsetting you."

"Yes, I am troubled, but it is not for my own feelings, sir. I am so very sorry for the suffering you endured, Captain." She squeezed his fist, and he opened it.

Helen did not remove her hand but nestled it into his. Her fingers were small and delicate.

He continued speaking to keep from focusing on the contact that, even thought they both wore gloves, was making his heart beat erratically. "But now I will skip ahead. As you can see, I survived." He gave her a wry grin. "But I was told my injury was too severe for me to continue in my military career." He glanced at her again. "And in the very same week, I received word that my father had died of a tropical fever. I'm afraid I became quite despondent. That time was the absolute lowest of my life. I could not walk, and I had no family—darkness took hold of my heart. I did not eat or sleep. I could not bear to keep living." He didn't look at her but felt her hand tighten in his again.

"One day the surgeon's aides fashioned a sort of chaise bed outside the hospital, thinking that fresh air and sunshine would improve my frame of mind. And as I sat, filled with despair and pain and anger, a mess of blood and fur climbed onto the bed and collapsed in my lap."

He heard Helen gasp.

"Upon examination, I found him covered with scrapes and deep cuts, surely from a fight with another animal. I called immediately for water and bandages, and even though the hospital staff thought I had lost my mind, I bound his wounds and fed him. Somehow, over the next days, I forgot my own sorrow as I cared for Badmash. I found a renewed desire to continue living because he depended on me. In time he recovered and I recovered, and . . . we carried on. It sounds foolish, but I believe Badmash saved my life." Michael leaned back against the rail of the gazebo, feeling exhausted. He turned his head to the side, wondering how Helen would react to his story. He'd never told it to anyone. Nobody had asked. What must she think of him?

Helen was silent as she studied their joined hands and then lifted her gaze to meet his. "You haven't told the story to many people, have you, sir?"

"You are the first."

She nodded, and a soft smile pulled at her mouth. "Thank you for trusting me with something so personal. I realize it was not easy."

Michael didn't dare to move in case she realized that he still held her hand.

"And I am indebted to Badmash too. I would be sorry never to have met you, Captain Rhodes. I am glad to have a friend here in—"

Her words broke off, and she stood when a servant approached on the path.

Michael rose with her.

The woman bowed as she neared. "Lady Helen, your mother sent for you."

"Thank you, Sita. I shall join her directly."

Sita bowed again and hurried away.

"Captain Rhodes, I am sorry to cut our visit short."

"Come. I will accompany you back to the house." He lifted her hand, placed it in the crook of his elbow, and led her back down the path. "I am sorry as well, but we shall have another opportunity I wager."

"Yes, I do hope so." Helen tipped her head toward him, smiling. Michael felt his heart lighten and his worry over whether he should reveal his personal thoughts dissipate. Time spent with Lady Helen was precious but far too short, and he feared that no matter how often they were in one another's presence, he would always be left wanting more.

Chapter 6

Helen bid farewell to Captain Rhodes, smiling as she made her way to the sitting room to meet her mother. As the youngest child, she had not often been taken into confidence, and she quite liked that the captain had told her his story, trusting her with something he hadn't shared with anyone else. She felt privileged that after such a short time he considered her a dear enough friend to confide in her. Other than her mother, and now Jim, very few people in Helen's life had made her feel valued the way the captain did.

In the sitting room, she found her mother dressed and waiting for her at the small table. "Mamá, are you certain you are well enough to be out of bed?"

She gave a quick nod. "Restorative herbs, a bit of extra sleep, and I am quite the thing. Thank you, dear." Lady Patricia lifted her cheek for a kiss and then motioned for Helen to turn and present her arm for inspection. Helen's neck grew warm at the idea that Jim had told her mother about the events of the night before. Her mother opened a small jar, and the aroma of witch hazel, lavender, and other herbs Helen couldn't identify filled the air.

Most would find the smell unpleasant, but to Helen the scent of her mother's herbs was comforting. The familiarity was bit of home in this faraway place. Lady Patricia gently spread some of the salve on Helen's bruise then nodded and wiped her fingers on a handkerchief.

"Thank you, Mamá." She twisted her arm to see she shiny smear spotted by bits of flora. Helen sat at the table and studied her mother. Lady Patricia did not look sickly in the least—in fact, quite the contrary. Her cheeks were rosy, and her skin glowed. The sight was a relief. "Have you eaten?"

"Yes, Jim sent for a tray before he left this morning."

Helen felt grateful for the level of concern Jim showed her mother. Lady Patricia was extremely practical and not at all given to drama or romantic fancies. She didn't dally when there was something to be done nor balk at unpleasantness. Helen had never known her to be ill; she simply did not have the patience for it. But in spite of her matter-of-fact temperament, Jim worried for her and even pampered her in a way Helen would have never thought her mother would allow.

"Jim told me you had quite an adventure last night." It was not like her mother to mince words, and Helen should have known she would approach the matter head-on.

"Yes. I am dreadfully embarrassed by how I acted. I was just so . . . frightened." Even just thinking about how she had felt when she'd seen the shadows flicker over the fanged beast made her heart beat faster. "Jim must have been very disappointed." She lowered her eyes, humiliated at what he must think. Jim was a soldier, commanding men in battles. How could he not think it ridiculous that a member of his own household would take such a fright from a mere decoration? The idea of disappointing the man she was coming to love as a father made her throat tight.

"He was not disappointed in the least." Lady Patricia touched her finger beneath Helen's chin, lifting her face. "One ailing uncle whose death provided enough money to purchase his army commission was all the family Jim knew. He did not think he would ever be a father and certainly has no experience caring for a young woman. It is good for him." She smiled, and her expression grew soft. "At first impression, Jim seems impatient and bad-tempered, but I believe his disposition is merely an act, a way he's found to protect himself. Can you imagine how difficult it must have been for a man to live nearly fifty years without being loved? Of course, he had the respect of his men and a few close friends." Lady Patricia blinked her eyes, which Helen noticed were shining. "But it is not the same as a family."

"I am glad he found you, Mamá. You love him so much, and he makes you happy." Helen thought about her mother's words. *A way to protect himself.* She wondered how much of her mother's independent nature was brought on by a need to be strong while married to the earl. Her own protection.

"With Jim, I am safe." Lady Patricia said. "Not simply safe from physical harm, but I trust him with my heart and know without a doubt he would never hurt it. I am safe to say anything or be anything with him, and he will not think less of me. That is what love is, my dear. And I did not know it until I met him."

Helen had never heard her mother speak so plainly about things of the heart. The words stirred up a confusing mixture of emotions. Hope and happiness but also sorrow. She knew her mother had not loved her father, but to hear it said so plainly made her shift in her seat, feeling ill at ease with the direction the conversation had taken.

Lady Patricia placed her hand on Helen's. "I hope you'll not settle for less, my dear. I have known both types of marriage. A title and a manor house are nothing compared to truly loving and being loved in return."

Helen nodded, still unsure how to respond. Her mother certainly had changed. In her entire twenty years, Helen had never known her to be so free with her emotions, and it was a bit frightening.

Lady Patricia straightened her lacy cap, clearly uncomfortable that she had shared so much. She turned toward the table beside her, spreading her hand to indicate the pile of calling cards and invitations from the entry hall. "We've had quite a few callers. Many even before our ship arrived and some yesterday while we were not receiving." She lifted a stack of cards and handed them to Helen. "And now to plan our return calls. Shall we begin?"

Helen knew the conversation was over and did not know whether to be grateful or disappointed. This new, expressive side of her mother would require a bit of getting used to. She took the cards and began to look through them, but her mind was on the words her mother had spoken. For the second time that day, she felt pleased that someone had shared something so intimate with her. Perhaps now that they were in India, Helen would not be simply the earl's shy youngest daughter but someone more notable. Perhaps others would treat her as an adult, sharing confidences, asking for her opinion, and taking into account what she had to say. *If* she managed the nerve to actually say anything.

"And you walked with Captain Rhodes this morning."

Helen glanced up as her mother spoke. "Yes. We explored some of the pathways of the garden. The grounds are lovely, a mixture between tended gardens and wild growth. The flowers are beautiful, and you know, the captain is very easy to talk to." She smiled, remembering her pleasant morning. It was a welcome change to the subject.

"He strikes me as very likeable."

Helen nodded. "Extremely so. I am glad to have made his acquaintance. Very likeable indeed."

They worked companionably together for a few moments, chatting as they sorted the cards into piles, indicating whether a visit or a note would suffice as a reply and which required immediate attention.

Helen opened a large envelope, removing the missive inside, then gasped with delight. "There is to be a ball on Saturday in honor of the brigadier-general and his family's arrival." She leaned closer so her mother could read the invitation as well. "Saturday. That is only three days away." Helen could not hold back her smile.

"And it is to be at the Raj Bhavan—the government house. Given by Lord Minto, the Governor-General, and his wife. What an honor."

Helen felt as if a bubble grew inside her chest. She had beautiful new ball gowns, any one of which would be simply perfect. And as a guest of honor, she would undoubtedly dance with nearly every gentleman in attendance. Captain Rhodes would surely ask for a set, and—Helen gasped and pushed aside the cards until she found the one she was looking for. Lieutenant Bancroft. How had she forgotten? Would he dance with her? The thought made the bubble expand, and her cheeks heated.

She held his note toward her mother. "Mamá, Lieutenant Bancroft requested a visit this afternoon, and I have already accepted."

Lady Patricia took the note. "*Loveliest young lady in all of India.*" She glanced at Helen, and a smile pulled at her lips. "Of course he is welcome, dear. Charming gentleman, is he not?"

"Very charming."

"And handsome too." She lifted her eyebrows, and Helen blushed.

"I thought to wear my new lavender gown."

"Then you shall indeed be the loveliest young lady in all of India." Lady Patricia winked.

"Mamá." Helen took the note and continued sorting the cards to prevent her mother from seeing the grin that grew on her face as she imagined dancing with Lieutenant Bancroft.

***

The midday meal, which Helen learned was called *tiffin*, was served at two o'clock in India. Afterward, she just had time to hurry to her bedchamber, change into her pressed lavender gown, and make her way to the drawing room, arriving at fifteen minutes before four. When she stepped inside, she found the room empty save for the punkawalla—a boy of about twelve—who sat in a corner, pulling on the rope that moved the large fan.

Helen nodded to the boy and looked around the room, smoothing her already smooth dress as she tried to determine the best place to sit in order to greet Lieutenant Bancroft when he arrived. If she sat near a window, he might get the impression that she had been watching for his arrival. But she did not want to sit on the sofa, or he might think she expected him to sit beside her. What if he *did* sit beside her? What if he didn't? Her heart was beating so loudly now that she was startled when someone behind her coughed.

Helen's heart jumped as she imagined Lieutenant Bancroft had arrived early and discovered her standing in the middle of the room wringing her hands. But when she turned, she saw a servant holding out a letter.

Thanking him, she took the note and opened it.

Dearest Helen,

I learned a new consignment of clothing arrived from London on our very ship. We simply must see them before the other women in Calcutta claim all of the best dresses. I would love it more than anything if you would join me at Taylor's Emporium tomorrow afternoon. What fun we shall have choosing gowns for Lord Minto's ball! As we are such dear friends, it would be a travesty if we did not plan our ensembles together.

If you are agreeable to the plan, Mother and I will collect you at three.

Yours,
Fanny

Hearing a step behind her, Helen's heartbeat skipped again. She turned and let out a breath as her mother entered the room.

Lady Patricia glanced down to the letter in Helen's hands, obviously believing it to be the cause of the nervousness in her daughter's expression. "Does the lieutenant send his apologies?"

"Oh no. This is simply a note from Fanny." Helen offered the letter to her mother. "She invited me to shop for gowns tomorrow."

Lady Patricia glanced over the note, and Helen did not fail to see her mother's nose wrinkle. Like her husband, she was not overly fond of Fanny. She stepped to the sofa and sat, patting the seat beside her. "And will you accompany her?"

Helen sat next to her mother, relieved that the matter of where to sit had been so easily resolved. "I suppose I shall. I do not need a new gown, but I should like to see more of the city."

"I worry that Fanny only wants to direct what you shall wear to the ball."

That same thought had occurred to Helen, but she did not like to think that Fanny was so small-minded. "Perhaps. Or she simply desires my company." Helen knew she sounded pathetic. Fanny was not the sort of person to do anything without a motive.

"Of course." Lady Patricia slid the note back into the envelope and held it toward her daughter.

Neither had an opportunity to comment on the shopping excursion or Fanny Cavendish further because at that moment the turbaned butler stepped into the room and placed his palms together, thumbs on his forehead, and bowed. "Lieutenant Bancroft and Sergeant Carter," he said then stepped aside to allow the two red-coated men to enter.

Helen's heart flew into her throat.

Lieutenant Bancroft strode toward them looking every bit as dashing as she remembered. "Lady Patricia." He swept up her hand, bowing elegantly.

"How very kind of you to call on us," Helen's mother said.

"A pleasure, my lady." The lieutenant turned his blue-eyed gaze to Helen. "And of course, Lady Helen." He took her hand and inclined his head. "Delighted to see you again."

Her mind had emptied at his touch, and her heart beat so loudly that she wondered if anyone else could hear it. "Lieutenant." She was amazed to have been able to force the word through her dry throat.

A slow smile spread over his face and melted Helen's insides into a puddle. He turned and held a hand toward his companion. "Ladies, if I might introduce my friend Sergeant David Carter."

Sergeant Carter stepped forward and greeted both women.

As Lady Patricia exchanged niceties and offered the gentlemen a seat, Helen took a moment to study Lieutenant Bancroft's friend. She could not help but compare the two men. Sergeant Carter was a shortish man with squinting eyes and red cheeks. His manners were not as graceful as Lieutenant Bancroft's. His hair hung limply as opposed to the thick curls of his companion. His coat did not fit nearly as well.

The men sat in armchairs across from the sofa. "How are you finding Calcutta, my lady?" Lieutenant Bancroft directed his question to Helen.

She let out a breath before answering, hoping to calm her nerves. "I . . . well, I have not seen much of the city, of course. I did walk a bit in the gardens around the house this morning, and they are splendid." She noticed that she was twisting her fingers and forced herself to stop, clasping her hands nicely in her lap as she'd been taught.

Sergeant Carter nodded. "Yes, this is the perfect time of year. In another month the heat will be unbearable. And of course, monsoon season will drive most of us to the hills." He leaned back in the chair, resting his ankle on his knee. "The general will no doubt be removing his family to Simla during the rains?"

Lady Patricia nodded. "That is indeed his plan; although I must say, I do not fancy traveling again so soon now that we have just arrived."

The hamal in her bright orange-and-red sari arrived with a tea tray, and Helen was glad to have something to occupy her hands as she poured the tea.

Leaning forward, Lieutenant Bancroft accepted the offered cup and saucer. His fingers brushed Helen's, sending a wave of heat over her skin. Helen set her own cup on her knees and stared down at it as she tried to calm her rapid heartbeat.

"With the weather so perfect, Lieutenant Bancroft and I have taken a short leave, beginning tomorrow." Sergeant Carter selected a small cake and took a bite.

"And where will you go?" Lady Patricia set her cup and saucer on the small table next to the sofa.

"The jungle, of course." Lieutenant Bancroft elbowed his companion. "Not much else for diversion in this country, eh, Carter?"

Sergeant Carter moved his cup away to prevent a spill when his friend's elbow hit his ribs. "Quite so. One thing India *can* boast is excellent game."

"And what type of animals are you hunting?" Lady Patricia asked.

Lieutenant Bancroft leaned forward. "You would not believe the diversity of game in these jungles. Carter and I are after deer, lions, wolves, leopards, jackals . . . of course, monkeys. We might even bag a tiger."

Helen let out a gasp. "Oh, no, you mustn't shoot any monkeys." The words slipped out before she had a chance to think, and she wished she could suck them back into her mouth, where they belonged.

One side of Lieutenant Bancroft's mouth lifted in a smile, and his brows rose. He shook his head as if looking at a darling child that did not quite understand the ways of adults.

"I . . . excuse me. I did not mean to . . ." Helen could not help herself thinking of Badmash and the way he had befriended Captain Rhodes. The monkey's dark eyes and mischievous manner. "Monkeys just seem . . . harmless . . . and clever."

Sergeant Carter's squinty eyes squinted even further. "Oh, of course this is upsetting to you, my lady. You have obviously seen a monkey now and then in London, wearing a vest and doing tricks with a street performer. I admit, they seem delightful, but when you've spent more time around the dirty beasts in their natural habitat, you'll not think of them as anything but disgusting pests." He sipped his drink, placing the cup back into the saucer.

Heat seared Helen's face. The officers must believe her to be a simpleton, a child who could not bear to hear anything that might upset her delicate feminine sensibilities.

Lieutenant Bancroft placed his cup on the low table. "Hunting monkeys in the jungle is a rare delight. Once the little beasts hear a gunshot, they spread out, chattering and swinging through the trees in a panic. That's the challenge—hittin' the wee devils while they're on the move. We've bagged twenty or thirty at a time, 'aven't we, Carter?"

Helen's stomach turned over as she imagined monkeys falling from the vines onto the jungle floor.

Sergeant Carter cleared his throat. "Delicious cakes, my lady."

Lieutenant Bancroft continued speaking as if he hadn't heard his friend. "Then the real fun begins; the leopards smell fresh blood, and if we're lucky even a tiger will come to—"

Jim entered the room, stopping Lieutenant Bancroft's words, and both men rose to their feet and saluted.

"Bancroft, Carter. Welcome. Please, sit down." Jim crossed the room to sit in the chair next to the sofa.

Helen poured a cup of tea for her stepfather, relieved that the conversation had been interrupted. She did not know how much more of the topic she could stomach.

"Good afternoon, General," Lady Patricia said. "Lieutenant Bancroft and Sergeant Carter were just telling us about the hunting trip they will be taking on their leave tomorrow."

"Aye. Thought I heard something about fresh blood and tigers." Jim nodded as he accepted the cup from Helen. "Hardly a discussion I expected to hear in my drawing room with the ladies of my family."

Helen glanced at the men. Sergeant Carter's mouth pulled slightly in a grimace, looking properly chastised.

But Lieutenant Bancroft did not seem to recognize the subtle reprimand. "Speaking of tigers, sir. You've one of the best specimens in the city right here in your library. Unless General Spencer took it with him. I've admired that big cat every time I've seen it."

"Yes, a very fine trophy," Jim said, darting a glance to Helen. "I'd thought to relocate that particular object. Perhaps it is better suited to my office at the fort."

Helen felt her face heat again, both at the reminder of her ridiculous overreaction the night before and also in appreciation to Jim for wanting to remove the horrid decoration because of the distress it had caused her.

"Surely you do not wish to be rid of it," Lieutenant Bancroft said. "I aim to have one of my own before I leave this sweltering country. Perhaps I shall make it into a rug. I have quite a few trophies myself—a few horned deer heads, a wolf skin, and a beautiful snow leopard."

"Quite a collection, then." Jim brushed the cake crumbs off his fingers. "Did I hear the new theater near Park Street is to be completed in a few weeks? I imagine there will be any number of musical performances. That should interest you, ladies."

Lady Patricia touched her fingertips to her breastbone. "I have certainly missed the theater since we left London. And, of course, Helen is so fond of music."

"A music appreciator, Lady Helen?" Sergeant Carter nodded. "I expect you shall be delighted with the small orchestra Lord Minto has engaged for the ball next week. You know, all of the officers are invited."

"Ah yes, the Governor-General is giving a ball. Another reason to be delighted at your arrival, Lady Helen." Lieutenant Bancroft's white smile and the cocky tilt of his head made Helen's blush return.

She stared again at her cup, heart racing as the lieutenant continued to speak.

"The ball will be a perfect opportunity to peruse the hunting trophies at the Raj Bhavan. Do you know Lord Minto has a mounted elephant head?"

Chapter 7

MICHAEL SHIFTED IN THE LEATHER chair, glancing up at the large bull elephant head that hung on the wall above the mantel in Lord Minto's library. Its ears flared to the sides, its trunk hung straight downward, and curved ivory tusks protruded from under its cheeks. The small glass eyes were a light blue, although Michael had only ever seen a brown or greenish color on the animals. He allowed his gaze to travel around the room. The sight of so many lifeless eyes watching him was unnerving. The Governor-General had an exceptionally large collection of hunting trophies from his time in India. Every animal Michael could imagine—and some he had never seen nor had a name for—prowled, snarled, crouched, coiled, or simply hung, bodiless and silent, on a wall or shelf.

Michael scratched his neck as his eyes lit on a large tiger rug that covered a good portion of the floor. The animal's head was full-size, posed with its mouth open, looking angry and defiant at the fact that the rest of its body was stretched out flat with a table leg resting on its left hip. The sight of the white, pointed teeth brought to mind Lady Helen and the story of her reaction to the stuffed tiger. He could imagine how in the candlelight, alone, this room would make even the bravest man uneasy.

Lady Helen. Michael closed his eyes and allowed his head to rest back against the chair as his thoughts returned to their visit the day before. The young lady was intelligent and compassionate and complicated in the way that made Michael want to understand every minute facet of her. Even something as simple as her smile evoked so many feelings that a day later the mere memory of it was utterly intoxicating and . . . confusing. What was so different about this woman that after only two days he could not stop thinking of her, analyzing the words she'd said, each variation in her expression, and the way she'd held his hand? The skin on his palm grew warm, as if it too remembered her touch.

The sound of voices caught his attention, and he stood at attention as General Stackhouse and Lord Minto entered the room. The general returned his salute, and the earl inclined his head.

"Captain, glad you're here." Lord Minto patted his hand over his white powdered wig held back by a strip of ribbon, which so many men over the age of sixty still considered fashionable. The earl eased into a chair and gestured for Michael and the general to do likewise. "General Stackhouse told me you're aware of our position as far as Shah Ahsan Ali is concerned."

"Yes, my lord." Michael sat straight on the edge of his chair and dipped his head once quickly as he spoke.

"And will you please explain to me how the situation has possibly progressed to this point without my knowledge?" Lord Minto's dark eyes bore into Michael. The contrast with his pale skin and white hair made them appear all the darker.

Michael paused for a moment. Telling the full truth would reflect badly on his former commander, but protecting General Spencer would make Michael look as if he had not done his duty.

General Stackhouse squinted. "We're not here to point fingers or accuse anyone of neglect, Captain. Speak freely."

"Very well, sir." Michael said. He blew out a breath. "A relationship was maintained between Fort William and the Shah's kingdom in Northern Bengal until the time of General Spencer's appointment."

"What kind of relationship?" Lord Minto asked.

"Friendly, diplomatic. The exchange of gifts and official visits. To an Indian ruler, such formalities are extremely important. *Durbars*, they are called. Leaders discussing policy and exchanging compliments. To us, it seems trivial, sir, but to the Shah, it is a display of his power for all his subjects. Unfortunately, General Spencer did not, uh, see the need to continue these customs, and it could not have come at a worse time." Michael resisted the urge to clench his fists and beat them on his knees. This had been a source of tension between him and his commander for years, and he wished the man were sitting here in this very room where he could hear the results of his unwillingness to recognize the significance of what he had called "ostentatious nonsense."

Michael cleared his dry throat before he continued. "The Shah is worried for his health, and his fear that he will not have a male heir and thereby forfeit his lands to the Crown has become all consuming. Another daughter was born just as diplomatic relations ceased. Paranoia as to the Crown's actual intent has led to the Shah's growing army and skirmishes on the borders."

"And do we have reason to fear this threat?" Lord Minto asked.

"Are you asking if we could defeat the Shah's army?" General Stackhouse asked. He raised his shoulders in a shrug. "I believe so. But at what cost? Heavy casualties, certainly. They know the terrain, and it would take an enormous amount of time to gather troops from all over India in order not to deplete our forces at any one position. We would be impeded by the summer rains. Not to mention the cost of launching an invasion—building roads, supplies, weapons. An expensive and unnecessary campaign when the entire situation could be diffused by much simpler means."

"What means?" Lord Minto patted his wig again.

General Stackhouse turned to Michael, raising a hand in an invitation to explain.

"An official visit. A friendly diplomatic call with gifts and an invitation for the Shah to do likewise. We offer our protection, provisions, should they be required. An alliance. The Shah will respond positively if we reopen the path of friendship. Show him we do not intend anything but to be good neighbors—"

"And let that barbarian believe we are afraid of his feeble display on our borders?" Red splotches grew on Lord Minto's neck. "We represent the most powerful kingdom in the world, and you are suggesting we grovel at the foot of a pitiful local prince with gifts and apologies?"

"Of course not." General Stackhouse's expression did not change, but Michael noticed a muscle in his jaw was clenched. "We are suggesting that, as the stronger power, we have no *need* to demonstrate our capability. The Shah is fully aware that these events could be considered acts of aggression, but by not reacting with force, we show that his display is of little matter to us. And as Captain Rhodes said, a simple diplomatic call will diffuse a situation before it grows. "

"I truly believe, my lord, there is nothing to fear. The Shah will treat his guests respectfully. It is a matter of honor to him," Captain Rhodes dared to interject. "And right now we have the perfect excuse. The new general is taking the opportunity to introduce himself, and I hear the Shah's newest wife is soon to have her first child. Strategically, the perfect time to show our friendship."

"*Newest* wife—disgusting . . ." Lord Minto muttered. "I shall certainly not miss the heathen lifestyle when I return to Hertfordshire." He tapped his thumb on his chin and stared across the room.

Michael glanced at General Stackhouse. Lord Minto was leaving? Permanently? What did this mean for the fort? For India? Michael hoped the Governor-General would expound on his statement—or that the general would ask for clarification.

"Well then, who shall we send?" Lord Minto sat up straight, seeming to bring his thoughts back to the present. He directed his dark gaze at Michael. "You, most certainly, Captain Rhodes. You speak the language and understand their customs."

"Yes, my lord."

And, General?"

"Of course." General Stackhouse nodded.

"I wonder if it would be advantageous for your wife and daughter to accompany the party." Lord Minto pursed his lips and tipped his head to the side. "If indeed the Shah's new bride is in a family way, perhaps the presence of ladies would further convince him that our intentions are charitable."

"Perhaps." The tight muscle appeared again in the general's jaw. "But I will not lead my family into any sort of danger."

"But as Captain Rhodes said, there is nothing to fear." Lord Minto flicked his gaze in Michael's direction.

Michael's stomach turned inside out. The Governor-General was throwing the words back in his face, challenging Michael's reasoning. Was Lord Minto trying to turn General Stackhouse against him? And what of Lady Helen? Michael didn't want her anywhere near a hostile foreign army or a power-hungry Indian prince.

"I trust the captain's judgment," General Stackhouse said simply. He turned toward Michael. "Do you believe they will be safe?" A hint of vulnerability wavered in the general's eyes.

At the sight, Michael swallowed hard. He had fully believed his position when he'd thought a group of soldiers would make the journey, but the stakes were suddenly so much higher. He had no reason to think the Shah would hurt a diplomatic group, especially one that included women. It would go against everything his people believed, but to take any kind of risk with Lady Helen and her mother . . . How could he agree to it? And how could the general be willing to trust Michael so readily?

The weight of his own conviction suddenly seemed heavy on his shoulders. He had been so certain until his fear for Lady Helen made him question his own judgment. But did her presence mean any greater danger? In truth, the women's presence lessened any likelihood of an attack. He turned to the general and held his gaze, hoping his expression showed nothing but surety. "I believe they will be safe, sir."

General Stackhouse nodded once then turned to Lord Minto. "And will you accompany us as well, my lord? And perhaps the countess? As you are the most powerful man in India, your presence would go a long way to establishing a measure of trust with the Shah."

"I have no desire to make the journey." Lord Minto rubbed his hands over his face and sagged back into the chair. To Michael, he no longer looked like a shrewd leader but an old man. "I am tired. Let my replacement attempt it next year."

"My lord?" General Stackhouse said.

"I am retiring, General, though I do not wish to make it common knowledge. My sons live in England, and I have yet to see any one of my grandchildren. My wife, bless her, has remained here with me, though I know she misses her family dreadfully. In a few weeks, a replacement will arrive and I will bid you and this dratted sweaty, insect-infested, dust-bowl farewell." He breathed out a sigh, patted his hand over his wig again, then sat up slowly, checking his pocket watch. "I'm sorry to call this meeting to a close, but I promised Anna Maria I would assist her today in planning for the ball. Something about china patterns or dance cards or linens or one of those trifling bothers that is so important to women."

He stood, and the men rose with him.

"Thank you for bringing this matter to my attention and for proposing a solution. I shall leave its execution in your capable hands."

Michael and General Stackhouse saluted as the Governor-General exited the room.

"Sir." Michael turned as soon as Lord Minto's footsteps faded. "I did not mean to put you or your family in this situation. If I had only—"

General Stackhouse held up a hand, stopping his words. "I know you did not, Captain. And while I am not happy about this, what is the alternative? Hoping the Shah doesn't attack? Hoping we can hold off his armies until reinforcements arrive? Hoping he doesn't intend to invade Calcutta? Given the odds, your plan is the safest for Patricia and Helen—diffusing the situation before our city becomes a war zone."

Michael hadn't even thought of the danger Calcutta would be in should the Shah's armies attack. He was not used to worrying about the families left behind and was grateful that the general had the presence of mind to consider that angle. He followed the general through the library toward the front hall. The marble floors of the grand entryway echoed with every step. "I thank you for your trust, sir."

Once they reached the main door, General Stackhouse turned to him. "I do not bestow it often, Captain, but something about you has convinced me it will not be misplaced."

Michael nodded, not sure what type of reply to make to a man he so respected who offered that level of confidence. "I will do all I can to ensure that your family is kept safe, sir."

The butler opened the door, and General Stackhouse glanced toward it and then back at Michael. "I have no doubt you will." He looked as if he would say more but turned instead and accepted his hat and gloves from a servant.

Michael followed suit, and the two men walked through the door and between the large columns supporting the roof. General

Stackhouse didn't seem to notice the stilted way Michael walked down the long flight of steps, and for that, Michael was again grateful to the man.

When they reached the general's carriage, the men separated, Michael walking toward the syce who was leading Ei-Zarka toward him. He took the horse's reins and mounted, then turned to bid the general farewell.

General Stackhouse stopped with one foot on the carriage step. Then, stepping back down, he turned toward Michael. "Captain, I wonder if I might ask a favor?"

"Certainly." Michael rode his horse closer.

"The item you arranged for was delivered just as I was leaving home this afternoon."

"I am glad that it arrived, sir. I hope everything was in order."

"It appeared to be." General Stackhouse squinted up at him and scratched his forehead just above his eye patch. "Helen has gone dress shopping with a friend. Taylor's Emporium, I believe she said. Perhaps you know the place?"

"I know it, sir." Michael's heart thudded into his ribs at the mention of Lady Helen's name, and he hoped his expression remained politely curious instead of betraying the madness that was happening inside his chest.

"Very good." The general clasped his hands behind his back as he looked up at Michael. "I hoped, Captain, if it is not inconvenient . . . Would you fetch Helen back to the house?"

Fetch Lady Helen? Michael wondered if he was suffering from heat stroke, or maybe the fish Naveen had prepared for lunch had spoiled and caused hallucinations. Had he imagined the general's request?

"I shall, of course, need to borrow your horse in order for you to take the carriage."

Michael stared at the general for another long second before his mind processed the realization that he had indeed heard correctly and the man was in earnest. He dismounted and attempted to act as if finding the general's stepdaughter at the dress shop were something he did every day. "Yes, sir. I will fetch Lady Helen right away." Handing the reins to General Stackhouse, Michael stood aside as the man mounted the horse. "His name is Ei-Zarka."

"Thank you, Captain." General Stackhouse saluted, and Michael returned the gesture, wondering at the strange expression that crossed the general's face. It seemed to be nearly a . . . smile.

Michael walked to the carriage as casually as possible under the circumstances and gave the driver instructions before climbing inside. As soon as the door closed behind him, Michael shook his head then leaned it back against the seat just as he'd done in Lord Minto's library. A smile spread over his face at the thought of what an agreeable task he had before him.

Chapter 8

"VERY PRETTY." HELEN FORCED A smile as Fanny held up yet another gown. Nearly two hours had passed since they'd arrived at Taylor's Emporium and began the task of finding Fanny a dress for the Governor-General's ball.

"Oh, no, no! This is all wrong!" Fanny tossed the dress on top of a growing pile, which the shopkeeper, dressed in a green-and-gold sari, was attempting to return to some semblance of order.

Helen looked down at the gowns Fanny had discarded. In her opinion there were quite a few that would do splendidly for the ball—one in particular that she might return for the next day without her companions. While Fanny was not satisfied with any of the dresses for herself, she did not hesitate to offer the very plainest gowns to Helen, pointing out various features and telling her how perfectly she should look in them. Helen wasn't fooled in the least by Fanny's attempts to outshine her at the ball. She did find herself feeling a bit disappointed. She had so wanted to believe Fanny had her best interests in mind when she'd proposed the shopping trip.

Fanny plopped down in to a chair, her lips pressed into a pout. "None of these gowns will do at all."

"There, there, my angel," Mrs. Cavendish soothed as she patted her daughter's shoulder. "We shall find the perfect thing." Fanny's mother was an older, plumper version of her daughter. She cupped Fanny's chin and lifted her face. "This shopkeeper must not understand that the most beautiful young ladies simply require finer gowns than her regular customers."

Helen looked at the shopkeeper, who met her gaze with raised brows. Helen rolled her eyes, and the woman smiled before schooling her face and offering another dress to the Cavendishes. It was rejected every bit as quickly as the others.

"I do not even wish to attend the ball." Fanny crossed her arms and bounced in her seat, much as a three-year-old child might do. Her eyes scrunched shut, and her pout turned into a trembling lip. Tears fell onto her cheeks, and she started to sob.

Her mother sat next to her, pulling her close and dabbing her cheeks with a handkerchief. "Do not worry, my dearest darling. We shall ask your father to employ a dressmaker. You will have a splendid dress, my love—the most splendid in the country, and that is all there is to it."

Fanny's weeping grew louder.

Helen thought it quite ridiculous that the daughter of an attorney for the East India Company should behave as though she were the queen of Sheba. Helen pulled her eyes from the embarrassing spectacle and looked around the emporium. The ceilings of the large warehouse were supported by columns that somewhat separated the room into sections. Dishes, linens, and clothes were all sold under one roof with native shopkeepers hurrying around to tend to mostly British customers.

"Lady Helen," Mrs. Cavendish marched toward her, pulling Fanny by the hand, "I am sorry, but we shall simply not be able to remain in this shoddy place any longer. Perhaps we will have better luck at Hogg Market." She lifted a spencer jacket from a display table, sniffed, and then tossed it on the ground.

"Of course," Helen muttered as the Cavendishes marched past her. She started to follow them but then turned and hurried back to the woman who was returning the gowns to their hanging rods. "I am very sorry." Helen reached toward her, but she pulled her hand back when she remembered what Jim had told her about religious differences and the offense some Hindis took to being touched by an outsider. Helen picked up the discarded jacket, returned it carefully to the table, then pulled the gown she had noticed earlier from under the pile. "This one. If you don't mind, I shall return for it tomorrow."

The woman smiled and bowed her head. "Thank you, Miss-Sahib."

"You keep a lovely shop." Helen gave her a last smile and hurried to join the Cavendishes.

Fanny, it seemed, had managed to stop her weeping once they stepped out of the emporium. "Oh, this filthy bazaar. It is disgusting."

Helen could not possibly have disagreed more. The street was filled with people in colorful costumes, calling out words that Helen didn't recognize as they held up their wares. Others perused, talking and laughing. Large burlap sacks held spices and fruit. Silk fabric hung from clotheslines. One man scampered up an enormous tower of watermelons. She was astonished to see cows walking through the crowd, folds of skin hanging under their necks. People simply moved aside to allow them to pass as if it was no trouble at all. She heard the clanging of bracelets, sounds of music, and syllables of languages that her own mouth would struggle to produce.

Trees with thin, winding trunks grew in clumps along the edges of the street; the branches were filled with noisy crows and other more colorful birds. The scents of spices and unfamiliar food wafted through the air and mixed with the smells of sweet fruit. It was all strange and a bit frightening, but Helen thought it fascinating.

A sound like a low-toned flute caused Helen to look around. The slow, lilting rhythm reminded her of the drone of bagpipes but much more nasal sounding and higher in pitch, with a scale system that was distinctly non-European. The man making the music sat on the dusty road with his legs crossed, blowing through an instrument shaped like a gourd. Helen gasped when she realized that in front of his bare feet a black cobra rose from a basket, swaying back and forth to the rhythm.

Fanny linked arms with Helen and curled her lip in disgust as she gazed around. She blew out a heavy sigh. "I do not know how I shall manage in this dreadful place. The bazaar is utterly filthy."

"It is wonderful," Helen breathed. "The colors and the smells. And did you see the monkeys?" She pointed to a rooftop where a group of monkeys sat chattering together and watching the crowds below. A group of women in beautiful saris embroidered with colorful detail walked past, the bangles on their wrists and ankles jangling with the movement.

"Helen, Mother and I have decided the only way we shall survive in this primitive land is to remember whence we have come." Fanny turned toward Helen, and her voice took on a scolding tone. "We are civilized British women and will not tolerate the ways of these dark-skinned heathens in the least. It would not do at all." She opened her parasol and pulled Helen along as she followed her mother toward the carriage. "You would do well to remember that we are to be an example of all that is refined and elegant. It is a service, really, to these primitive people who simply do not know any better."

"Fanny, do you not think, perhaps, we could appreciate the differences of this culture? Most of the people we know will never travel to India, and how fortunate that we have the opportunity—"

"Opportunity? Hardly," Fanny spat the words. "It is more of a punishment that is to be endured." They reached the end of the bazaar and turned, following the street to where the carriage waited. Mrs. Cavendish climbed inside.

"But—"

A familiar sound stopped Helen's words. Azān. She glanced up and realized the singing was coming from a tall tower with open windows at the top. The tower rose above a large mosque on the other side of the road. The sound was every bit as beautiful as the first time she had heard it. Helen breathed in, closing her eyes for a moment as she listened. When she opened them, she noticed men walking quickly toward the mosque.

Helen released Fanny's arm and made her way closer to the building to where she could see the courtyard filling with people. Men washed their hands and feet in fountains, unrolled rugs, and knelt to pray. Row upon row waited until the voice stopped and the prayer began. As one, they rose and knelt, prostrating themselves and kneeling again, saying the words of their prayer.

The sight touched something inside Helen, and she felt tears pricking her eyes. She pressed her fingers to her lips, feeling a hint of guilt at intruding on something that to these people was so sacred. She took a shaky breath through her constricting throat. The sight made her heart swell. The feeling of devotion was overwhelming and beautiful and—

"Oh, Helen, come away from here. This is hardly a respectable place for a Christian woman." Fanny's harsh voice contrasted loudly with the reverence around them, and she tugged at Helen's arm. "Completely ridiculous."

Helen kept her gaze down, both overcome by her surge of emotions and embarrassed by Fanny's brazen mockery. She brushed away the tears from her cheeks, hoping her bonnet provided enough shade that the other girl hadn't seen them.

Fanny pulled on her arm, nearly dragging her toward the carriage, but stopped abruptly.

"Pardon me, ladies."

The familiar voice sent a wave of relief over Helen, and she raised her eyes. "Captain Rhodes!" She did not think there was a person on the earth she would be happier to see at this moment. "What a surprise to find you here." Helen unwound her arm from Fanny's grasp. "Captain, may I introduce Miss Cavendish. Fanny, this is my dear friend, Captain Rhodes." Helen took a step closer to the captain as he and Fanny made the appropriate greetings.

Captain Rhodes turned to Helen. He squinted slightly, his gaze seeming to search her face, and she wondered if he saw the relief that his presence had brought or if he noticed the aftermath of her tears. "I am afraid it is not as much of a surprise as you would believe, my lady. The general sent me to the emporium to fetch you."

Helen grasped his arm. "Has something happened? Oh, Mamá! Captain, is she ill?"

"No, nothing of the sort." He patted her hand and then, taking hold of it, slid it around his arm to rest in the crook of his elbow. "It is no cause for alarm—quite the opposite in fact. He—a surprise awaits you at the mansion, and General Stackhouse is eager for you to return home."

"A surprise?"

Fanny bumped her shoulder into the captain's arm. "Oh, how very thoughtful of you to come all this way to collect our dear Helen, Captain." She batted her eyes and tipped her head, lifting her too-perfect lips in a too-perfect smile.

Helen felt a surge of heat roll through her stomach. *How dare Fanny flirt with Captain Rhodes!*

"And just at the right time too. I'm afraid dear Helen is starting to develop a tolerance for the barbaric native customs. Why, she was admiring the silly demonstration in the courtyard just now."

Helen's stomach sank. Fanny made her sound like a fool. What would Captain Rhodes think? She looked down at the dusty road beneath her feet and wished herself miles away.

"The heathens," Fanny continued. "Have you ever seen such a boorish display, I ask you?"

"I admit, Miss Cavendish, I have rarely witnessed an exhibition quite like the Mohamedan prayer."

Helen felt her stomach drop further. Tears pressed against the backs of her eyes, but they were not the tears of awe she'd felt before. She was ashamed and humiliated in front of the one person she'd hoped would understand. She didn't know why the captain's opinion had come to matter so much, but the thought of disappointing him was more than she could bear. She moved to pull her hand from his arm, but he held it tightly in place.

"The devotion shown by the faithful worshipers is beyond anything I have seen in my lifetime. It is inspiring to say the least. You have no doubt taken a page from Lady Helen's book and come to appreciate the sincerity of the ritual."

Helen raised her head and blinked. Had she understood correctly?

Captain Rhodes held Helen's gaze as he spoke. "A person with beauty in her heart is able to appreciate beauty in the world around her. Luckily for us both, Lady Helen is precisely that type of person. If you will excuse us, Miss Cavendish. We must be leaving."

Helen barely heard Fanny's stammering words as Captain Rhodes led her to the waiting carriage and held her hand as she climbed inside. He followed, sitting across from her and reaching out to offer her a handkerchief.

Helen took it and dabbed at her eyes. "Thank you, Captain Rhodes. I . . . I did not . . ." Her voice caught, and she looked down at the handkerchief, folding it carefully in her lap.

"My lady, there is no need to thank me." He pulled on her hand until she raised her eyes. "You were moved by the prayer. I saw it in your face. The ability to feel something, to want to understand people whose beliefs differ from yours, should never be taken for granted. It is what makes you special. Do not allow a person so shallow to tell you that your feelings are unimportant."

Helen squeezed his fingers, not trusting herself to speak. But she was coming to find that, with Captain Rhodes, words were not necessary.

Chapter 9

MICHAEL STUDIED THEIR JOINED HANDS. Lady Helen's white lace glove looked so petite and feminine in his large grip. A small pearl button was fastened at her wrist. He had never seen such delicate fingers, and his chest grew warm as he thought of what a privilege it was to sit quietly in a carriage holding this lovely young woman's hand. He wondered if he would ever again have the opportunity.

Lady Helen's face was turned downward. Her bonnet blocked his view of her eyes, but he could see that her lips were pulled tight. She ran her finger slowly over his handkerchief, which lay on her lap. Spots of gray against the white of the fabric showed evidence of her tears, and the warmth in his chest tightened as he thought of the spiteful Miss Cavendish and her attempt to show Lady Helen in the worst possible light. The pouting ninny really had no idea that what she considered to be faults, sure to turn him against Lady Helen, were actually the very things that most appealed to him.

Her interest in the native society was a welcome change from other British women in the colony. Most, like Fanny Cavendish, wanted nothing to do with the world around them. They went about simply pretending it didn't exist, content to live as if they were still in England, not experiencing India. He worried that this attitude of intolerance would cause the gulf between the British and the natives to grow too wide, leaving room for discontent and even rebellion.

That was why Lady Helen and her enthusiasm were such a breath of fresh air. He wanted to show her everything this country had to offer, from exotic animals to hidden temples to colorful festivals. He was certain she would be enthralled by it all.

When he'd arrived at Taylor's Emporium, he'd spotted Lady Helen right away, but Fanny Cavendish's tantrum made approaching the party awkward, and he'd waited for a better opportunity. Michael had seen her apologize to the shopkeeper and hurry after her friend, but before he could follow, he'd encountered Lord Minto and the countess choosing linens, so he stopped to exchange pleasantries. He made his escape a few moments later and searched the bazaar until he'd spotted the young ladies on the road near the mosque. Lady Helen had watched the prayer with a soft expression, and from his vantage point, he'd seen tears in her eyes as she pressed her fingertips to her mouth.

Fanny had jerked her away, and though he was not close enough to hear, he could tell she was berating Lady Helen for her reaction. Seeing Lady Helen's shoulders droop as Fanny marched her toward the carriage had lit a spark of anger inside him. The idea that a spoiled, ignorant person would cause a young lady he cared for to feel ashamed for her goodness was more than he was willing to tolerate, and it was with great restraint that he had kept from telling the blonde-haired half-wit exactly what he thought of her.

Glancing out the small carriage window, Michael could see that they were nearing Chowringhee. "My lady." He spoke in a quiet voice, not wishing to jar her from her thoughts.

Helen raised her face, and her gaze sent a jolt through him. Would it always be so when her eyes met his?

His collar felt tight, and he wondered if his face had reddened. "We are nearing your home."

She pulled her hand from his and clasped it with the other in her lap. "She really is terrible, isn't she?" One corner of her mouth pulled to the side.

He nodded his head once. "Thoroughly."

"I do not know why I care for her opinion at all. She only wished me to go to the emporium in order to ensure that I wore an uglier gown to the Governor-General's ball than she." She turned her gaze out the window. "She knows very well it does not matter what gown each of us wears; she will capture everyone's attention regardless."

"My lady, you are every bit as lovely. In fact, much more so than—"

Helen looked back to him, blinking and shaking her head. "Oh, Captain, I am not asking for a compliment. I did not mean for my words to come out that way."

"Then please tell me why you think Miss Cavendish will be the lady sought after at the ball." Michael had certainly never had so frank a conversation with a young woman and was at a loss as to what he should say.

"Because she is *Fanny*. Beautiful, a hopeless flirt. She always knows precisely what to say and how to tilt her head and bat her eyes. It would not matter if she were to wear a flour sack to the ball. Gentlemen would still want to be near her." She shrugged a shoulder and smiled shyly. "I, on the other hand, can never think of anything intelligent to say, and I turn into a complete featherhead when I speak to people."

"You are not a featherhead right now." It took every bit of his self-control to not allow his amusement to show on his face. Her brows were pulled together, her eyes turned downward.

"You are right." She tipped her head, and her eyes grew wide as if the realization surprised her. "But, you know, you are very pleasant to talk to. You set me at ease, Captain."

"I am glad of it."

"And will you attend Lord Minto's ball, sir?"

Michael hesitated. The idea of going to the Governor-General's ball turned his stomach hard. He studied her face. Her eyes were wide with a hopefulness that he could never in a thousand years turn to disappointment. "I will if you wish me to."

"You hardly sound eager, Captain. Do you not enjoy a ball?"

The thought of limping into a room full of dancing people, of gentlemen dancing with Lady Helen when he himself— "No, not particularly."

She raised a brow. "I take it you cannot endure the company of happy people or fine music. Or perhaps it is the abundance of delicious food that drives you away."

"I just . . . do not care for a ball."

Lady Helen drew her head back, and a smile grew on her face. "I know what it is! All of the beautiful ladies throwing themselves at your feet. It must be tiresome."

Michael allowed himself a smile at her lighthearted banter. "What makes you think ladies throw themselves at my feet?"

She shrugged again, and he noticed how bright her eyes had become. Did she have any idea how captivating they were? His heart stuttered when he realized he was the cause of her good cheer, that somehow he'd managed to raise her spirits.

"Because you are a handsome captain with broad shoulders and thick hair. You stand straight, and you are extremely kind." Her eyes twinkled. "And let us not forget, you have a monkey for a pet. Such a combination is more than any woman can resist."

"Lady Helen, are you teasing me? I do not think I have ever been teased in my life."

"Then you obviously have no brothers and sisters, Captain."

The carriage halted in front of the general's mansion.

"It is true; I do not."

"Sibling teasing is not always kind." Her eyes dimmed slightly, and she looked away for an instant then returned her gaze to his. She folded the handkerchief and held it toward him. "Thank you."

He took it, pushing it into his jacket pocket. The driver opened the door, and Michael leaned forward to climb down before her.

She placed her hand on his arm, stopping him. "I was teasing, but I assure you I was not being unkind. I did mean what I said, Captain. You are all those things, and I am fortunate indeed that you are my friend." Her eyes had regained their light.

Michael's collar had again grown too narrow. "As am I." He stepped out of the carriage and turned, taking her hand to assist her in alighting.

"And I do hope you will attend the ball." Her eyes met his again. Were they not the most perfect blue?

"I would not miss it, my lady."

Lady Helen kept hold on his hand, pulling him forward. "Come, then, Captain. Shall we see what surprise awaits?"

He followed her up the stairs to the main doors, trying not to wince with every other step. Stairs were particularly difficult for his leg, and when he was alone, he took them much slower, usually one at a time.

She hurried through the doorway, releasing his hand as she looked around the entry hall. "Mamá? Jim?"

"I believe you will find them in the drawing room." Michael found that the excitement of her impending surprise made him feel like a child on Christmas morning. He clasped his hands behind his back and nodded toward the doorway behind her.

She glanced at him, pulling her brows together as she removed her bonnet and gloves and handed them to a waiting servant. She waited for Michael to do the same, and then she moved toward the drawing room.

Michael stepped quickly behind her. He did not want to miss her expression when she saw the—

Lady Helen's gaze landed on the pianoforte, and she gasped. She clasped her hands beneath her chin. "I cannot believe it," she breathed. "I cannot *believe* it," she said in a louder voice. She turned, only now noticing the general and Lady Patricia inside the doorway beside Michael. "Mamá! Jim! What a surprise! Oh, thank you. *Thank you.*" She rushed forward to embrace her mother and then the general.

Jim smiled broadly. "The thanks goes to Captain Rhodes for locating the instrument in the Barrackapore station and arranging to have it delivered."

Lady Helen turned toward Michael. "Oh, thank you, Captain!" She clasped his shoulders and then stopped, seeming to remember herself before she embraced him and stepped back. She patted his arms and dipped in a curtsey.

The clumsy motion was so decidedly charming that he could not help but grin.

"I am just so delighted, I—" She clapped her hands and turned, spreading her arm to include her parents in the circle. "Shall I play for you?"

"I should hope so," General Stackhouse said. "Blasted waste of blunt otherwise."

Lady Patricia swatted him but smiled, overlooking his language. "We should love it, my dear."

Lady Helen hurried to the pianoforte. She sat on the bench and placed her fingers on the keys, breathing in deeply and then out slowly. She stilled for a moment and then began to play.

The music was beautiful, but it was the musician that held Michael spellbound.

As her fingers moved over the keys, Lady Helen swayed with the tune. Her eyes closed during soft notes, her brows lifted when the music slowed. Her wrists rose gracefully and lowered into place. He never would have imagined a piece of music could be so enthralling.

The song ended; Lady Helen held the final chord then slowly lifted her hands from the keys.

Michael blinked; a part of his mind realized the general had spoken. He shook his head slightly, turning toward his commanding officer. "Excuse me, sir?"

The general's brow ticked, and he tipped his head back slightly. "Perhaps, Captain, you would show Helen the music pages?" He flicked his gaze toward a box on the table near the instrument.

"Of course, sir." Michael thought General Stackhouse regarded him a little too closely, and he made a note to keep his feelings for Lady Helen from showing. He had been staring at her like a lovestruck moon calf, and the general had surely seen it. He did not imagine the shrewd man missed much, and he was undoubtedly even more aware of events taking place in his own household.

Crossing to the table, Michael lifted the box and offered it to Lady Helen. She scooted back on the bench to rest it on her legs then opened the lid. "Oh, this is splendid." She lifted pages out, looking each one over. Her smile grew. "Vivaldi, Bach, Mozart—all of my favorites." She looked up at Michael and then moved to one edge of the bench, patting the space beside her.

Michael sat, sliding his knees beneath the instrument.

Helen pulled out another page of music and sighed. "Truly, Captain, you do not know how very much this means to me. I am lucky to be so loved."

Michael's heart and stomach crashed together. Had he been so obvious? *What must she think?* He felt the blood drain from his face, and he searched his mind for something to say.

She placed the music onto the rack and glanced to where her mother and the general had taken a seat on a chaise across the room. "I am so happy that my mother found Jim."

His shoulders relaxed, and he blew out the breath he didn't realize he was holding. *Of course. Her* parents. *She meant she was loved by her parents.* He needed to rein in his irrational thoughts.

"My own father was much less . . . involved." Her fingers played absently on the keys while she spoke. "He was very busy with parliament and the estate, you know." Helen glanced at him, and the music stopped. "Are you well, Captain? You look a bit pale."

He coughed through his dry throat. "Very well, thank you."

"I am glad." She smiled and continued playing a melody as her gaze moved to her parents and then down to her hands.

"If you will forgive my ignorance, my lady—I am not an expert in the least—but it does not sound as though you are playing Beethoven's 'Moonlight Sonata.'" He motioned to the music she had placed on the rack. "Although I am sure you know the music better than I."

She blushed and looked down at her fingers. "I am going to tell you a secret, Captain, because you shared something very personal with me. And because I know you will not laugh at me even when I'm ridiculous."

"I never would."

Helen nodded and glanced across the room before lowering her voice. "This is Jim's song."

"Jim's . . . ?"

She lifted her eyes to his and lowered them again. "I told you it is ridiculous, but ever since I was a child, I have thought everybody has a song. I hear it sometimes in my head when I am with a person." She continued to play the melody, and Michael heard a marching beat beneath low, warm tones. The melody was not lighthearted but still had a feeling of contentment to it.

"It is . . . nice."

"I sound foolish, don't I?"

"Not at all."

"Well, I should tell you this was not always Jim's song."

"No?"

She shook her head, and the song changed. The melody retained its original tune, but the chords were minor—discordant and much harsher sounding. "I was afraid of Jim when I met him." Lady Helen's voice was low. She continued to play, and the song evolved into the pleasant one she had started with. "Jim's song changed."

"And what brought about the change? Was it the person that transformed or your feelings toward him?" Michael asked.

She stopped playing and looked at him for a moment with her eyes squinted. "I believe both." She placed her hands back on the keys and began a staccato rhythm with precise notes and scales. "This was my mother's song." Helen said. She continued to play the clippy tune, and Michael wondered at the lack of warmth in the song. He did not know Lady Patricia at all. Was she a compassionate mother? A moment later, the tune changed, or rather the melody stayed the same, but it slowed, deepening into something much softer.

"Mamá's song changed when she met Jim."

Michael watched her, fascinated. With her music, Lady Helen had revealed so much about herself. "And the rest of your family. Do they have songs?"

She glanced at him from the side of her eye and changed the tune again. The song was loud and the melody fast; low notes rumbled beneath a steady beat. "My father." A higher, shrill-sounding song took its place with harsh notes and a swift rhythm. "My sisters." The song changed to a low, slow tune with a rough sound—strong notes against an agitated drumming. "My brother," she nearly whispered.

Michael didn't have to be told that her childhood hadn't been pleasant. Through her simple songs and the things she had mentioned before, he realized that being the youngest child had been difficult for Lady Helen. She had been overlooked and dominated by aggressive siblings and unhappy parents. It was no wonder she struggled to find the words to say in front of people. She had likely been chastised and put down so often that she'd not had the confidence. He'd seen the same thing when she was with Fanny Cavendish today. If only Lady Helen could see what he saw when he looked at her: her kindness when she spoke to the shopkeeper, her excitement about the painted elephant, her tears at the mosque. She was a compassionate, fascinating person but did not believe in herself. His throat constricted as he watched her, realizing that the instrument was a means for an unheard child to express what was in her heart.

"And what is *your* song, my lady?"

She stopped playing but did not look up from the keys. "I do not know, Captain. I think it is the reason I wished to come to India. To find my song." She darted a glance at him. "How silly does that sound?"

He longed to bolster her plunging confidence, to tell her he understood everything, that he knew what her heart was saying, that she was important and perfect and, that with him, her opinion would always matter. He ached to pull her into his arms, but instead he brushed his fingers on her wrist. "Do not believe this search is any other but the most important thing you will ever do."

She looked up at him, her gaze seeking assurance, and he hoped above anything that she saw it in his eyes.

The sound of a throat clearing pulled him to his feet.

"And remember, you must always keep the music sheets inside this box." Michael's words came out in a stammer. "Tin will keep white ants from eating the paper." He turned and found that Jim and Lady Patricia had moved closer without his notice. Michael could feel his heartbeat in his temples, and he knew his face must be red as a beet.

The general studied him with an eye that seemed to see through him.

Michael swallowed.

Lady Patricia touched her fingertips to the pianoforte. "Beautiful, my dear. I have missed your playing these months. It makes this place seem like home, does it not, Jim?" She smiled at her daughter and her husband and then turned her gaze to Michael. "It is nearly time for supper. Captain Rhodes, will you join us?"

"Thank you, my lady, but I'm afraid I must decline. I have some duties to attend to this evening."

"Well, then, we will see you at the ball on Saturday, Captain." Lady Patricia offered her hand.

"Yes." Michael took her fingers, bowing stiffly. "If you will excuse me. I . . . uh . . . should return to the fort."

"Good evening, Captain." Helen stood; her eyes squinted, and her head tipped slightly.

"Yes. Good evening, my lady. General." He bowed and saluted and hurried from the room before he could make a bigger fool of himself.

A syce brought his horse as he left the house, and Michael turned Ei-Zarka toward the strand, hoping a long ride would clear his head.

He needed to get ahold of his emotions before he allowed them to get away from him. Lady Helen considered him a friend—a *dear* friend—and he needed to accept that was all he would ever be. Allowing himself to think of her as any other than his commander's daughter or a delightful acquaintance would be a disservice to both of them.

But he could not keep his mind from pondering the things she had said. *A handsome captain with broad shoulders and thick hair.* A smile tugged at his lips, but he quickly stopped it. She was obviously teasing or, more likely, being polite.

He thought of her reaction to Lieutenant Bancroft's letter, and the image helped quell his fantasy of anything between himself and the young lady.

Lady Helen was young and clever and beautiful, while he was a crippled man with no future. He sighed, bouncing a fist on his thigh. Perhaps it was time to apply for a transfer. He'd been in Calcutta for a few months shy of two years, and there must be another station where his particular linguistic skills and local knowledge would be useful. But as soon as he had the thought, the idea of leaving Lady Helen behind shot a jolt of pain through his heart. Would it hurt worse to never see her again or to see her every day and know she could not be his?

Chapter 10

THE EVENING OF THE BALL, Helen sat before her changing table, watching in the mirror as Sita arranged her hair, weaving a string of pearls artfully through the light brown curls. Not for the first time, Helen wished her hair were not such an uninteresting color.

"Thank you, Sita," Helen stood once her ayah was finished and brushed her hands down over her skirts. She was truly thrilled with this gown her mother had discovered in a dress shop before their voyage. The satin fabric was dyed a beautiful shade of peach. The skirt was pulled up in places, nearly to her knee, revealing a lace trim beneath. Each gathered point was adorned with silk roses, and more sat at her waist and neckline, dangling curling ribbons beneath them.

She pulled on her gloves and hurried down the stairs, where she found Jim and her mother waiting in the entry.

"Oh, my dear, you look beautiful." Her mother gave a satisfied nod and held out her arm for Helen to join them. "Isn't Helen's dress lovely, Jim?"

"Yes, a fine dress." Jim looked uncomfortable, and she knew he was searching for the right words to say. "Very good, uh, flowers and . . ." He cleared his throat. "Well done."

Helen smiled at his attempt. "Thank you."

Lady Patricia scratched a spot on the back of her shoulder, her face squeezing in a wince.

"Are you well, Mamá?"

"Yes, I think it is just an insect bite. Only a bit of an itch. Shall we be off, then?"

Jim offered an arm to each lady and led them outside to the waiting carriage.

As they drove through the city, Helen's confidence waned. She had no idea what to expect at a ball in India. Was she dressed properly? What if the dances were different than those in England? She did not want to look like a fool making the wrong movements. And she knew very few people. What was the Calcutta society like? What did one talk about with the other members of the Raj? She clenched her hands in her lap and watched the city of Calcutta through the window.

Jim motioned toward the other side of the carriage. "We are passing Eden Gardens."

Lady Patricia leaned forward on the bench, looking past him out the window. "Oh, how lovely! We should take a walk through the paths some evening."

Helen studied the beautiful gardens and continued to watch as the carriage passed through a large, wide, grassy plain.

"On the other side of the garden is Hogg Market, and here in front of the fort is where the troops drill," Jim said. "In the morning, you'd see cavalry lines and marching regiments."

Helen followed Jim's pointed finger to a flat expanse of ground. She recognized barracks and spotted dark-skinned Sepoys with exposed legs and red regimental jackets as well as British soldiers moving between the buildings.

"The park here—the *maidan*—used to be a tiger-infested jungle separating Chowringhee from the river until His Majesty's forces needed a fort," Jim continued. "And on the other side of the park, you can see Nabob mansions. The East India Company has made men rich as kings with the spice trade."

Helen twisted to look out the other window at the large houses lining the far side of the maidan. She appreciated Jim's efforts to distract her from her nervousness. He seemed able to read her moods better than even her mother.

The carriage passed between a triumphal arch guarded on each side by soldiers. When Helen looked up, she saw a large stone lion on the top. She thought the real animal wouldn't be happy with the many birds who had decided to make the arch their roost, building nests and covering the monument with grass and sticks and other messes birds bring with them.

Carriages, horses, and servants crowded the wide tree-lined road in front of the Raj Bhavan. Jim held her hand as she stepped out of the carriage, and Helen raised her eyes to the enormous building where the Governor-General lived and entertained. The building, she knew, had been built by the Marquess of Wellesley when he'd arrived in India and found his living conditions unsuitable.

Situated on spacious grounds, the yellow-painted building was shaped like a U, giving the area in front of the main steps the feel of a vast courtyard. The large stairs led to an impressive columned entrance that had a decidedly classical feel. The Raj Bhavan stood out as the largest and most commanding structure in the city. The style was definitely British, not Indian, and Helen believed that was the point. It left no question as to who was in charge.

She followed Jim and her mother up the stairs, glancing at the people making their way inside. She saw many red-coated soldiers; other men in tails and waistcoats mingled among them. The lack of women surprised her.

They walked through a wide entry hall and into a grand ballroom with high ceilings and mirrored walls. A small orchestra played at one end, and vases filled with exotic flowers were arranged on tables, giving a heavy perfumed scent to the room.

A tall man in a white powdered wig and a matronly woman in a plum-colored gown greeted them near the doorway. "Welcome, General Stackhouse," the man said.

Jim inclined his head. "Ladies, this is our host, Lord Minto."

Lord Minto bowed his head and introduced the countess, who offered her hand to Jim and the ladies.

Jim continued the introductions. "My wife, Lady Patricia Stackhouse, and her daughter, Lady Helen Poulter."

"A pleasure." After Lord Minto greeted them, he patted his wig.

Helen wondered if his head itched in the heat of the crowded room or if the wig had slipped when he bowed his head.

"What a lovely ballroom," Lady Patricia said. "And it was so very gracious of you to invite us tonight."

"Of course. It is not every day that two titled ladies arrive from Home." Lady Minto lifted her hand in the direction of a group of women. "I shall love to introduce you to our small circle of friends here in Calcutta." She nodded her head at Helen. "And if you would like to accompany us, Lady Helen, there are plenty of people you simply must meet."

As she followed the women, Helen's eyes scanned the crowd in the ballroom. Even when she'd attended the first assembly of her season last year, she'd been able to find others of her acquaintance or at least see familiar faces.

Though she did not recognize any of the people, she did recognize their expressions of interest as they watched her and Lady Patricia. Helen and her mother were new to this society, and she felt that everything about them was being assessed—from their hairstyles to their gowns to the way they walked.

From across the room, Lieutenant Bancroft caught her eye, and she stopped as he approached. "Oh, Lady Helen, how exceptionally lovely you are tonight." He swept his arm to the side as he offered a deep bow then took her hand.

Lieutenant Bancroft was so very handsome. Helen's palm sweated beneath her glove, and she forced herself not to drop her gaze from his. "Thank you." She tried to think of something to say that would not sound ridiculous.

He brushed a curl from his forehead with a flick of his writs. "I do hope your hand has not already been taken for the first dance. I'd hoped to find you as soon as you arrived."

Helen managed a smile. "It is not taken, sir."

He grinned, showing his deep dimple and setting Helen's heart beating faster. "Good, good. I would consider myself the luckiest man in the room to have the pleasure of claiming it."

"Thank you. I should love to dance with you, Lieutenant." Helen was spared from having to come up with anything further when she heard her name followed by a familiar-sounding giggle. She closed her eyes and let out a breath, arranging her face into a smile.

Fanny joined them, wearing a green gown covered with layers of lace. "Helen, is this not a fine party?"

"Very fine. Fanny," Helen said, "will you will permit me to introduce you to my friend?"

Fanny turned to look at the lieutenant, and her eyes widened as if she had not noticed him. "Oh, by all means."

Helen wasn't fooled by Fanny's surprised expression. Meeting the handsome lieutenant was undoubtedly the precise reason she had approached in the first place.

"Lieutenant Bancroft." Helen nodded toward him. "Fanny Cavendish. Miss Cavendish and I arrived on the same ship from England."

The lieutenant leaned forward in a bow. "A pleasure, Miss Cavendish."

Fanny turned her charm in his direction, batting her eyes and pulling her lips into a perfectly executed moue. "Lovely to meet you, Lieutenant."

"Lieutenant Bancroft enjoys hunting," Helen said, nearly rolling her eyes at how daft the sentence sounded. Why could she not carry on a simple conversation?

Fanny placed her palm to her chest. "How exciting, Lieutenant. Will you tell me about it?"

Helen didn't want to hear any more about the lieutenant prowling around the jungle shooting at things. She glanced toward where her mother stood chatting with a group of women. "Pardon me," Helen said. "I must join my mother."

She walked away, certain Fanny's flirting would keep the lieutenant occupied and that he would love an enthusiastic audience for his stories. Once she reached her mother's side, introductions were made, and Helen's mind swirled as she tried to remember all of the new names.

Her mother scratched her shoulder again, and when someone asked, Lady Patricia told about the insect bite that was bothering her. The women all had stories to tell and remedies to share. They explained to Lady Patricia that it was common practice for ladies to tie pillowcases around their ankles on warm nights like this one to prevent insect bites on their legs.

"And you must remember to tell a servant to put your bedposts in saucers of water to prevent creeping things from climbing onto you from the floor while you sleep," a woman said. "They can crawl under the mosquito netting."

While they talked, Helen stood quietly listening. She was reminded again how much she still needed to learn about India. The idea of insects crawling on her while she slept made her skin tickle, and she shivered. She glanced around the room. Her heart skipped, and a smile lit her face when she saw Captain Rhodes. The sight of him was a relief, and she felt her earlier worries dissipate.

She waved, and he approached, greeting her with a bow.

"I am so glad that you decided to come after all, Captain."

"I told you I would be here."

His manners seemed stiff, and she wondered if something was wrong. The last time she'd seen him, he had left abruptly. A pit started to grow in Helen's stomach. Had she said something to offend him? Was the captain irritated with her silly confession about assigning songs to people? Perhaps she was reading too much into his mannerisms and he was simply tired.

Captain Rhodes glanced above her head and pulled on her elbow, leading her to a pillar a few steps away from the wall.

Helen looked back and saw moths and mosquitos and other insects swarming around the candle sconces she'd been standing beneath.

"And is the ball as terrible as you anticipated?" She hoped her lighthearted question would produce his smile. For some reason it seemed extremely important to ensure that the captain felt contented.

"It is not terrible since I have the privilege of seeing you. You look very beautiful, Lady Helen."

Helen smiled. "Thank you, Captain." She knew he was not one to toss out insincere compliments, and knowing that he spoke genuinely warmed her insides like a drink of hot tea.

The music changed, indicating that the dancing would begin.

Helen looked up at him when she recognized the song. "I love a cotillion, don't you?"

Captain Rhodes clasped his hands behind his back and nodded. "Very nice." He did not look at her but kept his gaze on the partners that had begun to fill the dance floor.

Helen looked away. He was obviously unhappy with her. Perhaps he thought she was hinting that he should ask her to dance. Heat flooded her face. What must he think?

Lieutenant Bancroft approached and took her hand. "Excuse us, Captain, while I dance with this exquisite young lady."

Captain Rhodes nodded his head and made a grunting sound that Lieutenant Bancroft must have taken for an acknowledgment.

Helen glanced back as Lieutenant Bancroft led her away. Captain Rhodes met her gaze, but she could not decipher his expression. He did not look pleased in the least, and Helen felt miserable. Why did she always say the wrong thing? Now even the man she considered a dear friend didn't want to talk to her.

The lieutenant faced her as the dance began, and Helen knew she should think of some conversation. She had already disappointed one man tonight. "How was your hunting excursion, Lieutenant?"

She had found just the topic to keep from having to speak further. Lieutenant Bancroft described his journey, the animals they had found, and how exciting the hunt had been. "My only regret is that we did not bag a tiger," he said.

"I am sorry, sir. I know you hoped to find one."

"There is always next time, and if I *should* find one, the striped beast will not know what hit it."

Helen nodded, not knowing exactly how to reply, but it didn't deter him at all. He continued to describe more of the animals he had killed and how exciting his leave of absence had been.

She glanced to where she had left Captain Rhodes. He met her eye again but did not smile. His mouth was tight and his eyes hard. Helen drew her gaze away, blinking at the tears that threatened. Of all people, she never expected the captain's displeasure to be directed at her. Why had she insisted he come tonight? And why had she babbled on about silly topics that were undoubtedly of little interest to a man of his position? She always said the most ridiculous things.

When the dance ended, Sergeant Carter approached and asked for her hand. Then Ensign Porter and Sergeant Jacks from the ship. The night progressed, and Helen was introduced to more gentlemen. Some were officers, and others employees of the East India Company.

She looked again to the pillar where the captain had stood, but he was gone, and though she was dressed in a beautiful gown and receiving more attention from handsome gentlemen than she had at any occasion in her life, a gloom settled over her heart. She had to force herself to stop thinking of Captain Rhodes and how unhappy he'd been. She turned her attention back to her partner, a son of a nabob, who wore a brightly colored waistcoat with peacock feathers embroidered on it. She smiled and nodded and tried to focus on the words he was saying.

Helen hardly had time to catch her breath between sets, and before she knew it, the dinner dance was announced. Lieutenant Bancroft hurried to claim her hand, and after the quadrille ended, he escorted her to the dining room.

She scanned the crowd for Captain Rhodes but was beginning to suspect that he had not just abandoned his position by the pillar but had left the ball altogether.

Though she tried to keep a pleasant face, her melancholy grew. The ball no longer seemed enchanting and beautiful. She noticed the moths flitting near the candles and the sheen of sweat on the faces around her. The perfume coming from the flower arrangements on the dining room tables was nearly overpowering. The punkah on the ceiling swayed but did not seem to be stirring the air enough to prevent the room from feeling oppressively hot and stuffy.

Lieutenant Bancroft led her to the Governor-General's table. Jim stood on the other side of the table, speaking to Lord Minto as the men waited for their wives.

Helen found her place, and Lieutenant Bancroft held her chair and then sat next to her saying something about perhaps visiting the room where Lord Minto kept his collection of hunting trophies.

She nodded as he spoke, but she didn't give the lieutenant her full attention. Her mother had arrived at the table with Lady Minto, and Helen noticed Lady Patricia's face was flushed. Jim stepped toward her, obviously concerned as well. He touched her arm, and his eyes grew wide. He pulled his glove off and touched it again and then placed his fingers on her forehead. Although Helen could not hear his words, she saw alarm on his face.

Helen stood and made her way around the table.

Lady Patricia began to sway, and Helen broke into a run. She pushed past the people blocking her way and reached her mother just as Lady Patricia crumpled into Jim's arms.

Chapter 11

Michael set his bicorn hat on the table in his bedchamber and worked at the row of gold buttons, removing his jacket and then the vest beneath it, laying them over the open door of his wardrobe. He sank into a chair, letting out a groan as he removed his boots. Then, loosening the strap just beneath his knee, he eased off the wooden leg, rubbing the painful, scarred skin where his own leg ended.

Basu Ram entered the room, setting a candle on the table, and then picked up the discarded clothing. Brushing off the red jacket, he hung it in the wardrobe. "Rhodes-Sahib, you should not spend so much time on your feet." He shook his head in disapproval.

"My *foot*," Michael said, surprised by the bitterness in his voice. He kicked the wooden limb across the floor, sending Badmash screeching from the room. Anger and frustration boiled up. The ball had been worse than he'd imagined. *Utterly miserable.* If only he hadn't promised to attend. He scrubbed his hands over his face, furrowing his fingers into his hair as he rested his elbows on his knees.

He thought of Lady Helen in her ball gown. She'd been beautiful. No, *beautiful* did not begin to describe how she'd looked. *Radiant. Exquisite. Perfect.* No term came close to a description. Though she was not tall, she stood straight and walked with a grace other woman should envy. Her honey-colored curls had framed her face and lay against her neck, and her bright eyes had shone with nervous excitement as she entered the ballroom. The sight had made his knees weak.

When she'd made small talk with Lieutenant Bancroft, Michael remembered her reaction to the man's note a few days earlier. He clenched his teeth. She had blushed and lowered her eyes when the lieutenant spoke, and smiled shyly as he held her hand to walk onto the floor. Just the memory of Lady Helen dancing with him felt like a blow to the gut.

Michael had been able to do no more than watch, wishing above anything that it was *his* hand she held, that *he* was on the receiving end of her smiles. A wave of self-loathing and jealousy washed over him, but it soon simmered down to regret. He adored Lady Helen and knew he had hurt her feelings by acting curt to her this evening. But it was for the best. She deserved a man like Lieutenant Bancroft. A *complete* man who could dance with her and had the hope of rising in his career instead of a one-legged cripple who only remained in the army because of his commander's pity. The thought of applying for a transfer came into his mind again, and he pushed out his breath in a gust.

Basu Ram set the boots next to the bedroom door to blacken and polish. He picked up the wooden leg, carefully leaning it against the wardrobe. "Have you need of anything further, sahib? Are you hungry?"

Michael did not like his servant's scrutinizing gaze. Basu Ram had known him since he was a boy, and in spite of the casual words, his narrowed eyes and the twitch of his curled mustache indicated that he could tell that Michael was troubled.

"A drink," Michael said. "Rum, if you please." *Though I'd much prefer something stronger.*

"Yes, sahib."

He rubbed the rough spot below his knee where the strap dug into his skin. Basu Ram was right. He should have rested his leg more today. He would be feeling the stiffness in his muscles tomorrow morning when he supervised the soldiers' drills.

The man returned with a bottle and a glass, setting them on the table. Even though Basu Ram didn't say a word, Michael sensed his worry.

Badmash followed behind, climbing up to sit on the arm of the chair. Michael poured the dark liquid into the glass and scratched behind the monkey's ears as the captain leaned his head back to take a drink.

A pounding on the door jarred him from his contemplations.

He and Badmash shared a glance before the animal jumped down and scampered out of the room to see what the commotion was all about.

He heard the door open.

"I am looking for Captain Rhodes. Is this his home? Is he here?"

The voice was Lady Helen's, and she sounded frantic. Michael jumped up and hopped to the doorway of his bedroom.

Basu Ram pulled the main door open wide, bowing and sweeping his hand in an invitation for her to enter.

She stood with a servant on the threshold of his bungalow. Something was wrong. In the light of the servant's lantern, he saw that most of her hair had fallen from the pins and hung around her shoulders. Her eyes were red and panicked.

"Lady Helen, what's happened?"

"Captain! Oh, thank goodness." She hurried toward him.

He wobbled and steadied himself against the doorframe.

Helen stopped, and her eyes dropped to the floor beneath him where only one foot stuck out of his trousers. Her brows rose, and her mouth opened as if she was about to say something. She looked back up at his face and paused.

Michael could see the parade of expressions move through her eyes, and humiliation twisted hot in his belly. The sight of his missing leg must disgust her.

Her hesitation lasted only an instant before she seemed to remember herself. "Captain, please. My mother—you must help. She is burning with fever, and the doctor wanted to bleed her, but Jim sent him away, and you told me you have a friend, a native healer who uses herbs. He must come to her directly."

Michael called for Naveen, sending him off to find the *hakim* and fetch him to the general's house. Once the servant was gone, he turned to Helen. "Do not fear, my lady. We will go at once. I only require a moment if you please."

"Oh yes." She darted a glance at the space beneath his knee. "Thank you, Captain."

Basu Ram followed him into his bedroom and closed the door. He wordlessly handed Michael the wooden leg and his boots. Michael could not push away the image of Lady Helen's face when she had seen the truth. It made his stomach sick as he imagined her repulsion. He nestled the end of his leg against the cushion, tugged the strap tight, and buckled it, then he thrust the wooden leg into his boot. He pulled on the other boot and stood, balancing for a moment to make sure the leg was on properly.

A moment later, he found Lady Helen crouched down near his front door, scratching Badmash under his chin. Her servant and the insect-attracting lantern remained in the doorway. The monkey wore an expression of supreme satisfaction, and Michael thought he would feel exactly the same if he were in Badmash's place.

She stood when he approached and waved her fingers at the monkey. "Good-bye, Badmash."

A carriage waited in front of the bungalow. Michael sat on the bench across from her and banged his hand on the roof to signal the driver. "My lady, if you please, explain the situation again, more slowly."

In the dim carriage, she twisted her hands together. "I do not know what is wrong with my mother. She seemed fine earlier today, but at the ball she was suddenly burning with fever. She fainted, and Jim carried her to the carriage and then sent for a doctor. The doctor met us at home and insisted that Mamá had too much blood, but as I told you before, my mother does not allow herself to be bled. I do not know how much she overheard—she seems to drift in and out of sleep—but on that point, she was adamant."

Though Michael could not see her clearly in the darkness, he could tell that Helen was making an effort to keep her voice steady.

She wiped at her cheeks. "Jim was furious with the doctor for not having a remedy and threw him out. He is worried it is ague, and he told me he had seen men sick with fevers in the West Indies and the jungle, and we did not know what to do. But I remembered you mentioned a healer, and I knew you could help, Captain."

He found her shaking hand in the darkness and clasped it, only now realizing that neither of them wore gloves. Her hands were soft, and her fingers trembled. Heat moved up his arm from the feel of her warm skin. "You did the right thing. Lal Singh is the best healer in this city. He will know what to do."

Lady Helen shifted, and he thought she might pull away, but instead she scooted forward on the bench, laying her other hand atop his. He lifted it off and grasped it tightly, holding both her hands in the space between them, hoping she felt comforted and hoping the pounding of his pulse was not apparent beneath her palms.

The carriage ride ended much sooner than he was ready for. Michael reluctantly released her hands then followed Lady Helen into the entry hall. "The hakim will be here soon; do not worry."

She glanced at the stairway and then nodded, rubbing her hands up and down her arms. "Captain, I wanted to tell you—"

A knock at the door interrupted her, and the butler admitted Naveen and Lal Singh. Michael thanked Naveen and dismissed him then greeted the hakim.

Lal Singh was a small, thin man wearing white cotton clothing and a red turban. He carried a small bag. Deep wrinkles creased the dark skin around his eyes, and he wore small, round spectacles. Michael had no idea of the man's age, but by the amount of gray in his mustache, he appeared above his fiftieth year.

"Thank you for coming so quickly," Michael said in Hindustani.

Lady Helen took a step closer, and Michael made introductions, explaining that the hakim did not understand English.

"Please tell him thank you." Helen's smile didn't fully ease the tightness in her face. She lifted her hand toward the stairway. "If you will follow me, my mother is in her bedchamber."

Lady Patricia lay on the bed, covered with blankets, shivering. Her skin was flushed, and her damp hair stuck to her face. Michael did not have to touch her to know her body was extremely heated.

General Stackhouse sat on a chair beside the bed. He stood as they entered, and when he turned toward them, Michael saw pure panic in his eyes. "This is the doctor?" He motioned to Lal Singh.

"Yes. Lal Singh," Michael said.

"She has hardly moved." The general swallowed hard. "She is mumbling incoherently. It looks very much like the ague."

Michael understood the general's fear. Ague set in quickly, and most who were afflicted did not survive. During jungle campaigns, he'd seen healthy men drop with no warning and burn with fevers until they were buried a few days later.

Lady Helen slid her arm around General Stackhouse's waist, and he pulled her against him, resting her head on his chest. Her lip trembled, and the sight was nearly more than Michael could bear.

Michael translated the general's words for Lal Singh. He explained what Lady Helen had told him about her mother collapsing at the ball and the general sending away the doctor when the man had wanted to bleed Lady Patricia.

The hakim tapped his finger on his mustache, nodding as he listened, then spoke to Michael, who translated for the general. "Sir, Lal Singh asks your permission to examine your wife."

"By all means," General Stackhouse said.

The hakim started to lift away the blankets, and Helen left her stepfather's side to assist him. Michael saw that Lady Patricia still wore her ball gown—and the garment was soaked.

When the bedding was pulled off, she shivered more violently.

Jim pressed a fist against his tight lips.

Lal Singh touched Lady Patricia's forehead with the back of his fingers, then lifted her eyelids, bending close to see her eyes. He muttered to himself and laid his ear against her chest to hear her heartbeat. He pressed gently on her stomach and then pushed his fingers against her neck. Straightening, he spoke to Michael then picked up his bag and sifted through it, finally pulling out a small parcel.

"Lal Singh says Lady Patricia should be examined thoroughly for a sting. He suggests the men leave the room while her lady's maid and daughter search her body."

"The insect bite!" Lady Helen hurried to her mother and lifted her shoulder off the bed, pointing at a dark patch of inflamed skin. The hakim bent closer, peered at it, nodded, and spoke again.

"She should be examined for more," Michael translated. He knew all too well the seriousness of a scorpion bite. Over the years he'd had a number of them, with varying degrees of illness following. Some had merely left an itchy bump, and others had caused fevers and hallucinations that lasted for days.

"He does not think it is ague?" General Stackhouse asked.

"No," Michael said, "but it is imperative that the fever is brought down as quickly as possible. He will make up a tea, and she should be dressed lightly and cool water used to bathe her skin."

With Michael's help, Lady Helen sent a servant for a teakettle and another for cool rags. Then she made a shooing motion with her hands in the direction of the men. "We shall do it immediately."

Lal Singh spoke again as he walked toward the door. Michael translated his words. "He says it is lucky you did not allow her to be bled." The hakim kept talking. "She needs her strength, and the loss of blood might harm—" Michael turned back to Lal Singh, asking if he'd heard his words correctly. Receiving an affirmative answer, he cleared his throat, feeling extremely uncomfortable at the message. "Might harm . . . the baby," Michael finished.

Lady Helen and General Stackhouse froze midmotion and stared at him. They looked at the hakim with wide eyes then to Lady Patricia.

In the silent room, Lady Helen's gasp seemed like a blast from a cannon.

"What did you say, Captain?" General Stackhouse's voice sounded like he was being strangled.

Michael turned to Lal Singh, speaking in Hindustani. "Are you certain?"

"I felt the growing womb, Sahib."

Heat flooded Michael's face at the man's direct terms and was grateful the general and Lady Helen could not understand the words. "He says he is certain, General." Michael looked away, completely mortified at having to deliver the surprise news to his superior officer that his wife was increasing. He did not dare to look at anyone and instead studied the pattern of the silk wall covering.

Hearing a crash, Michael turned his gaze quickly back. General Stackhouse leaned with one hand pressed against the wall, the other rubbing his forehead. He looked as if a dizzy spell had overcome him. On the floor beside him, a small table lay on its side, and pieces of a vase were scattered among the water and flowers it had held.

"Jim, you must sit down," Helen moved toward him and clasped his arm with both of hers. "Captain, please help him."

Seeing that the general's legs were in danger of giving way, Michael slung the man's arm across his own shoulders as if escorting someone home who had drunk too much at the tavern.

General Stackhouse looked at him with a dazed expression that would have made Michael laugh if he'd had any less respect for the man.

Helen called for a servant to get the general a drink and for another to clean up the broken vase. She pushed the three men from the room, closing the door behind them.

"Apparently the baby is a shock," Lal Singh said.

Michael saw humor in the man's eyes and held his lips tightly to keep from smiling. He eased the general into a hallway chair. "Of that, I think we can be fairly certain."

***

Lady Patricia was examined, and no other stings were discovered. Lal Singh and Lady Helen spooned the herbal tea—which Michael thought smelled like bitter tree bark—into her mouth and supervised the process of cooling her fever.

Michael tried to assist at first but found that he and the general just seemed to get in the way. After a while the two men sat in the hallway chairs just outside the bedchamber—one waiting anxiously for news of his beloved and the other ready to translate when needed.

General Stackhouse held his head in his hands and occasionally muttered the word *baby*.

The hours slipped by, and the voices inside the room became murmurs. General Stackhouse left to tend to his wife, and Michael found it difficult to keep his eyes open. He rested his head in his hands, allowing his thoughts to wander where they would, and of course they drifted to Lady Helen—the way she'd come to him for help, fully trusting that he would assist her. Had they only known each other less than a week? The warmth of her hands and the concern in her eyes. Her hair falling loose around her shoulders. Her voice when she said his name.

"Captain Rhodes?"

He lifted his head and, for a moment, tried to detach his dreams from reality. Lady Helen was standing before him tapping his shoulder. "Pardon me, my lady, I must have dozed off." His mouth felt thick, and his words sounded sluggish. He shook his head to wake himself.

"Mamá's fever has broken."

Her eyes were tired, and her entire body seemed to droop with fatigue, but there was a relief in her expression.

"I am so glad."

She pulled on his arm, helping him to stand. "Come, it is nearly dawn. Lal Singh is leaving, and you need your sleep. The carriage is waiting to take you home."

He winced as he followed her. Falling asleep in the hard hallway chair had done his leg no favors.

From the doorway of the bedchamber, Michael saw Lady Patricia sleeping soundly and the general holding her hand as he slept in the chair next to her. Lal Singh stepped into the hallway and handed Lady Helen the parcel of herbs. Through Michael, he instructed her to give her mother a cup of tea every four hours. He would return tomorrow to check on Lady Patricia's progress.

"Thank you," Lady Helen said to the hakim, and then to Michael, "How do I tell him *thank you* in his language?"

"*Dhanyavaad.*" He said the word slowly, drawing out the syllables.

"*Dhanyavaad*, Lal Singh." Lady Helen's brows pulled together as her mouth struggled to produce the unfamiliar sounds. Her accent was heavy and the word hardly understandable, but her effort was endearing. "Thank you for helping my mother."

The hakim bowed with his palms together and his thumbs touching his forehead then took his leave.

Michael glanced at the long flight of stairs. His stiff leg ached just looking at it. "I will see myself out, my lady. Return to your family."

"Thank you, Captain," she said and turned back into her mother's room.

Michael grasped the handrail and took the stairs one at a time, grunting with every other step. He reached the entry hall and started toward the door.

Lady Helen called his name, and he stopped. She held her skirts as she hastened down the stairway. "Captain, I cannot let you leave until I speak to you." She joined him and looked suddenly nervous, as if she didn't know what to say. Her eyes moved to the side then looked up at him, a line of worry forming between her brows. "I must apologize, sir, for how very rudely I reacted tonight at your house, when . . ." She glanced down at his foot.

Michael's stomach twisted. "I completely understand, my lady. It is a repulsive injury and must have disturbed you greatly to see it. Think of it no more." He inclined his head and turned away before his expression could betray the hurt he felt. He swallowed at the thickness in his throat.

Lady Helen moved around in front of him, holding on to his arms to stop him. "Captain, I am not disturbed in the least, and I definitely *shall* think of it because I consider my friends' pains instead of ignoring them." The nervousness had left her expression, and her bright eyes flashed in the candlelit hall. "I was surprised, Captain. That is all. Until tonight, I did not know to what degree your leg had been injured, and I must tell you, I do not think it repulsive in the least."

She stepped back and folded her arms, looking at the floor and then to him. "I assumed you thought better of me, sir." Her lip trembled slightly as her voice softened. "I am not the sort of person who requires a man to have two feet in order to be considered my friend. And I only wish you had told me earlier so I would not have been hurt when you did not dance with me." Her brows drew together. She balled her hands into fists at her sides. "Blazes! I would never have persuaded you to attend the accursed ball in the first place!" Lady Helen clamped her hands over her mouth, and her eyes opened wide. Then she rushed past him and up the stairs before Michael could call her back.

He stood in the entry hall and stared after her, stunned by her words. Not just her use of coarse language—which in itself made him want to laugh aloud—but the things she'd said shocked him. Did she mean them? She was hurt that he had not danced with her? And was she truly not disgusted by his missing leg? He stepped out into the early morning air to join Lal Singh and thought through the events of the night. Had he assumed the worst of Lady Helen? That she was a faithless friend who would snub a person who was damaged? Her actions since he had met her spoke otherwise.

He climbed inside the carriage and considered if their roles were reversed. If she were deformed in some way, would he think less of her? He shook his head. It would not matter to him in the least, so why had he assumed it would be such with her? He had been so blinded by his own self-doubt that he had not given Lady Helen his trust.

At his bungalow, he climbed out of the carriage, bid farewell to Lal Singh, and waved to the driver, but he did not go inside, choosing instead to walk. He clasped his hands behind his back and thought again of Lady Helen's expression. Hurt and anger had raised color in her cheeks and made her eyes look as if they could melt metal.

He owed the lady an apology, and in spite of her anger, he smiled, thinking of what she'd said. She considered him a friend. She had rushed to him in the late hours of the night when she needed help and felt hurt because he had not danced with her.

He knew he would have to think of a way to make it up to her. But at this moment, he felt very contented, and the pain in his leg was not bothersome at all.

Chapter 12

HELEN AWOKE, FEELING FAR FROM rested. She'd not gone to her own bed until past dawn, and her head ached. Lying beneath her mosquito netting, she threw an arm over her eyes to block the sunlight. She was mortified by the way she'd behaved to Captain Rhodes. The frustration of the ball, the worry about her mother, and her lack of sleep had all seemed to expand inside her until they'd burst out in a gush of words. She groaned. Had she truly resorted to obscenities? If the captain did not have a low opinion of her before, he certainly must now.

She rolled onto her stomach and pulled a pillow over her head. What exactly had upset her so badly that she'd lashed out? Had she been so offended that he did not dance with her? She thought through the evening. While she'd felt disappointed at the ball and concerned about Lady Patricia, the moment that flushed her with emotion was when she'd seen the empty space where the captain's foot should have been.

Even thinking of it now, her heart ached for him, and accompanying the ache was hurt that he had not disclosed the secret to her. And atop it all was a hot wave of embarrassment. She'd been so selfish, teasing him about the ball and insisting he attend. Certain that she knew what was best, she must have humiliated him by making him promise to attend an event that only drew more attention to his inability to participate.

But why had he not told her? His story of despondency in the hospital suddenly made more sense. A soldier without a leg must certainly feel inadequate. *Poor Captain Rhodes.* She understood completely why he would not want to make his disability known, and her eyes burned with sympathy. But what had hurt more than anything was Captain Rhodes thinking that she would be repulsed by his injury. Did he truly think she was such a shallow friend?

Sita entered the room with a tray of breakfast, and the smell of warm eggs and toast roused Helen from her contemplations. She rose and moved to the small table in her bedchamber.

Helen knew that in spite her own hurt feelings, she owed Captain Rhodes an apology, and she would offer it at the first opportunity. She only hoped she had not offended him too badly to repair their friendship.

Sita told her that Lal Singh and Captain Rhodes had paid a call earlier in the morning to assess Lady Patricia's health. Helen was a bit disappointed she had missed them and realized that the men must have had only a few hours' sleep. She herself had no more than five, and it was nearly time for *tiffin*.

Once she was dressed, Helen peeked inside her mother's bedchamber. Lady Patricia was asleep, and when Helen touched her mother's forehead, she found no fever remained. She breathed a sigh and sat in the chair next to the bed. Her mother slept peacefully— a welcome sight after the night before. Helen studied her face and thought of the other revelation of the night.

A baby.

Jim had not been the only one to nearly collapse at the news. Did her mother know? Or, when she woke, would it be a surprise to her as well? Helen smiled as she thought of holding a small pink brother or sister, but at the same time a tendril of apprehension worked its way into her mind. Lady Patricia was in her forties and had grandchildren. Was she healthy enough to carry a child? Would the child be well? She brushed a strand of hair from her mother's face and kissed her forehead before quietly exiting the room, heading for the pianoforte. Music had always been her comfort, and right now she needed to sort through and understand her confusing range of feelings.

As she walked through the entry hall, she saw a large arrangement of flowers on the table. When she lifted the card next to it, she found that it was addressed to her.

She opened the envelope.

Dear Lady Helen,

Dancing with you was the high point of the ball.

I am very sorry about your mother's illness and regret that your early departure prevented you from visiting Lord Minto's trophy room. If you are so inclined, I would be pleased to accompany you to see it another day.

Lieutenant Arthur Bancroft

Helen put the letter back on the table and studied the flowers for a moment. Large, white, trumpet-shaped flowers with tinges of violet on their petals sprang from the center, attached to thorny fruits that reminded Helen of hedgehogs. Other colorful flowers surrounded the white blooms. The display was grand and a bit gaudy for the entry hall. Besides, Helen didn't like the bitter smell of the blossoms. Perhaps it would suit the drawing room better.

She lifted the vase and thought of the handsome lieutenant. Dancing with Lieutenant Bancroft had been quite enjoyable. He was very skilled, and of course his dimpled smile and the curl that fell onto his forehead turned her insides to melted butter. How very considerate of him to send flowers. Helen placed the arrangement on a table near the window, far enough away that the smell wouldn't bother her at the pianoforte. In spite of the thoughtful gesture, she had no inclination whatsoever to visit Lord Minto's trophy room.

***

Jim ordered every inch of the house to be searched for scorpions. The servants found and killed three before showing the creatures to the general and Helen. One black scorpion was quite large, and the sight of it gave Helen a shudder.

But it was a much smaller specimen that made Jim's face go pale. "Come near, Helen. I want you to see this."

She leaned closer and studied it. A servant held a wad of cloth with the smashed remains, but she could see the shape of it quite clearly. Its body was a reddish-brown, the legs and pincers a lighter tan color. The long tail curled around and ended in a pointed barb.

"A red scorpion," Jim said. "That creature is why you must always shake your shoes before putting them on, and if you do see one, get away, Helen, and call for help. You'd likely not survive a sting."

A cold finger of fear slid down her spine as she looked back at the red scorpion. It had been found in their house? Helen did not trust herself to speak and only nodded.

"I do not mean to frighten you," Jim said, "but you must understand."

"I understand, sir."

"Good." He waved his hand at the servant. "Now get that blasted devil out of my house."

Over the next days, Helen saw Captain Rhodes briefly in passing, but an opportunity to speak in private did not preset itself. Lieutenant Bancroft and Sergeant Carter had called each afternoon, but Helen only received them once for a short visit.

Lady Patricia grew stronger, and Helen found her one morning at the sitting room table with Lal Singh, making notes in her sketchbook. Her ayah stood close by. Helen was disappointed that Captain Rhodes was not with the hakim.

"Good morning, Helen, dear," her mother said.

Lal Singh stood and bowed.

"Mamá, are you well enough to be out of bed?"

Lady Patricia brushed away Helen's concern with a wave of her hand. "Lal Singh and I are discussing herbal remedies. He has quite a knowledge of plants and their use. I thought it would be helpful to know the local names for the herbs, should I ever find myself in need."

She turned the page of her book and pointed at a star-shaped plant. "Morning glory, or bindweed" she said. She pointed to the notes beside the sketch. "Tea from the flower can induce vomiting."

The ayah said something to Lal Singh, and he nodded. He leaned closer to the sketchbook. "*Hirankhuri*," he said once and then more slowly so Lady Patricia could transcribe the word.

"Hi-ran-khu-ri," she muttered.

Lal Singh spoke to the ayah.

"He says the tea from the leaves can treat spider bites," the ayah said.

"Very interesting." Lady Patricia wrote in her careful script.

"Mamá, please make sure you rest," Helen said as she excused herself.

***

A week after the Governor-General's ball, Helen sat in the morning sunlight playing "Robin Adair." She knew her mother loved the song, and Helen felt happy to be doing something to make Lady Patricia's recovery more pleasant.

She held the last notes and lifted her hands slowly, resting them in her lap the way her music instructor had shown her. At the sound of clapping, she snapped her gaze to the doorway.

Captain Rhodes stood, leaning his shoulder against the door-frame, applauding. Helen felt a burst of nervous energy skitter over her at the sight of him. Her heartbeat quickened. She breathed deep to give herself courage and stood, walking toward him on weak legs. The captain had every right to reject her apology after the way she had treated him, but she did not think she could bear it if he did.

"Captain, I have something I must say to you."

"If you please, my lady, I should like to speak first." He spoke without a hint of a smile.

Helen felt as though she was sinking through the floor. The captain's grave expression did not bode well, and her eyes began to prickle. Why did she always say the wrong thing? Now her words had ended a treasured friendship. She nodded her head and lowered her eyes, ready for the reprimand the captain was certain to give. She didn't want to see the disappointment in his face.

"My lady, I ask your forgiveness for the deplorable way I treated you."

Helen looked up. "But, Captain—"

He shook his head and continued. "I hold your friendship in the highest esteem, but by my actions have failed to show it. I should never have made you feel as though you were not trusted. The thought that your estimation of a person would be based upon his appearance is beyond offensive, and you have never shown yourself to be anything but genuine. I am afraid my actions toward you were based on my own insecurities, and I offer my deepest apologies."

"But, sir, I should apologize to you. It was I who became angry and said—" Heat rushed into her cheeks at the memory of her outburst. "I am sorry for insisting that you attend the ball and then for allowing myself to be offended by something that I assumed instead of understood." She lowered her eyes again. "I am particularly sorry for the way I spoke to you. My language was filthy and shocking. You have no need to apologize, Captain."

He did not respond, and Helen glanced upward through her lashes to see a strange expression on the captain's face. He seemed to be trying to hold back a smile.

"Well, if that is the case, my lady, I guess I shall have to keep the gift I brought for you."

Helen raised her head to look at him. "A gift?"

"Yes, I'd thought a token of my apology would . . . Well, it is of no matter since you assure me I have no need to apologize." He took a step toward the door.

He was definitely trying not to smile.

Is he teasing? "Perhaps I spoke too hastily, sir."

Captain Rhodes's brows rose. "You do accept my apology, then?" His eyes twinkled.

He is *teasing*. "Yes. If you will accept mine." She lifted her shoulders. "I will find it in my heart to forgive you for neglecting to inform me of your injury and for keeping your promise to attend the ball." She allowed a smile of her own.

"No, it is not enough." The playfulness left his eyes. "You must forgive me for assuming that you would think any less of me because of . . ." He motioned toward his foot. "You are a true friend, Helen, and I should not have hurt you with my petty assumption."

The sincerity in his expression took her by surprise. "I forgive you, Captain." She spoke solemnly, realizing how very important this was to him.

He nodded, and the brightness returned to his eyes.

Had his eyes always been a light gray? She wondered why she had never noticed. It was a very nice color, and in the beams from the windows she could see hints of red highlighting his hair. How had she not seen that before either?

He offered his hand, and Helen shook it.

"Then I shall also forgive you—for your surprisingly skillful usage of vulgarity." His face broke into a grin, and Helen snatched her hand away.

"It is very ill-mannered of you to mention it, sir." Her face, neck, and ears felt unbearably hot.

Captain Rhodes laughed, and the sound warmed Helen's insides. He reached into the pocket of his jacket and pulled out a wrapped parcel roughly the size of teacup and held it toward her. "Lady Helen, you can say anything you like or behave in any manner that suits your mood, and I would think no less of you."

She studied his face. Something in the solemnness of his tone told her he wasn't simply saying kind words. He was sincere. She took the package and turned it over in her hands. Her heart was beating, undoubtedly with the anticipation of a gift. She could think of no other reason for her hands to be trembling.

Sitting on the sofa, she untied the string, carefully pulling the paper away to reveal a small wooden elephant. Intricate carvings decorated the gold blanket on its back, and the figurine was painted with colorful designs. Helen was amazed at the amount of detail on something so small. Even the delicate eyelashes and toenails were carved and painted.

"Oh," she breathed, running her finger over the bumps on the trunk. "It is so beautiful." When she looked up at Captain Rhodes, she saw that he watched her with soft eyes and a tilted head. The sight made her heart beat strangely again, and she wondered if it was the growing heat of the day that was causing her curious reactions. Or maybe she needed to eat something. "Thank you, Captain Rhodes. It . . . I love it."

"I thought you would. Although it is hardly a substitute for the real thing."

He had remembered the silly fancy she'd shared with him not long ago. Helen's heart felt hot and tight. "It is a good deal easier to carry around in one's pocket, I would think."

He smiled, and she thought how handsome he looked with such a tender expression on his face.

"I am sorry that I do not have a gift for you, Capt—" Helen cut her words short when she saw Captain Rhodes gaze past her.

His eyes widened, and his face paled. With quick steps, he crossed the room to the flower arrangement. "Dhatura. Where did this come from?" He studied the flowers, then his gaze darted back to her. A crease had formed between his brows.

Helen thought he looked worried or frightened. What could possibly have made him so? "I—Lieutenant Bancroft sent the flowers."

He nodded slowly. "My lady, I apologize. Dhatura flowers are . . . The Indian people believe them to be an evil omen." He glanced at the arrangement. "I cannot believe the servants did not dispose of this immediately. They would certainly have noticed."

Helen lowered her shoulders, feeling suddenly defensive. "The lieutenant was only being thoughtful. Surely he did not know."

"No, I am certain he did not." Captain Rhodes shook his head, and a portion of his pleasant expression returned. "Pardon me. My ayah—my nursemaid—instilled superstitions in me that are sometimes difficult to forget. I have no doubt the lieutenant sought only to bestow a beautiful gift."

Helen smiled and lifted the elephant. "As did you, sir. And I thank you again for it."

"You must think me silly with my irrational worries."

"You are hardly silly. And as you know, I quite like learning about the native traditions."

"I admire that about you, my lady."

He held her gaze, and Helen's breath caught at the intensity in his face. Just as she was beginning to think her cheeks would light into flames, Captain Rhodes blinked and took a step back. He cleared his throat and glanced at his pocket watch then snapped it shut. "If you will pardon me, my lady. I am sorry to cut our visit short, but I have a meeting with the general."

"Yes. Of course. I did not mean to take up your time." She was both relieved that the tension of the moment had ended and disappointed, though she could not for certain say why. She held the elephant in both hands as she curtsied.

"Talking with you is never a misuse of my time." He inclined his head and started toward the door then glanced back. The softness had returned to his gaze, and the sight of it caused Helen's heart to feel light. "I do not think the sound of your playing would be unwelcome as we discuss dull business matters, my lady. In fact, it should make the meeting nearly enjoyable." He nodded once more and left the room.

Helen sat back onto the sofa and studied the beautiful figurine. She did not know what had come over her. Her erratic moods might be attributed to the relief she had felt at Captain Rhodes's extraordinary kindness and unexpected apology. *Yes, that is undoubtedly the case.* She nodded to herself as she walked to the pianoforte. She called to a servant and requested that the flowers be disposed of. Then she set the elephant carefully on the instrument and, with a smile on her lips, started to play for Captain Rhodes.

***

It was just over an hour later when she noticed a servant enter and politely cough. She stopped her song and twisted on the bench. "Does my mother send for me?"

"The general, Miss-Sahib. He requests your presence in the library."

Helen handed the elephant to the servant. "Please, will you place this in my bedchamber?"

He took the figurine and bowed before hurrying away.

Helen left the room, wondering why Jim had sent for her. Had he discovered another scorpion? Did he require her to make a special request to the cook for their supper? Had her mother taken a turn for the worse?

Jim and Captain Rhodes stood when she entered the library.

"You sent for me, sir?"

"Yes, Helen, please join us." He gestured to a chair next to Captain Rhodes and then sat back down behind his desk, facing them. Helen saw piles of papers and a map spread out on the desk as if the two men had been discussing it. She wondered what any of it could have to do with her. She glanced to the captain, who nodded and then turned his gaze back to Jim.

Jim leaned forward, resting his elbows on the desk. "Helen, nearly two weeks ago, we made arrangements to send a company on a diplomatic mission to the palace of Shah Ahsan Ali. He paused as if waiting for her acknowledgement.

Helen nodded, and he continued, "The group was to be made up of military commanders, heads of state, and their wives. But in light of . . . events with the Governor-General and your mother's health, the party has dwindled. Captain Rhodes and I feel it would hurt relations if we were to cancel the visit, and if we delay, we shall run into the hot season and the rains will make the journey nearly impossible."

Helen glanced between the men, still unsure why they were involving her in the discussion.

Captain Rhodes picked up the conversation. "Having women in the party gives the appearance of a friendly visit—not a military detachment marching in formation but a group of diplomats paying a call to another head of state. In India, such niceties are important to maintain relationships. *Durbar* is what the Indians call this type of visit, and it is simply a matter of showing respect to a neighboring dignitary. Not a formal event or procession."

"But the matter is entirely up to you," Jim said. "If you feel uncomfortable in the least, simply say the word, and we will discuss it no more."

Helen looked from Jim to Captain Rhodes and then back. An excited fluttering was happening inside her ribs. "Are you asking if I will go to the Shah's palace?"

"Yes." Jim nodded.

"And who would accompany me?"

"I will, of course," Jim said, "and the captain here and a few other officers. And of course, soldiers, for protection. Including servants, we shall not likely be more than thirty in our party."

The fluttering grew more intense, and Helen could not help the grin that burst on her face. "Oh, I would love to see an Indian prince and a palace. Yes, please, may I go on the journey?" She clenched her hands in her lap to keep from clapping. "Thank you for—" Her heart plummeted as she thought of Lady Patricia. She felt herself sag but tried to maintain her composure so the men did not know. "But Mamá. I cannot leave her alone." Helen's throat clogged. It was a disappointment, to be sure, but other opportunities would arise.

"Utter nonsense!" Lady Patricia's voice rang through the library.

The men rose to their feet, and Helen hurried to the doorway to help her mother to a chair. "Mamá, you should be resting."

Lady Patricia gently lifted her arm from her daughter's grasp. "I plan to see to my herb garden. A bit of fresh air and exercise will do more good for my recovery than lying around all day." She moved to stand next to Jim but kept her gaze on Helen. "I am so grateful for your attention during my illness, but it is unnecessary any longer. I am a grown woman and perfectly capable of caring for myself for a few days. My fever is gone, and it is not as if I have never carried a baby before."

Helen stifled a gasp at her mother's indelicacy. She glanced at Captain Rhodes and saw that his face had gone red and he was looking with great interest at the map on Jim's desk.

"Patricia, it should be Helen's decision. I do not want her to regret—"

"I absolutely insist," Lady Patricia interrupted. "Helen, you came to India to experience the world, not to care for your mother.

"But, Mamá—"

"Enough. I shall be just fine while you are gone, and you must tell me all about it when you return." She smiled. "Every detail."

"Thank you, Mamá." The excited flutter started again.

Jim held his wife's gaze for a moment before he offered Lady Patricia the chair behind the desk and stood next to her. He turned back to the map. "The terrain will be flat for the majority of the journey. In the interest of speed, we shall use packhorses instead of carts, and, Helen, I can arrange for a palanquin, or you will have to ride."

"Of course I can ride," she said. The idea of lounging in a box carried on men's shoulders sounded dreadful. "I am a good horsewoman. I'll not slow the group."

She turned her head to see Captain Rhodes studying the map. He traced his finger along an invisible path. "If we can cover forty miles the first day, we should only have to camp for one night." He looked up at her. "For a person who is unused to being on horseback for such a long time, forty miles can be quite . . . uncomfortable."

"Do not worry. You shall not hear me complain once, Captain."

Chapter 13

TWO DAYS LATER, THE COMPANY departed well before dawn in order to get as many miles behind them as possible before the heat of the day. Helen didn't mind rising so early. In fact, she'd hardly slept as she anticipated what awaited her—an expedition through the Indian countryside, a visit to an Eastern prince's palace. Both equally terrified and thrilled her. Would she be able to endure the journey? Sita did not know how to ride a horse, and though Helen told Jim she did not mind traveling without a maid, she worried about sleeping alone. She had never slept out of doors. The thought of tigers or snakes coming into her tent at night tied her insides into a hard knot.

The knot loosened somewhat, and she allowed a shiver of anticipation to tingle over her skin as she thought of the Shah's palace—the White Palace, Jim had told her. What would it be like? Helen had been to Saint James's Court when she was presented in the Queen's Drawing Room, but she did not imagine the White Palace would resemble the king's at all. She had seen drawings of local maharajas sitting upon golden, jewel-encrusted thrones, wearing elaborate silk headpieces decorated with pearls and feathers. Were the representations accurate? Or simply fanciful? She couldn't wait to find out.

Helen's eyes began to adjust to the darkness, or perhaps the sky was lightening. She rode next to Jim, though only his outline was visible. The other men and horses were still merely shadows. Aside from the sound of horses and an occasional cough, the group remained silent.

Aside from the noises of their own party, Helen heard the creaks of wagons, the sounds of animals, and the hushed voices of other travelers. Occasionally she saw the glow of a fire beside the road and smelled the aroma of cooking food. Once, she even heard the sound of a *pungi*—the gourd-shaped instrument she'd seen in the bazaar—and shivered, imagining someone playing for a trained cobra in the dark. She shifted her position, stretching her back as well as she was able while she rode sidesaddle. She didn't think she'd been on the horse for longer than a few hours, and already her spine felt stiff.

The sky gradually turned purple with streaks of gold, and Helen noticed a change in the company's movement. She reigned in her horse, wondering at the disturbance, and looked back to discover what had caused it. It seemed some of the servants and sepoys at the rear of the party were dismounting and leading their horses from the road.

Jim stopped next to her. "Prayer for the Mohammedans. Come, we do not need to wait. They will catch us when we stop to water the horses."

The sun burst into view on the company's right side, and the road came to life. It seemed the light was a signal for travelers to call greetings to one another and urge their animals forward with yells. Camels plodded along the road with lazy-looking steps. Children ran among the parties, and men wearing bright turbans and loose clothing rode donkeys laden with large loads that looked as though they should cause the animals to topple over.

Helen saw camps on the sides of the road among the trees. Birds called, goats bleated, and monkeys chattered. Shrines with flowers and brightly painted deities stood along the road. She glanced back, hoping Lieutenant Bancroft was not in a hunting mood this morning. The colorful road with its noises and smells lifted Helen's spirits, and she could not help smiling at the people they passed.

A group of women with sticks piled high on their heads walked in the other direction, somehow managing to converse while they balanced the cumbersome bundles. Other women walked barefoot, holding the silk fabric of their richly colored saris in front of their faces, covering all but their eyes. She noticed men away from the road kneeling on prayer rugs the way they had done at the mosque, and she wondered how they could possibly concentrate on their worship with all the noise and smells and dust surrounding them.

Captain Rhodes rode at the front of the company, and she wondered if he would turn around now that it was light enough to see one another. Would he meet her eye and smile? Would his face light up and his brow rise in a teasing expression? She planned the perfect expression to make in return. Would he motion for her to ride next to him? What would they talk about?

Her mind turned to the carved elephant that sat on her bedside table. The captain had known the perfect gift. Helen's chest warmed as she remembered the softness in his face when he'd given it to her. She wondered if she'd have the opportunity to see that expression again.

Captain Rhodes didn't look back, however, and Helen had to be content with noticing how straight he sat in the saddle. From her position, she thought he looked both alert and at ease as he rode. A true soldier. Just the sight of him scanning the road ahead left her feeling safe as they journeyed farther from the city.

Jim turned toward her. "What do you think of the Grand Trunk Road, Helen?"

Helen drew her eyes from Captain Rhodes, disappointed that he had not turned his head just a bit to meet her eye. "I have never seen such a wide road. And it is as busy as the marketplace in Calcutta, yet we are miles from the city."

He nodded. "Remain close while the road is congested. Thieves and highwaymen hide among the crowds."

Helen drew in a quick breath, darting her glance at the people around her. "But surely we are safe with all the soldiers."

"Let us hope we don't meet a band of *Crim* or *Dacoit*. They'll have no qualms about slaughtering the lot of us and seizing the gifts for the Shah." He spoke in a low tone, his eye squinting as he looked over her shoulder toward the jungle.

"Sir?" Helen's mouth had gone dry. She glanced from side to side as they rode between the trees. The sounds of the birds took on a sinister tone, and the morning did not seem so bright. She wondered if Jim was truly worried or if something else bothered him. His jaw seemed unusually tight, and the lines around his eyes were deep. Perhaps he was remembering something unpleasant. "Does our journey remind you of a Spanish campaign, sir?"

He shrugged, and his lip curled the slightest bit. "The dust is the same, but it lacks the fear, the smell of death, the cold, the vultures picking apart men who—" Jim blinked and grimaced. "Pardon me,

Helen. I am used to soldiers on a campaign, not young ladies. I did not mean to speak so crudely." His expression looked pained, as if he were attempting to smile but could not manage it. "I do not believe we are in any danger. It is just best to remain on guard."

Helen nodded her head, unsure of how to respond. She had never known him to act so sullen, and she wondered what had brought this mood on. *Oh, but of course.* The reason came to her mind so suddenly that she was surprised she'd not realized it before. "You miss Mamá, don't you, sir?"

Jim swallowed and nodded. He kept his gaze directly ahead. "More than I'd have imagined. 'Tis the first time we've been separated, and in her condition . . ." He cleared his throat again.

"I worry for her too, but she is strong. I wouldn't be surprised if she is looking through her sketchbook at this very moment or pouring water over her herbs." Helen smiled and leaned to the side to catch Jim's gaze.

"Or comparing foul-smelling concoctions with the skinny hakim," Jim said.

Helen's smile grew. She was starting to recognize Jim's crotchety manner as an attempt to disguise his deeper feelings. "I expect she is. She would be furious to know that we spent the journey worried about her."

"Aye, and Patricia's distemper is every bit as frightening as any danger India can produce." His gaze remained soft, but his mouth turned up the smallest bit.

Helen laughed.

Jim's smile grew. He studied her for a moment. "I am not used to campaigners attempting to keep my spirits up. Usually my experience has been very different." He glanced forward. "Ah, Captain Rhodes has halted. Shall we have breakfast?"

Ahead was a grassy clearing among the trees. She thought it was probably near to fifty meters in each direction. Down a slight hill in the middle of the clearing flowed a stream. Helen dismounted, and a man took away her horse, binding its front legs loosely with a strip of cloth so it could feed and reach the water but not run away.

Helen saw the servants had built a fire near the road and were unloading the implements to make a meal. Her legs and back were stiff. It might be the only opportunity to walk and stretch she'd have for hours, so avoiding the trees and anything that might be hiding within, she walked across the space toward the stream. As she walked, she listened to the sounds of the birds and the water trickling over the rocks. She noticed white flowers that looked like balls of cotton growing in patches throughout the clearing. She wondered if she should pick some to take home to her mother, but remembering what Captain Rhodes had told her about the innocent-looking dhatura, she did not touch any plants.

She looked back toward the group, hoping to see Captain Rhodes. Why had he not sought her out before now?

Lieutenant Bancroft caught her eye, lifted his hand in a wave, and made his way across the field toward her. When he reached her side, he gave a small bow. "Fine day to be out of doors, isn't it, my lady?"

Helen took his offered arm, and they began to stroll. "Very fine, Lieutenant."

"A welcome change from drilling. And I'd not be surprised if we meet with a fair bit of game as we travel north. Much less civilized that direction. We might even see a rhinoceros in the lowlands beneath the mountains. Or a bear."

"That sounds very nice." Helen glanced nervously toward the tree line. She didn't know whether the idea of *meeting* wild animals or of Lieutenant Bancroft *shooting* them made her cringe.

"And I noticed there is no palanquin accompanying us. Smashing young lady you are to ride the entire way. I'd not have thought—"

"Lady Helen!" They both turned at the sound and saw Captain Rhodes hurrying in their direction. His brow was furrowed, making him appear angry or frightened. "My lady." He was breathing heavily. "Do not venture into the tall grass." He moved his gaze over the ground near her skirt. "Cobras, my lady. They dwell near the water's edge."

"Oh." Helen clung tighter to Lieutenant Bancroft's arm and whipped her head around, looking for any sign of a snake. "I did not know." Her heart was racing.

Captain Rhodes tugged on her other arm, pulling her from Lieutenant Bancroft and leading her quickly away from the stream and the tall grass. He did not glance back at her.

She felt as if she were a child who had behaved badly and was to be punished. A lump grew in her throat. She'd been a fool earlier to believe the captain would have caught her eye and smiled as if they shared a sort of secret bond. This journey was work, not leisure, and she was extra trouble.

"If you'll excuse me, my lady. I must speak with the lieutenant," he said.

Helen rushed away. Her skin burned, and her ribs squeezed.

Behind her, she heard Captain Rhodes's voice. "Lieutenant, Lady Helen is not wearing thick soldiers' boots. Have a care when . . ."

She found Jim sitting on a thick root in the shade of a tree with large red blossoms. She joined him. Her throat was tight. After only a few hours, she had managed to disappoint the person she'd looked forward to impressing on the excursion. Helen did not have an appetite but managed to take a few bites of the food the servant brought her.

She glanced up when a group joined them. She recognized the men who had stopped to pray and saw that one of them was Captain Rhodes's servant. The man moved directly toward the officers, and Helen turned her eyes away, not wanting to meet the captain's gaze and not knowing why she felt so embarrassed over the exchange near the stream.

The meal was finished and the horses rested before the group started off again. Helen felt sick inside that she'd become such a bother to the captain, and she resolved not to be a burden on him or anyone else on the journey.

The road was still crowded, but it seemed less cheerful now. People did not raise their hands or call out greetings as they passed. The midday heat and the dust were taking a toll on all the travelers.

***

They stopped again, hours later, on a patch of hard-packed earth, finding bits of shade from the midday heat for a rest and tiffin. Helen joined Jim beneath a tree with many thin trunks that wound together as if they'd been braided. Little striped squirrels darted over the twisting branches and moved in and out of the roots. Helen was too tired to watch the animals or move away from them. A servant handed her a water skin, and she drank gratefully.

She glanced up once as she ate and saw Captain Rhodes studying her, but she quickly turned her gaze away. The memory of his face when he'd marched her away from the stream made her feel heavy.

The journey was much more difficult than she had imagined. She hurt all over from riding, and the dust churned up from the road became so thick that she kept her head down, using her bonnet to shield her eyes and holding a handkerchief in front of her nose and mouth. She hoped the horse would follow the others since she could hardly raise her eyes long enough to see their direction. But the factor that caused the most discomfort was the heat. The air she breathed was hot in her lungs. Her hair was damp. She thought the mixture of dust and sweat must be making a muddy mask over her skin and clothing.

The men rode silently, their laughter and conversation gone as if the cheerfulness had been baked out of them by the Indian sun.

She felt a touch on her arm and looked up. Jim squinted at her. "Are you well, Helen?"

She could only nod.

"Captain Rhodes informs me we've only an hour or so until we reach the *dâk* bungalow where we'll spend the night."

Helen nodded again and tried to form a tired smile, but she knew it didn't look convincing in the least. Another hour seemed like an eternity.

"Haven't complained once. That's my girl." Jim patted her arm again.

Helen turned her burning eyes back downward. A swell of pride grew in her chest at his praise.

The evening was growing dark when the company reached their stopping point. With Jim's help, Helen dismounted and nearly collapsed. Her legs shook as she tried to stand. He put an arm around her and led her up the stairs of a small wooden building with a large porch.

Captain Rhodes spoke to the owner of the inn—the dâk bungalow—and a moment later a servant woman appeared. Helen might have bid the gentlemen good evening, but she did not remember for certain. The servant led Helen into a room and helped her undress and wash. Helen found that her eyes would not remain open as she went through the motions of preparing for bed. The servant brought food, but Helen couldn't remain awake long enough to eat. She spent her first night in the jungle deep in a dreamless sleep, where worries of tigers and frustrated military officers could not bother her at all.

Chapter 14

MICHAEL KICKED A ROCK ACROSS the dirt road, hearing a satisfying crack when his wooden foot made contact. Another hour remained before the men would break camp, but sleep had not come easily, and after a frustrating night, he'd finally risen. He paced back and forth in front of the dâk bungalow, working the stiffness out of his back and leg. He did not look forward to another day in the saddle. And he didn't think any of the men did. Perhaps Lieutenant Bancroft was the exception. That man was decidedly a member of the Corinthian set. A sportsman before all—even before his duties as an officer and a gentleman, Michael thought. He was furious with the lieutenant's negligence when it came to Lady Helen. Sending her dhatura flowers—not only were they extremely poisonous but also a sinister omen. The sight of them in Helen's drawing room had chilled his blood. Michael's ayah would have cast them out of the house and burned an offering to her gods, begging for protection from the evil the dhatura foreshadowed.

A twist of guilt tightened in his gut. He was being unfair. Lieutenant Bancroft was a fine soldier who had no idea of the superstitious connotations of Indian flowers. He'd likely thought they were beautiful, and how could he be blamed for ignorance?

Michael blew out a breath. He knew whence his ill feelings were derived. It was physically painful to see Lady Helen in love with the lieutenant.

His heart ached as he thought of her clinging to the lieutenant's arm when Michael had warned her of cobras. And she'd brought the arrangement of flowers the lieutenant had sent into her drawing room so that she might look at them while she played the pianoforte.

It was not Lieutenant Bancroft's fault that Lady Helen was smitten with him. Michael hoped the man knew how extremely lucky he was to have that young lady's affection. He himself would give anything for the pleasure. But seeing the flowers and their placement in the drawing room had been a sharp reminder that he needed to keep his feelings in check. Allowing his regard toward her to develop into something deeper would only end in heartache.

He rubbed his eyes and blew out another breath. Lady Helen was beyond his grasp, and he had known it all along. If only his heart understood, and if only his mind would not return to thoughts of Lady Helen's smile, her laughter, or her bright eyes, perhaps he would manage to sleep one of these nights.

He looked up, watching the swooping bats that filled the sky. The sight of the large wingspan was typically a source of surprise for new recruits, but for Michael it was just another part of life in his homeland.

Although Michael knew he should hold no ill feelings toward the man, it was, however, completely unacceptable for Lieutenant Bancroft to place Lady Helen's life at risk as he had done by allowing her to walk through the tall grass near the stream. When he had a gift so precious as Lady Helen's heart, he should protect her as she deserved.

A movement at the corner of his eye caused him to look toward the veranda in front of the bungalow. Lady Helen stepped down the stairs, stretching her arms out to the sides as she breathed in the early-morning air.

His heart skipped as he watched her. She was just a shadow, but he could see the grace of her movements. Even when she did not try. Did she have any idea how lovely she looked? Her figure was silhouetted against the lightening sky, and he did not think he'd ever appreciated how very feminine her curves were. He checked himself, taking a step back and shaking his head. What had gotten into him? Staring at a young woman without her knowledge? Now who had forgotten his place as a gentleman?

She started walking toward him, and he knew she could not see him in the shadows near the side of the bungalow. He cleared his throat in order not to frighten her. "Good morning, my lady."

She twirled around at the sound of his voice and pressed her hand to her breastbone. "Oh, Captain Rhodes, it is you."

"I am sorry if I frightened you."

"Not at all. I was hoping to find something to eat. I fell asleep as soon as we arrived last night. Perhaps sooner. It is all a bit hazy."

He smiled at her honesty. "Come. I will ask my servant to fetch some breakfast." He took her hand and slipped it beneath his arm, leading her toward the camp behind the building. The soldiers had begun to awaken, and the grunts of tired men preparing for the day sounded around them. "Did you sleep well?"

"Yes. Very well." Helen's voice sounded distracted. She stopped walking but did not release his arm. "Captain?"

"Yes, my lady?" He wished he could see her face clearly in the darkness.

"I am sorry I made you angry yesterday. Overseeing an entire company must be difficult enough without a young woman who does not know—"

"Angry?" He didn't allow her to finish. He would not permit another apology when she had done nothing wrong. "I was most certainly not angry. Not with *you*, in any case. Terrified. But not angry."

She did not make any response, but she did not move away, which he took as a sign that she was contemplating his words.

The feel of her hand on his arm—or perhaps the darkness—made him bold. "I worry about you, my lady." He spoke in a low voice, meant only for her ears.

"You do?"

"Yes. Constantly."

He saw her tip her head to the side as if trying to read the expression on his face, but he knew she could not see him any better than he could see her.

"I did not know that." Her voice was nearly a whisper. She placed her other hand on his arm. "I will try not to do anything else to cause you to worry."

"I fear I will always—"

The sound of something moving through the trees caused them both to jump. Michael stepped in front of Lady Helen, wishing he had a weapon of some sort, but he knew a shout was all it would take to bring a dozen armed soldiers running.

He squinted, trying to make out a shape in the darkness.

"Good day, Sahib." Naveen stepped from the tree line.

Michael allowed his shoulders to relax as his heartbeat slowed back to its normal pace. He turned to Lady Helen. "It is only my servant returning from performing his *pujah*."

"Please bring some breakfast for Lady Helen and myself," he told Naveen in their shared language. He took her arm again, leading her toward the area where the men were gathering to eat.

Helen sat on a low rock near the fire. "What is *pujah*?"

"A Hindi prayer ritual. Some, like Naveen, perform it daily."

Helen pulled her brows together. "And your other servant, he prays with the Mohammedans?"

Michael was surprised that Lady Helen had noticed the habits of the servants, but he knew she was interested in the rituals and customs of the Indian people. Her curiosity was one of the things he admired about her. She did not look at the practices with distaste, as did so many British women. "Basu Ram is a Mohammedan, yes."

Michael squatted down next to her.

Helen jumped up and motioned to the rock. "Please sit, Captain. That position must hurt your leg dreadfully."

Her concern touched him. "Not at all," he said, though he did not speak the truth. The strap pulled tightly, and the wooden leg dug into the sensitive skin under his knee. "I'll not sit while you stand, my lady."

"I insist. There is room for both of us on this stone." She sat on one edge and patted the flat space next to her.

Michael would have been a fool to refuse such an offer. He stood and moved to the spot, stretching his legs before him. "Thank you."

Naveen brought fruit and bread on large banana leaves.

They thanked him and ate in silence once he departed. Michael watched the firelight move over Helen's face and tried not to stare at the light flickering in her eyes.

Helen set the makeshift plate down on her legs and took a bite of the bread. She twisted her body slightly toward him. "Does it cause discord, Captain? Having so many beliefs in one household? Or do you all get along together in spite of the differences?"

It took him a moment to realize she was still speaking of the religious practices of his servants. Lady Helen was not one to be distracted for long when something piqued her curiosity.

"Oh, they argue constantly, but they respect one another, and I admire them for it. Many wars have been fought over religion—luckily none under my roof."

"I do not imagine for a moment that Badmash would put up with any disharmony."

"You are quite right." Michael grinned. "That bag of fleas keeps all of us in line."

Helen looked up, and Michael stood as General Stackhouse approached.

"Good morning, Helen. Captain. Ah, good, you've found breakfast. We depart soon." The general continued past toward the other side of the fire, where the servants were preparing food. Michael looked behind him and saw that the majority of the camp had been dismantled and the horses were being saddled.

"Very well." Helen's shoulders slumped. "I should see to my things. Excuse me, Captain. I do not want to make the party wait on my account."

Michael felt heavy inside at her expression. The journey was not easy. Last night he'd heard enough grumbling from seasoned soldiers to fill a book. A swell of pride warmed his chest. Lady Helen had not complained once, even though he could see from her expression and her exhausted form that the general had nearly carried into the dâk bungalow the night before that an entire day on horseback had been extremely difficult for her.

He squeezed her fingers. "Today's ride will be easier and shorter. We leave the main road and take a course through the mountains. Much less dust, and it will not be so hot."

Helen did not pull her hand away. "That is a relief."

"You have not complained at all," Michael said. He hoped if he kept her talking, she would remain a bit longer. "Just as you promised."

"I have not complained *aloud*. It is a good thing you cannot see into my mind. I fear you would see a different attitude completely."

"I cannot imagine anything but loveliness in your mind, my lady."

Lady Helen smiled and cast her gaze downward. He thought that if it was light, he would see a pink blush spreading over her soft cheeks. She gently released his hand. "Thank you for breakfast, Captain."

"My pleasure." He watched her retreating figure as she walked around the side of the building, wondering if he should have offered to see her safely inside. But since it was only a few meters, he thought the proposal would have seemed silly. An ache welled up from his toes, growing in intensity until it stung his eyes and burst out of his mouth in a sigh that left him limp. If anyone would have told him he'd ever feel so strongly about another person, he would not have believed it possible, yet here he sat, mourning the empty space on the stone next to him and swallowing hard in an attempt to quell the pain in his heart.

***

Michael led the party from the Grand Trunk Road northward to the mountains. As he'd promised, the ride was cooler beneath shady trees. The men's spirits seemed to rise with the variation of the terrain, and he heard laughter and occasional singing behind him as the day stretched on.

Where there had been crowds and a wide dusty road the day before, today they passed through wide meadows interspersed between patches of green jungle and rocky hills.

They rode through a grove of banyan trees, leading the horses around the strange roots that grew down from the branches. Nearing a wide river, Michael did not hesitate to cross, knowing that the crocodiles would have moved to deeper pools this late in the season. The horses splashed through the shallow water and up the grassy hill on the other side. The land on the far side of the river was much more mountainous with thick vegetation growing over the rocky hills.

Michael scanned the hilltops and saw a glint as light shone on metal. He turned in the saddle and caught Jim's gaze. Jim nodded, indicating that he'd seen the glint as well. Now that they were in the Shah's lands, his soldiers were watching.

Although he did not consider the party in any danger, Michael fell back to ride next to Lady Helen. She greeted him with a large smile that set his heart thumping.

"This view is marvelous, Captain. The flowers are so colorful, and the birds and deer . . . If I'd known how pleasant the ride would be today, I would have not begrudged a moment of the heat and dust yesterday."

He followed her gaze across green hills. Butterflies flitted between small yellow flowers, and creeping pink and orange bushes sprang from mounds of rocks. He'd always thought the jungles and mountains beautiful, but seeing them through Lady Helen's eyes gave him a new appreciation for the diversity of the land. A herd of deer sprang through the tall grass, and they both turned their attention to watch the animals.

"Spring is the best time of year in India. The flowers are in full bloom but not yet withered by the hot sun. And of course, the rains have not started."

"I have heard of the monsoon season. Is it dreadful?"

"A constant downpour for weeks at a time. Roads flood; buildings flood. Everything is wet and muddy; even the walls are covered in mold."

Lady Helen grimaced. "It sounds terrible."

Michael shrugged. "Uncomfortable, but between the rains the sky is the brightest blue and the sunsets are more magnificent than you could imagine."

She turned her head to look at him fully around her bonnet's brim. "You love it here, don't you, Captain?"

"I do."

"And did you not enjoy living in England?"

He hesitated, not wanting to offend. "I was young when I went to England—young and alone in a land covered by fog, trying to find my way among a people that I apparently belonged to but did not understand."

"It must have been difficult. I am sorry I did not know you then." She turned her gaze toward her horse's ears. "You would love Somerset. We could have attended garden parties and played croquet. Springtime there is marvelous. I know you would have found it to be splendid. I wish your time in England had not been so lonely. If only we had known one another . . ."

"I am certain my experience would have been vastly different if I had been acquainted with you, my lady, but I do not think you had yet been born when I was in England. And if you had, you must have been very small indeed." He attempted to smile as the discrepancy in their ages became all the more apparent. She must think him a stuffy old man blathering on about sunsets.

"Captain, are you saying you would have been opposed to playing with dolls? I had a beautiful dollhouse at Hawthorne House, I'll have you know. And I would have entertained you quite well. Although I would not have shared Molly with you. She was my favorite. So do not even ask." She wagged her finger at him.

"I would not dare." The corner of his mouth twitched.

Her smile dimmed slightly. "I cannot imagine leaving home without my mother and Jim. You must have felt so alone."

He could not maintain his smile as he thought of the years away from India. While he'd made friends and enjoyed his schooling, the entire time he'd longed for home, for his family. "I did indeed."

"Do you think you will ever return to England?"

"I do not know. I must admit my life's plans are rather undecided at the moment." He didn't tell her he planned to transfer or that he could not imagine leaving her behind when he did. The memories of his time in England were dark and lonely, but thinking about his future without Lady Helen seemed even more bleak. Yet how could he remain and watch her love another?

Chapter 15

HELEN RODE IN SILENCE, WORRIED that she had upset Captain Rhodes. His entire carriage had seemed to wilt as he'd spoken about his time in England. And about his future plans. She wondered why he had seemed so unhappy and why the pall over his mood spread a shadow over her own. She tried to think of something else to talk about, something that might return the sparkle to his eyes, a task which suddenly seemed extremely important.

"Will you tell me about pujah?"

He raised his brows and tipped his head. A small smile drew over his face as he studied her expression, and Helen found that it warmed her down to her toes.

"I do not know fully what the ritual entails. It is very sacred and involves washing and praying. And an offering of food to a chosen deity. Naveen is typically gone for hours every morning."

Helen thought about what he said. Hours every morning? The Mohammedans praying five times a day? A twist of guilt pulled inside her. She thought of her Sunday meeting at St. Mary's Church in Somerset, how she allowed her mind to wander, glancing around the congregation while the bishop read from the prayer book. In London she'd paid more attention to the fashions and the stained-glass windows of Westminster Abbey than to the sermon. Her devotion to her own beliefs was definitely lacking, and she felt a surge of motivation to do better in her personal worship.

Helen rode beside Captain Rhodes in a comfortable silence, gazing around at the countryside. The land had changed from untamed hills to orderly cultivated fields. A cluster of structures—whitewashed buildings with thatched roofs, surrounded by a bamboo fence—was nestled back against the trees. She thought it must be a small farming village. People dotted the vast landscape. She heard bleating as a boy herded goats toward an enclosure. Another child chased a flock of birds that rose into the sky like a white cloud. Men and women bent at the waist, working in a wide green field.

"What are they growing?" she asked.

"Rice."

Helen blinked her eyes. She'd never known the origin of a food that was such a staple of her diet.

He lifted an arm to indicate the other side of the road where trees grew in orderly lines. "Mango and date trees. And over that way are mulberry bushes."

Helen looked closer and saw people squatted down among the rows of bushes. "Are they picking mulberries?"

Captain Rhodes shook his head. "Tending the silk worms. Silk is much more valuable than sour berries."

Children ran along the side of the road, some holding hands of smaller children, others driving laden bullock carts. Their white smiles shone as they waved at the company. Helen could not contain a grin as she waved back.

Tall coconut trees shot straight up, and Helen stopped to watch a young boy wearing only a cloth around his hips attach a rag to his feet and use it to step on as he shimmied to the top of a tree, well over thirty feet high. Children brought the coconuts to the road for the soldiers to purchase.

Captain Rhodes sliced off the end of a coconut and indicated for Helen to drink the juice inside.

She took a sip and offered it to him, but he shook his head, indicating for her to finish it. "My ayah gave me coconut water for every small injury or childhood illness," he said. "The taste has lost its appeal."

The company wound through the farmland and then on through green hills. Captain Rhodes told her the mountains were covered in tea farms. When they crested a rise, Helen saw that the land dipped, and in the distance the road passed between two rocky cliffs.

On one of the nearby hills, Helen saw an animal moving and peered closer. Through the tall grass, she couldn't make out what it was. It appeared to be a deer, but the neck was too short. A dog?

With a gasp, she realized it was a bird. A peacock.

Helen pulled on the reins to halt her horse.

His eyes wide, Captain Rhodes turned his horse around to join her.

She pointed toward the peacock.

He looked toward the hill and then back at her with a smile.

When Helen squinted, she could see that what she'd taken for rocks or mounds of dirt were other large birds not so brightly colored. They must be the females. While the birds adorned the gardens of the Prince Regent and other British nobility, seeing them in the wild was much more exciting. The male peacock continued to preen. Its neck and body were a vivid blue, and a long train of feathers bearing characteristic "eye-spots" trailed behind.

"Can we move closer?" she whispered.

"Certainly," Captain Rhodes said.

The birds did not pay any attention as the horses walked slowly toward them. The male stretched its neck up and let out a piercing, discordant call. For such an elegant bird, its call was surprisingly harsh. It turned its head with jerky motions, causing the crest of feathers to shake.

Helen grinned at Captain Rhodes. "Have you ever seen a more beautiful shade of blue?"

His mouth pulled in a slow smile. "My lady, your own eyes are precisely the same color."

Helen felt a wave of heat rise up her neck, and she turned back to watch the bird. She had no idea why Captain Rhodes's words affected her in such a way. Obviously, she was fully aware that her eyes were blue. But the fact that *he* was aware of it was so much more noteworthy.

They continued to ride slowly closer but were still well over a hundred meters away when the peacock fanned his tail feathers into a grand display. Helen wanted to clap her hands.

Captain Rhodes raised his eyes to study the sky. "His dance means rain is coming."

Only a few white clouds hovered in the distance. Helen opened her mouth to tell Captain Rhodes that she didn't think they were in any danger of rain, but a commotion behind her stopped the words.

Some of the officers had approached and were pulling muskets from their saddles. Lieutenant Bancroft pointed his toward the birds.

Helen's breath stopped when she realized they meant to charge at the birds and shoot them. She met Captain Rhodes's gaze, shaking her head. "No, they cannot . . ."

He dipped his chin then rode back toward the others. "I'll speak to the entire company, please." His loud voice boomed through the hills.

Captain Rhodes led them toward the road, where the remainder of the group waited.

The men exchanged looks as they followed.

Helen squirmed uncomfortably in her saddle as she rode behind them. She broke off and joined Jim where he waited a bit apart from the remainder of the company.

What would Captain Rhodes say? Would they be angry that their hunting plans had been terminated? Was it her fault for allowing her distress to show?

Captain Rhodes halted his horse and waited until the entire group had gathered. "There will be no hunting on the Shah's lands."

A few officers made noises of complaint but stopped when the captain glared at them.

"We will give the people and their ruler no reason to be discontented with our presence here." He allowed his gaze to travel over the men, who eventually all nodded their agreement. "The peacock, in particular, is sacred to these people. Its death would not go unnoticed."

Jim watched Captain Rhodes speak. His face bore no expression, although Helen got the impression that he approved of the captain's orders.

Captain Rhodes turned toward Jim. "If General Stackhouse has no objections, we will rest the horses and take tiffin where the road flattens out in the shade of the rocks."

When they reached the designated spot, Helen dismounted and followed Jim toward the other officers. Her legs burned, and her spine felt as though it had been compressed. She spread her palms against her lower back and leaned from side to side, unable to stop a grimace.

Captain Rhodes hurried toward her. "Lady Helen, would you like me to send someone ahead to arrange for a palanquin? Or perhaps we could retain a cart from the village we passed."

She shook her head, frustrated that he had seen her soreness and hating that he would notice another weakness of hers. "I would not hear of it. I have only to walk around for a moment, and I shall be just the thing."

He nodded, but his brows remained furrowed.

Helen walked away, deliberately putting as much energy into her steps as she could to alleviate the captain's worry, though doing so caused her stiff muscles to cry out. With every bit of her energy, she held a pleasant expression on her face as she made a wide circle around the group of men and horses.

Making sure to watch where she walked and avoid any sort of high grass or wet places, she turned away from the road and climbed a gentle, rocky slope, hoping to watch the peacock and his lady companions as they moved among the hills. All around her, birds sang and vivid flowers swayed in the soft breeze. The sky was a clear blue, and tall trees grew in clumps around the clearing. Helen turned in a circle to watch the group of men.

She spotted Lieutenant Bancroft and Sergeant Carter studying a musket between them, apparently discussing the firing mechanism. Her eyes moved over the company. The dark-skinned sepoys spoke and laughed together, the officers rested in groups, and servants prepared food. A quick movement caught her attention. Jim jerked his head to the side and walked a small distance away from the company. Captain Rhodes followed him.

The men stood close to one another as they looked toward the pass between the cliffs. Although they were not facing Helen, she could see their actions. Captain Rhodes lifted his chin in a swift movement toward the top of the cliffs, and Jim followed his gaze then nodded.

They turned, and she saw that both men wore sober expressions. Helen studied them for a moment, trying to understand what caused their concern. She looked at the cliffs but saw nothing out of the ordinary. Perhaps the route posed some sort of threat she didn't recognize. Were they afraid of bandits? Dangerous animals?

She looked at the pass again, noticing how the cliffs shadowed the road, which suddenly seemed dark and menacing. In spite of the heat, she shivered. Helen glanced around and realized that, though the hills were low, they blocked visibility of the surrounding area. Anything could be hidden just over a rise. With swift steps, she walked back toward the group.

When she drew near, Lieutenant Bancroft hurried to intercept her and offer an arm.

Helen took it, glancing at his face. "I am sorry your hunt was banned today, Lieutenant."

"'Tis a pity, of course, but Captain Rhodes is my commanding officer." He lifted his shoulders in a shrug, and Helen saw that his expression was open and friendly, not upset in the least. A small crease appeared between his brows. "I'd have given you some feathers for your hair. I hear the style is all the rage in London." His forehead smoothed out as quickly as it had creased. "Well, no bother. There will always be other days and other birds to hunt. Eh, Lady Helen?"

"I imagine so," Helen said.

He turned his gaze toward the cliffs. "Captain says we're close. On the other side of the pass. We've less than half a day until we reach the Shah's city. We should be lounging on silk cushions, sipping cool fruit juice by this evening."

Helen remembered the captain's quiet exchange with Jim. "And do you think we're in any danger, Lieutenant?"

Dimples appeared in his cheeks as he smiled and patted her hand. "Not at all, my lady. The countryside is safe, and the Shah's an ally. Do not worry yourself."

Helen thanked him for escorting her then moved to sit on a blanket that had been laid out over the ground. She ate cold meat and cheese, and listened to the conversations surrounding her. Hearing nothing to indicate that there was any reason for concern, she relaxed and enjoyed the sunlight and the sounds of the birds.

Too soon, it was time to continue. Helen mounted her horse and joined Jim. Once the group had spread out and she did not worry about being overheard, she turned to her stepfather. "Sir, can

I ask what concerns you and Captain Rhodes about the pass? Is it dangerous?"

Jim turned his head and squinted his eye as he studied her. "Don't miss much, do you?" He lifted his gaze to the cliffs in front of them. "The Shah's soldiers are hiding on the ridge." Jerking his chin slightly, he indicated the tops the cliff walls.

Helen squinted as she looked up but saw nothing. "But they are friendly, are they not? You are not concerned?" She spoke the words, hoping only for reassurance; the shaded area between the cliffs looked foreboding.

"We are safe, Helen. It is just wise to be aware. If a foreign power was making a journey to Calcutta, we'd do the same." He rotated fully toward her and laid a hand on hers where it held the horse's reins. "I would not have brought you if your safety was the smallest bit in question."

Helen nodded, wondering why his words did not reassure her.

They were nearly inside the pass now, and she estimated the walls were roughly twenty meters high, with a jagged ridge high along the top. It looked as though some attempt had been made to clear loose boulders from the road beneath, but smaller rocks still dotted the passage.

Captain Rhodes signaled with his hand, and the party moved forward into the shady corridor. Helen did not like the feeling of the high walls looming over her, especially now that she knew soldiers were watching from above. The space between the walls was probably as wide as the Grand Trunk Road, but the rocks clogging the space and the surrounding cliffs made it seem much more narrow.

"It must be very difficult to bring carts along this route," Helen said in a low voice to Jim.

"Excellent defensive strategy." His lips tightened.

Helen was grateful when they emerged into the sunlight a few moments later. Before her, encircled on all sides by lush green mountains, was a wide valley. A walled city with white buildings and tile roofs was situated on a slight hill. Tended farmland surrounded it like a bumpy patchwork quilt. Even though they were still miles away from the city, all eyes were drawn to the largest visible structure, which sat alone on the tallest hill in the center of the buildings: the White Palace.

"It is beautiful," Helen breathed. The palace was made of white stone that seemed to glow in the light. Large windows with carved Arabian-style arches decorated the facade. Onion-shaped domes adorned the top of the structure, with the largest in the center. Tall minarets rose from the corners.

She looked at the other members of her company. From the expressions and noises the soldiers around her were making, she knew she wasn't the only one enraptured by the splendor of the view. Glancing around her, she met Captain Rhodes's gaze and smiled, giving a little shrug to show how excited and nervous she was.

He raised his brows and smiled in an encouraging expression that set her at ease.

***

The valley was much larger than it appeared, and three more hours passed before they neared the city.

"And here's the welcoming committee," Jim said, pointing toward the city walls. A company of horsemen rode toward them in formation. A few carried banners.

Captain Rhodes watched them approach and turned his horse to draw close to Jim and Helen. "I think it would serve us well if we do not reveal my understanding of the native language." He spoke in a low voice that betrayed a hint of worry.

"Wise," Jim said, tapping his finger on his lip. "Give us the upper hand." He motioned a soldier near and told him to convey the information to the others.

Helen felt a prick of unease. This visit was purely friendly, so why bother with subterfuge? Perhaps Jim and Captain Rhodes were just being cautious.

"And your servants, Captain," she said. "You should remind them to speak to you solely in English."

"You possess a very sharp mind, my lady." Captain Rhodes's mouth twisted in a joking smile even though his eyes remained serious. "I am a bit worried that you so readily grasp the finer points of espionage; however, you are very wise to have thought of it. Overlooking the smallest detail could reveal us." He motioned for

Basu Ram. "The servants would not speak in the presence of a member of the court, but they might perhaps speak to other servants."

Helen felt proud at his compliment, but the unease remained. Why was deception even necessary?

Basu Ram joined him. He listened to Captain Rhodes then nodded and moved back to his place.

A shadow fell over the valley as gray clouds gathered in the sky. The peacock had been correct, and Helen hoped they would be indoors before the rains started.

Most of the approaching horsemen stopped fifty meters away; only three continued to advance.

Jim ordered the men into a line facing the Shah's soldiers, and he rode forward with Captain Rhodes and Helen on either side of him, and a servant behind.

Now that they were closer, Helen studied the men moving toward them. She knew right away that one was a servant. He was dressed plainly and rode behind the others. Another, she was certain, was a soldier. He sat tall and proud in the saddle, his eyes scanning them and his face unmoving. A red silk sash stretched from his shoulder to waist, and hanging from it was a golden-hilted sword. His wide silk trousers were tucked into leather boots, and a black turban wound around his head, held in the center by a gleaming red jewel.

The other man was much smaller and did not appear as easy on horseback. He wore an embroidered cap that coordinated with the vest that hung open over his long, collarless shirt. Instead of boots, he wore slippers with pointed toes that curled upward, and he carried no weapon.

When the groups were close to twenty feet apart, Helen followed the others' example and dismounted. The servants held the horses' reins, and the two groups approached each other on foot. When they met, the smaller man bowed, greeting them with flowery phrases and a stream of compliments that Helen thought were as insincere as the public facades of two rival debutantes. He introduced himself as a minister of the Shah's court but did not provide a name for either himself or the soldier next to him. The minister's voice was high and slightly squeaky, and he spoke in English with strange inflections that Helen had to concentrate on in order to understand.

"Yes, uh . . . thank you." Jim looked uncertain as to what to say in return. "Your valley is very beautiful, and it is an honor to be permitted to visit with Shah Ahsan Ali."

The small man nodded his head with a serene smile at the mention of his ruler's name.

Jim cleared his throat and plunged ahead. "I am Brigadier-General Jim Stackhouse, and this is Captain Michael Rhodes, and my daughter, Lady Helen."

The man nodded again, and Helen wondered if that was part of his duties as a minister of the Shah's court. He motioned to the mounted group behind him, and a man rode forward. When he reached them, he dismounted and placed long, flowered garlands on Helen's, Jim's, and Captain Rhodes's shoulders, one at a time, pressing his palms together and leaning forward in a low bow to each of them.

Helen thanked him but noticed none of the men looked at her directly, so she moved her attention to the beautiful, fragrant flowers that hung around her neck. The blossoms were spectacular—red, yellow, pink, purple—and they were arranged in lovely patterns. Their perfume was exquisite, and Helen thought she wouldn't mind wearing a floral necklace every day of the week.

When the man had finished distributing the garlands, he returned to the others, and the small minister in the cap spoke again. "You must be very tired. Please allow us to escort you and your men to the palace, where rooms and refreshment await after your journey. If it pleases you, the Shah will allow you to rest this evening and meet with you on the morrow."

"Thank you. That is very hospitable. We appreciate it very much." Jim motioned for the company to follow. When they crossed the space between them, the other soldiers moved to ride on both sides and behind the British soldiers.

Helen looked nervously at the formation. They were surrounded. But she took comfort in the fact that Jim and the captain did not appear worried.

The procession rode through a maze of narrow streets. Just like in Calcutta, the markets were colorful and full of life and noise. People stopped their conversations and watched as they passed, shutters in high windows opened, and eyes looked down on them. The roads sloped gradually upward until they reached the high stone walls and heavy wooden gate.

Syces led away the horses, and the British soldiers were politely disarmed before being led through the palace gates.

She followed Jim, who walked directly behind the Shah's minister, with the remainder of the company following. The hair on the back of Helen's neck prickled as they continued through a stone corridor lined with men in boots, red silk sashes, and black turbans. Torchlight glinted off the shining swords that hung from their sashes and the pistols tucked into their belts.

Helen pressed closer to Jim. Although she could not see his face, she could tell by the way he walked that he was tense.

They emerged into a courtyard, and the Shah's minister proceeded forward along a path that led through the center of the open space toward a large door beneath a wide balcony.

Jim walked behind him.

But Helen could not follow. Her legs felt as though they were made of lead. Pacing along the edges of the courtyard were six chained tigers.

Chapter 16

MICHAEL NEARLY PLOWED INTO LADY Helen, she stopped so suddenly. When he looked ahead, he realized why. Enormous Bengal tigers paced or lounged against the walls, taking advantage of the scant shade. Thick chains were attached to collars around their necks, and each chain was looped around a metal post to limit the animals' reach. But the chains could easily be loosened to allow them to access every bit of the courtyard.

He stepped closer to Helen and could feel her trembling where his arm brushed against her shoulder. "Do not worry; they cannot reach us on the path." He kept his voice low. He was certain the Shah watched from behind the carved screens on the balcony or windows. The man was no doubt anxious to see how frightened the British soldiers would be when they saw his pets.

Lady Helen still did not move, and the men behind them began to make noises, obviously wondering why they had stopped in the dark passageway.

Michael found her hand and squeezed, leaning forward so only she could hear him. "I will walk with you, my lady. Nothing shall harm you while I am near."

He could hear her quick breaths. Lady Helen took a step forward into the sun, and Michael stepped beside her. When she turned toward him, he was startled by how white her face looked against the light-gray bonnet. Her eyes were wide, and her expression one of sheer terror.

He felt a wave of anger toward the Shah and cursed the man for causing such distress to a young woman. Michael lifted her hand onto his bent arm and gently pulled her forward.

The tigers watched them pass; occasionally one made a growling sound. From the way the animals paced and strained against their chains, Michael knew if they had not been restrained, the courtyard would be a killing field.

With slow steps, Helen kept pace though he felt as though he was practically dragging her. He felt her entire body shaking and thought if he was not holding on to her, she might collapse. Ahead of them, Jim stopped and turned. He looked at Lady Helen, and his face tightened. He was also obviously angry with the Shah's show of "hospitality" and its effect on his stepdaughter.

When they reached the other end of the courtyard and stepped past the guards into a wide hall, Michael felt Helen droop. Jim held on to her elbow, and Michael reluctantly released her.

The minister called to a servant, ensuring that the rooms were in order. The servant assured him they were and that supper awaited the travelers. Accommodations had also been made for the servants.

Michael kept his expression impassive as if he had not understood the exchange.

The minister excused the servant. "I will show you to your rooms, and if you like, perhaps the young lady would prefer to remove to the women's quarters for the night."

Michael's muscles compressed at the suggestion. Although he knew she would be treated well, he did not want Lady Helen taken where they couldn't find her. Aside from queens, a prince's harem consisted of concubines and dancers and other less-than-refined women. He didn't think Lady Helen would be comfortable at all.

"Thank you," Jim said, "but I think my daughter would prefer to remain near to me."

Michael could have embraced the general for his perfect answer.

The minister showed the officers to their rooms; then, when he was certain they had everything necessary for their comfort, he told them he would return for them in the morning and took his leave.

Michael took a bit of refreshment from the common area then claimed a bedchamber in a suite shared by a portion of the officers. He stepped through the door and threw his jacket and garland onto a chair. He'd not realized how tightly he'd been holding his shoulders nor how the ups and downs of the day had taken their toll on his nerves. He was exhausted. He lay down on the bed, and it seemed only moments later that a servant knocked on the door, bearing a candle and note.

Michael heard a thunderclap and glanced at the screened windows, then looked at his pocket watch. The time was well into the evening. He must have slept longer than he'd realized. The servant lit more candles and left.

Michael looked at the note.

Captain Rhodes,
Please join Lady Helen and me in our quarters for supper.
Brigadier-General Jim Stackhouse

There was no flourish, greeting, compliment, nor anything that would make the note more than an order from his commander, but at the sight of it, Michael felt a surge of energy and knew a foolish grin spread over his face.

He shaved, drew a comb through his hair, and changed his shirt in record time, arriving at the general's rooms less than twenty minutes later.

Lady Helen rose when he entered the sitting room. Michael noticed she had also changed her gown and freshened up. Her face looked radiant in the candlelight, and none of her earlier anxiety showed as she greeted him. "Captain, I am so glad you came to join us." She held out her hand, and Michael took it, marveling that something as simple as the touch of her fingers could send a wave of heat up his arm. "Jim will join us in a moment. Please have a seat." She motioned toward a sitting area.

Michael sat on a carved wooden divan with silk cushions, and she took a chair beside him. He glanced around the room, admiring the silken window hangings with golden embroidery that shone in the candlelight. Tapestries and paintings hung on the walls, and a thick Persian rug spread over the floor. The furniture was beautiful, carved in excessive detail from dark wood and embellished with colorful pillows. But as magnificent as the palace decor was, it did not compete for his attention in the slightest with the young lady next to him.

"Captain Rhodes, I am grateful for your assistance today. I was so very afraid, and you—you set me at ease." She looked down at her hands that sat gracefully curled in her lap. "I could not have walked through that horrible courtyard with anyone else."

Her words hit Michael's heart with the force of a musket ball. He took a breath as heat filled his chest, certain that she could hear his pulse pounding in his ears. "I am glad to have helped. I was quite nervous myself."

"You disguised it admirably." She lifted her gaze to his. "You always seem so steady, Captain."

If Lady Helen had any idea what was happening inside his heart and mind at this moment, *steady* would be the last word she'd choose to describe him.

"I—" Michael was spared from finding a suitable reply when Jim entered the room.

"Good, you're here. We've much to discuss."

A servant set a steaming tray on the dining table. Michael's stomach rumbled at the smell of curry, steamed fish, and tomato chutney.

"Perhaps it should wait, sir." Michael looked pointedly at the man setting out the dishes. The Shah would undoubtedly have spies listening everywhere. Michael had already warned the other officers to watch what they said.

Jim nodded. "You are right, Captain." He led them to the dining table, and Michael studied the beautiful dishes. Gold trim wound through the detailed painted patterns. It was a pity that all of the tableware would be destroyed as soon as the *ferengi* left, he thought. What a waste of beauty.

A bolt of lightning lit up the sky, followed by another clap of thunder. The smell and the cool of the rain floated in through the screens, making the room feel cozy and bringing the temperature to a comfortable level.

The meal was delicious, and they kept their conversation to neutral topics. Lady Helen seemed to understand right away the wisdom of not discussing anything they would not want to reach the ears of the Shah.

Of course she did, Michael thought. She was much more clever than most.

Helen tried each of the dishes. She took a small bite of curry and rice, and her eyes opened wide. She swallowed and coughed then reached for a drink of juice.

"It is very spicy, my lady." Michael laughed.

"You should have warned me." She dabbed her watering eyes with her napkin. "I think I will stick with the fish."

She told him stories about her youth in Somerset, and she asked Michael about his own childhood in Bombay, listening with rapt attention as he described the cave temples on Elephanta Island.

"And the festivals, my lady . . ." Michael continued. "My favorite is *Janmashtami* after the rains end. The festival celebrates the birth of Lord Krishna, and in Bombay, pots of butter are strung up high above the streets, and people build human pyramids to reach them."

"But why?" Helen asked. She squinted her eyes and pulled her chin back, her face a mixture of amusement and curiosity.

"Krishna was a trickster. And the custom is an imitation of his childhood pranks. You would enjoy watching."

Helen laughed. "Or perhaps I should climb to the very top and snatch a pot myself."

Both Michael and General Stackhouse laughed at this.

If he did not think too hard about the circumstances surrounding their situation, Michael could almost imagine himself to be enjoying a dinner party with old friends. Lady Helen was engaging throughout the meal, and Michael believed her laughter capable of softening the cruelest of hearts. He was disappointed when the servers brought a plate of *Mango Sandesh* and *Jalebi* for dessert, for he knew the meal was nearly over.

Lady Helen sampled a bit of the Bengali sweets and then laid her napkin next to her plate. "Supper was delightful, Captain Rhodes. I am so glad you joined us." She moved to rise. "If the two of you would excuse me. I am very tired."

The gentlemen stood and bid her farewell as she exited the room. The light seemed to dim and the warmth to disperse with her leaving. Instead of remaining at the table, they moved to the sitting area while the servants cleared the dishes.

Michael and the general spoke of mundane things as they leaned back in their seats, sipping their after-supper port—the repair on a wall of the fort, a proposed advancement for a junior officer, and the weather—until finally the last servant stepped into the hall and closed the door behind him.

General Stackhouse leaned forward in his chair, his hands dangling between his knees. "What do you make of—"

Michael held up a hand to stop him. He crossed the room to the door leading to the hallway and opened it quickly. Seeing no one there eavesdropping on their conversation, he returned to his seat but made certain to keep his voice low. "We could still be overheard, sir. Better to speak quietly."

The general nodded. "What do you think about the reception we received, Captain? Is it typical native courtesy to intimidate one's guests?"

Michael scratched the side of his face, glad that the noise of the rain would help keep their conversation from being overheard. "I don't like it at all, sir. The man who greeted us is a junior minister at best. The Shah thinks to insult us by not sending a high-ranking member of his court."

Michael stopped speaking when he heard a commotion outside— shrieks and bleats followed by loud roars. He recognized the sound immediately. Hurrying to the window, he unlatched the screen and pushed it open. General Stackhouse joined him. The general's rooms faced the courtyard they'd crossed when they arrived. The rain made visibility nearly impossible, but it was not difficult to deduce what was happening. It sounded as if goats had been loosed in the courtyard and the hungry tigers given slack in their chains to fall upon the smaller animals.

The appalling noises made by the predators as well as the prey rose from the ground below, and Michael hurried to close the screen. Though it did nothing to keep the sound out. Or the musky smell of wet cats and the tang of blood.

"What is happening?"

Michael spun around and saw Lady Helen standing in the doorway of her bedchamber. Her hair hung over one shoulder in a loose braid, and she clutched a silk shawl around her shoulders. To say she looked frightened was an understatement of immense magnitude.

He started to move toward her, but Jim hurried past, and Michael remembered his place. Embracing Lady Helen while she wore her nightdress was not in the least appropriate. Just the idea started Michael's heart pounding, and he kept his gaze toward the window in order not to glance down at her bare feet or to notice how errant locks of her hair curled around her cheeks and neck.

"Do not worry," the general was telling her as he patted her shoulder. "We are perfectly safe. The Shah is simply feeding his . . . pets."

"Why is he doing this? It is horrifying." Helen's voice shook, but it was much stronger than Michael would have imagined, based on the paleness of her face. "I thought the Shah was friendly. It seems as though he is deliberately trying to frighten us."

The general and Michael shared a glance. Lady Helen was very perceptive.

"It is simply posturing, my dear," the general said. "You should go back to bed."

Lady Helen glanced at the window. The sounds had not fully quieted, and even the rain could not drown out the loudest of them. Occasionally a tiger would growl or make a chuffing sound, and even worse was the intermittent goat's panicked bleat. She looked between the general and Jim. "Please, can I remain here with you? Just for a short while?"

Her expression was so vulnerable, with wide eyes afraid and pleading, that Michael balled his fists to keep himself from rushing to her.

"Of course." General Stackhouse led her to a chair in the sitting area and motioned with a bend of his head for Michael to join them.

Once Michael was seated, the general leaned forward again, keeping his voice low. "Intimidating display." His eyes darted to the window. "But he's chosen to offend the wrong people."

Michael nodded. It was true. With just an order, the general could mobilize an entire army, and few came out on top when they challenged the Crown. "It is a pathetic display from a person who has no real power," he said. "Rather like a child playing cruel jokes on the stronger children he envies."

Though he did not allow his gaze to move toward her, Michael was completely aware that Lady Helen had pulled her feet up onto the chair and scooted down to lay her head on the armrest.

Jim stood and paced back and forth, no longer keeping his voice low. "I hate feeling like a prisoner. There is only one path in or out of this blasted valley. We are without weapons, and I doubt any of us could find our way out of this palace. If we did, we not only have tigers to deal with but the Shah's armies and a city that's like a maze. Not to mention the wide-open farmland and the heavily guarded pass awaiting us. We're in a highly vulnerable situation here, and the Shah knows it."

Michael blew out a breath. "He knows it. But his situation is the more vulnerable."

"True." Jim sank back into the chair. "What is our strategy for meeting the prince tomorrow?"

"We refuse to act at all intimidated and do what we came here for: present gifts, share wishes for his health and a friendly relationship between our nations, then get out. The quicker, the better," Michael said. "With any luck, we will be through the pass and far from this place before nightfall."

"Good plan," Jim said.

They continued the discussion for nearly half an hour longer. Michael knew the instant Lady Helen fell asleep by the sound of her breath deepening. He fought the entire time to concentrate on the general's words and ignore the sighs that escaped her lips. Forcing himself not to glance over when her arm dropped was a feat of unparalleled willpower that would impress a *fakir* holy man who fasted weeks at a time.

Finally the general declared that he would retire. He rose, and Michael followed suit.

"Good night, Captain. If you don't mind letting yourself out, I'll see Helen gets to her bedchamber."

"Of course."

General Stackhouse helped Lady Helen to her feet.

"Jim?" Her voice was soft and sleepy.

"Come, Helen. You can sleep in your bed now. All is silent." He slid an arm around her and helped her toward her room.

She rested her head on his shoulder as she walked. "Is Captain Rhodes still here, Jim?" Her speech was slurred.

Michael's hand froze in the air as he reached for the door handle.

"I feel so safe when he is near."

"Of course you do," Jim soothed.

Michael hurried out into the hall and pulled the door closed behind him. He didn't believe that any words in any language or context could have the impact her drowsy statement had on him. He thought his heart might explode from his chest, and he quickened his pace in case the general should call him back. He knew he would not be able to control the grin that was so large it hurt his cheeks—even for his commanding officer.

Chapter 17

HELEN AWOKE TO SUNLIGHT STREAMING through a carved wooden screen onto the silk bedding surrounding her. The bedchamber was much more beautiful in the sunlight. She studied a painting that hung near her bed—an array of bold colors in a geometric design. A perfect symbol of India: color. She had never seen such vivid hues, and they were everywhere: clothing, plants—even the peacock they'd seen yesterday was bright and colorful.

Her eyes moved to the garland lying on a table near her bed. The fragrance was still strong, and she smiled at the memory of Jim wearing a necklace of flowers. He had removed the garland with a look of long-suffering the moment they'd entered their suite the night before. Apparently floral decorations were not his choice of accessories.

A servant entered and helped her dress in the gown she'd chosen to wear to meet the Shah. Helen loved the creamy yellow color and the lace trim around the neck and sleeves. Embroidered flowers in green and pink flowed down the sides like vines. Helen attached a simple necklace of coral beads and slipped a long silk shawl over her arms, allowing it to trail behind her. She did not wear a bonnet, so the servant helped pin curls loosely on Helen's head, and she pulled on long gloves that reached past her elbows. She emerged from her room a few moments later and found Jim seated at the dining table.

He stood when she entered. "Good morning. I hope you slept well."

"I did, sir. After the . . . excitement . . . was finished."

"And how do you feel?"

"Nervous." She sat at the table across from him. "What do you think the Shah is like?"

"I cannot begin to guess. But something I've learned is that no matter their station or importance, beneath it all, men are just that—men."

Helen accepted a dish of fruit a servant offered. "*Dhanyavaad*," she muttered then smiled at Jim's surprised expression. She lifted her shoulders in a shrug, and he turned the edges of his lips downward as he nodded. Helen wondered if Captain Rhodes would be impressed that she had remembered the word.

She thought of the captain and their interactions over the journey: watching the peacock, worrying about her near the stream, riding next to her and sharing stories, holding her hand when she was afraid. Being with Captain Rhodes felt more comfortable than being without him, and she pondered over the fact that she missed his company even though it had been only a few hours ago that they'd eaten supper together. It was a comfort to know that she'd see him again when they met with the Shah.

Her mind returned to the upcoming meeting, and she thought about what Jim had said. The Shah was a man, just like any other. She should not harbor ill feelings toward him for frightening her the day before. Perhaps he had only wanted to show off his beautiful animals, not knowing it would be upsetting to a British lady. Since she did not fully understand the customs of these people, she could not expect that he would fully understand hers, and she should approach this meeting with an open mind.

Glancing around the room, she nodded. Yes. She was in a magnificent palace and had the opportunity to meet an Indian prince. The experience was one most people would never know, and she resolved to enjoy herself and to learn everything she could about the Shah. With the sun shining, it was difficult to feel anything but cheerful.

***

Not long after breakfast, the prince sent a servant to summon them for an audience. Jim and Helen followed him through passageways and beautiful gardens until they arrived at a large courtyard where the rest of their company awaited them.

The minister from the day before entered the courtyard accompanied by another man. The stranger's clothing was much finer than his companion's, and Helen thought he must be more important. Perhaps he was the Shah? Both bowed a greeting, and the minister introduced the other as the Shah's *diwan*, or prime minister.

The diwan spoke for a moment, and the minister translated in his high-pitched voice. "He is very sorry to have been unavailable to greet you when you arrived yesterday. An error, I'm afraid. His secretary confused the day of your arrival, but the person responsible has been suitably punished."

"Completely understandable," Jim said. "No offense taken."

Helen darted a glance at Captain Rhodes and saw that his face remained impassive. The light-gray of his eyes had taken on a darker hue that reminded Helen of storm clouds. She didn't think he believed the diwan's flimsy excuse in the least.

The diwan spoke again, spreading his hand to the side.

"His Majesty, Shah Ahsan Ali, awaits you in the Hall of Public Audience. Please follow me."

As they entered the antechamber, Helen saw columns running along both sides, leaving the hall open to the outside and allowing a breeze to move through the vast space.

Servants and soldiers mingled throughout the room, many wearing the same black turban Helen had seen on the soldier the day before. Other people Helen thought were courtiers wore a mixture of bright-colored clothing, though she noticed no women present. The people in the chamber stood aside and watched with unreadable faces as the British group made their way across the marble floor along a carpeted pathway lined with soldiers to the far end of the room.

Steps led up to a platform where servants waved fans of peacock feathers and more soldiers stood serving as guards for the man who sat cross-legged on a raised cushioned dais. The Shah.

Trying not to appear as if she was staring, Helen studied Shah Ahsan Ali. He was close to Jim's age, she thought. His skin was much fairer than any Indian's she had seen thus far. A pointy mustache curled beneath his nose, looking too small for his face and a bit comical. Helen was reminded of her sisters making similar mustaches with curls that had fallen to the floor after her brother's hair had been cut. The Shah's clothing was elegant: Flowing silk made up his trousers and shirt, and he wore a long embroidered vest. His turban was decorated with a cluster of jewels from which rose long feathers. Gemstone rings adorned every finger. Even his slippers were decorated with pearls.

Helen followed Jim's and Captain Rhodes's lead; she curtsied when the men bowed.

The diwan and his interpreter stepped up onto the platform. "Brigadier-General Jim Stackhouse," the minister said to the Shah.

"Your Highness, it is indeed an honor." Jim stepped forward. "I thank you for your excellent hospitality in this magnificent palace. I bring greetings of Lord Minto, who regrets that he could not accompany us himself." He spread his arm to the side. "This is my second-in-command, Captain Michael Rhodes, and my daughter, Lady Helen."

The interpreter spoke to the Shah, but he did not seem to be listening. Helen wanted to shy away when she realized the Shah's gaze was firmly settled on her. He held up his hand, and the room fell immediately silent. He continued to watch Helen as he spoke in a quiet voice to the interpreter.

The man replied, and Helen heard her name. She glanced at Captain Rhodes and saw his jaw was clenched.

The minister stepped to the edge of the platform. "Please, General Stackhouse, His Highness asks if he may speak to your daughter."

Jim cleared his throat and moved his gaze between the Shah and Helen and then to Captain Rhodes. "What does—"

The Shah spoke again, cutting him off.

"You, of course, will remain with her, General."

Jim looked to Helen, and she nodded permission, her curiosity overcoming any trepidation. Why would the Shah wish to speak to her?

Shah Ahsan Ali motioned for Helen to step up onto the platform. Jim stayed close behind.

"I have never seen eyes this color. They are extraordinary," the Shah said through the interpreter.

The Shah said something else, but the interpreter did not expound.

"Thank you, Your Highness. Dhanyavaad."

The Shah smiled when she used the word, but his eyes remained thoughtful.

Helen was surprised, and a little shocked, to see that his red-tinged teeth did not look at all healthy, and now that she was closer she noticed his skin was a bit yellow. She hoped the Shah was not unwell.

"Do you like the palace, Lady Helen?" the interpreter asked for the Shah.

"Yes, very much." Helen's palms were damp, and she could feel them sticking to her gloves as she struggled to find words to say. She thought repeating Jim's compliments was a wise course of action. "The palace is more beautiful than I could have imagined. Thank you for allowing our visit. It is quite a privilege."

The Shah listened to the minister translate and then studied Helen again. "I rarely have women in my court. It is strange to me that your father would allow you to travel with a band of men who are not relatives. Our women are considered precious and are kept hidden from the eyes of other men." He waved his hand to the carved screens that lined the upper story of the wall behind him.

Helen raised her eyes and saw movement behind the carved wood. She realized the screens were in place to insure the women's privacy as they watched the proceedings in the chamber below. She looked back to the Shah.

"Do you think this custom strange?" he asked.

Helen considered for a moment before she answered. The Shah appeared to be testing her. Did he think his words might offend her? She did not feel as though Jim considered her less precious just because he did not keep her hidden behind a screen. The thought surprised her. She had not realized how much she had come to love Jim and felt his love for her in return.

The Shah's statement had not made her feel insulted but interested. "Not strange, Your Highness. Different. I enjoy learning about such customs. And I find it extremely admirable that you hold women in such high regard."

A sound like a cough drew the Shah's gaze toward the British soldiers, but he returned it to Helen as he listened to the interpreter. He studied her for a moment longer, and Helen thought there was perhaps nothing more uncomfortable than standing on a platform in a room of silent men while being stared at. She felt self-conscious and did not know what to do with her hands, so she clasped them behind her back.

"I wonder . . . would you like to visit the women's section of the palace?"

Both the Shah and the interpreter watched her expectantly.

Helen looked at Jim, wondering how to possibly answer such a proposal.

"It is your choice, Helen," he said through tight lips. "You do not have to go anywhere."

She glanced at Captain Rhodes and saw that his eyes had darkened further to nearly the color of charcoal. She raised her brows in question, and he gave her a tight nod. Even though he looked angry, she took his gesture to mean she would be safe to accept the offer.

The decision was up to her, and Helen felt nervous with the weight of it. She was curious about the palace, and the idea of seeing more of it—perhaps seeing the queen—was nearly too tempting to pass up. But she remembered the tigers from the night before and did not know if she could fully trust the Shah. Before she could answer, she heard her mother's voice in her head. *Helen, you came to India to experience the world.* Was she brave enough to do just that?

Helen turned back to the Shah. His expression had taken on a hint of impatience, and she realized he was not often in the position of waiting for others to make up their minds. "Thank you for your gracious offer, Your Highness. I would enjoy it very much."

Helen did not know what to expect as she followed a servant through the crowd of people. It was frightening to leave the security of her group. She glanced back once to see Captain Rhodes watching her. She gave him a smile, and he tipped his head slightly. His face did not have any of his cheerfulness or teasing, and the sight of him looking so solemn cast a shadow over her mood.

The servant brought her to the bottom of a flight of steps where a female servant waited to accompany Helen upstairs. When they reached the upper landing, Helen was startled and a bit unnerved to find the most enormous men she'd ever seen standing guard on either side of a heavy door. The men looked strange. Though they were well-muscled with broad shoulders, something about their mannerisms seemed nearly feminine—perhaps their hairless faces.

They both studied Helen as the servant spoke to them. One man produced a key and opened the door, and Helen followed the woman inside. The sound of the thick wooden door closing sent a feeling of dread over her, and Helen looked back, wondering if it was too late to run back to the safety of Captain Rhodes.

The woman spoke, nodding and motioning for Helen to follow her through a passageway. When they reached a doorway, the servant scratched on the doorframe and, hearing a voice within, slid the door to the side. She bowed and indicated for Helen to precede her.

Helen stepped over the threshold into an open, airy chamber with billowing soft curtains. Two women were in the room, and one rose and bowed a greeting. The other remained as she was, lounged on a long divan and propped up with pillows. Helen saw that her belly was swollen. This woman must be the queen.

Helen stood in the doorway, uncertain of what to do. She knew the women would not understand her if she spoke, but she couldn't very well just stand here looking at them all day. She stepped into the room, glancing back when she heard the door slide shut. "Hello," she said, putting on a smile. She pressed a hand against her chest, feeling extremely foolish. "My name is Lady Helen." She looked back and forth between the women.

The lounging woman spoke to the other, who stepped forward. "Welcome, Lady Helen."

"Oh, wonderful. You speak English." Helen smiled in relief.

The woman inclined her head in acknowledgement and motioned toward the other. "This is Rani-Sanjana."

Helen dipped in a deep curtsy, bowing her head forward as she'd been taught when she was presented at King James's Court.

The Rani lowered her eyelids and tipped her head forward slightly. She motioned for the other woman to bring a chair closer. Helen sat, obeying another elegant gesture. It seemed the Rani was accustomed to giving orders with the slightest wave of her hand.

Helen did not want to be rude and gape at the Shah's wife, but she could not help herself. Rani-Sanjana was young—much younger than Helen would have imagined. She thought the queen could not have been older than sixteen. Her appearance reminded Helen of a doll. Her hair was woven into a braid thicker than Helen's arm and so long Helen thought it must reach nearly to her knees. She wore a headpiece of gold chains from which dangled pearls and, in the center of her forehead, a red gemstone. Gold bangles adorned each arm. Large brown eyes painted in kohl and surrounded by thick lashes blinked from the heart-shaped face. Her mouth was small and smiled softly. Helen got the impression that if the Rani was angry, her face could just as quickly turn from gentle to fierce.

The Rani spoke to the other woman, who listened closely before turning to Helen. "My name is Prema. I am ayah to Rani-Sanjana. She is very happy that you came to visit."

Prema's accent was heavier than the Shah's minister's, and Helen had to listen closely to her words. Her voice rose and fell, making her sentences seem almost like she was singing. Her *v*'s she pronounced as *w*'s, causing the word *visit* to sound like *wisit*.

"Pleased to meet you, Prema. How is it that you speak English so well?"

"I was a servant in a British household for many years before I was brought to the palace."

She did not embellish, but Helen thought there must be more to the story. She did not press for details.

The Rani spoke to Prema again, and Helen took the opportunity to study the ayah. Prema was not as beautiful as the Rani. Her teeth poked out beneath her upper lip, and she had harsh cheekbones, but her smile seemed genuine. Helen liked her right away.

"Her Highness has never met a British woman, Lady Helen, and she wishes to ask you questions, if she may."

"Of course." Helen smiled at both women.

"Are you married?" the Rani asked through Prema.

"No."

When she heard Helen's answer, Rani-Sajana tipped her head, allowing her gaze to travel over Helen—much as her husband had done half an hour earlier.

"You are not ugly. Engaged, then."

"No, I am afraid not."

The Rani's eyes opened wide. "But you must be nearly twenty. Has your father not settled upon a bride-price?"

Helen shook her head. "I have had no offers," she said. "And the man I will marry will be my choice, not my father's."

"How can you choose your own husband?"

"I suppose by meeting different men and becoming acquainted with them to see if we are a good match."

"This cannot be so." The Rani sat up on the divan and shook her head. "I have never heard of such a thing."

Helen darted a look at Prema, worried that she was being offensive, but the ayah did not look as though anything was wrong. "Rani-Sanjana has lived in *purdah* her entire life," she explained.

"I do not know what that means," Helen said.

"She has never left the women's quarters. The only men she has ever spoken to are her brothers, her father, and now her husband. She cannot imagine what it must be like to 'court,' as British women do."

"Oh." Helen glanced around the Rani's rooms. They were beautiful, and through a door behind her, Helen could see a walled garden that must be a pleasure to walk through. But never to leave?

"How long have you lived in the White Palace?" Helen asked, hoping to change the topic.

"I arrived from Bihar fifteen months ago," Rani-Sanjana said.

Helen did not know where Bihar was but hoped it was not far. The Rani seemed so young to be away from her parents. Especially with her condition. Helen suspected she would want her mother near. "And do you miss your family?"

Prema did not translate her question. "Her parents both died this past year."

"Oh, how terrible. I am sorry. And the Shah's parents? Is his mother—"

"They are both dead as well." Prema darted a nervous look toward the Rani, who watched the exchange with narrowed eyes. "I am going to tell her you inquired about her health."

"Thank you." Helen cringed inside at the reprimand in Prema's voice. She felt such pity for the young queen, who was alone in the world, but gratitude that she had a woman like Prema to look after her.

When the Rani heard Prema's words, her face lit up.

She placed a hand on her swollen belly and smiled as she spoke.

"She says she will bear a son who will grow to be a great Shah," Prema said.

"Or perhaps a daughter?" Helen thought it was extremely naive for the Rani to believe that just because she wished for a son her child would not be a girl.

Prema translated her words, and the Rani's face clouded. Helen had been correct when she assumed the young woman was capable of producing an extremely fierce expression. She spoke quickly, and Helen could tell her words were angry.

"A son," Prema said simply. Her eyes pleaded with Helen not to argue.

"A son will be wonderful. And I am sure you will be an excellent mother to him." Helen was worried that she would feel the displeasure of the Rani, but the young woman's face softened when she heard Prema's words.

Rani-Sanjana nodded her head and ran her hands gently over her belly.

"Perhaps, Lady Helen, you may tell the Rani about your journey to the White Palace?" Prema said.

"I would love to."

The tension left the air as Helen spoke of peacocks and rolling hills covered with flowers, Prema translated, and Rani-Sanjana listened to the descriptions of a world outside the palace walls, a world which she would only ever see through another's eyes.

Chapter 18

MICHAEL STARED ACROSS THE COURTYARD at the Shah, hardly able to disguise the enormous amount of disgust he felt for the man. They had removed from the Hall of Public Audience to a small patio spread with cushions and shaded by leafy trees. The setting was magnificent but the company repulsive.

Believing none of his guests could understand him, the Shah had maintained a battery of insults and crude jokes at the expense of the British officers. Michael didn't believe the Shah was paying the junior minister enough for the skillful way he manipulated his ruler's words into polite compliments. The man was invaluable. Michael was tempted to reveal himself numerous times when the Shah or his diwan said something particularly insulting. Especially when he spoke crudely about Lady Helen.

When the Shah had made a particularly offensive comment about the lady, Michael had nearly leapt onto the platform and delivered the mustached ruler a facer, though such a thing would undoubtedly lead to him losing his head or being fed to the tigers in the courtyard.

The suggestion for Lady Helen to visit the women's quarters had sent darts of panic through his veins, but he realized that, while he didn't like the idea of her being where he could not reach her, it was preferable to her remaining where the Shah could ogle her.

And how often had the Shah mentioned her eyes? Just hearing another man admire the feature that Michael himself so adored made his gut hot.

The Shah's mouth and teeth were red from chewing tobacco, and Michael could see the damage an opium addiction had wrought on the prince's health. He knew the man was speeding himself toward an early death with the habit.

The meeting was filled with false flattery and insincere compliments. Though Michael sensed that the Shah was intelligent, he was also petty and spoiled. It would not take more than a loss of his temper to send his armies over the hills into Calcutta. The thought was disturbing. While the smaller kingdom was no match for the British army, there would be losses on both sides. The meeting didn't last long, and within twenty minutes the Shah left them, ordering refreshment be served to his guests. His religion forbade him to remain and eat with them.

Glancing around, Michael could see he was not the only one to have lost his appetite. It was difficult to eat while every move was being scrutinized by intimidating guards.

Finally, Jim rose and thanked the junior minister and the diwan for the excellent hospitality and delicious food. He sent for Helen, who, much to Michael's relief, arrived a moment later.

She smiled and held out her arm to show Jim a golden bangle that the Rani had apparently given her. Michael noticed that her coral necklace was gone, and he assumed she had given it in exchange. It seemed that she, at least, had enjoyed her time at the palace.

Returning to their rooms, the group hastily made ready to depart. Thankfully they were escorted to a different gate than the one they'd entered on their arrival. Their horses, weapons, servants, and provisions awaited there.

Lady Helen had changed into her riding habit, and she smiled and thanked the servant who assisted her to mount her horse. They started through the gate, but when they heard a shout behind them, they halted.

Michael's heart froze. What was the Shah up to? Had he changed his mind and decided to keep them prisoner? He moved his horse close to Lady Helen's.

"Is something wrong?" she asked.

"I do not know." Michael kept his eyes on the approaching figure.

As the man drew near, they recognized him as the junior minister. He made his way directly to Lady Helen. "From the Shah." He bowed and handed her a small silk purse then, bowing again, departed.

Lady Helen watched him leave. She looked at Michael and then Jim with her brows pulled together; slowly she loosed the strings to open the purse. Turning it over, she gasped when she drew out a golden chain. The pendant hanging from it was a single jewel, nearly the size of an acorn. The gemstone was the vivid blue color of a peacock, or . . .

Michael resisted the urge to snatch it away from her. The Shah had not kept his admiration for Lady Helen's eyes a secret, and now he'd given her a costly jewel the precise vivid hue.

She held it up, watching the sun play through the magnificent stone. "It is so beautiful. I cannot accept something like this." Returning the stone to the pouch, she fished out the rolled bit of parchment from the small bag.

From their position upon their horses, Michael and Jim both leaned closer to read the writing.

This jewel appears pale when compared to the brilliant blue of your eyes.

Jim jerked straight in his saddle. "Move out!" He pulled on the reins of Helen's mount to get the horse walking. Helen looked confused but tucked the small purse into the reticule that hung from her wrist and tapped her riding crop on her horse's flank to match Jim's speed.

They left White Palace at a trot, and Michael hoped they would never return.

The group rode swiftly and silently through the valley and didn't stop until they reached the far side of the pass.

"I hope we never see that accursed place again," Jim muttered to Michael. "And what does the man mean, sending my daughter a jewel like that?"

"Let us hope he is simply being generous," Michael said.

"Did he seem at all generous to you?"

"No."

"Helen is never to go near to that place again. Do you understand?" Jim said. His face was red, and his eye squinted in a scowl.

"I could not agree more, General."

He fell back to ride near Lady Helen and listened with a smile as she described her time in the White Palace to Lieutenant Bancroft and Sergeant Carter. She had been enchanted by the palace and the queen, and Michael felt his worries dissipate as he listened.

"The Rani is more beautiful than you can imagine. She lives in elegant rooms surrounded by silk and flowers, and she has her very own lovely gardens with fountains and tame doves."

"A gilded cage," Sergeant Carter said.

"Pardon me?"

"She is a prisoner. She cannot leave," Lieutenant Bancroft said.

"No, I do not think she sees it that way. She is not unhappy." She glanced up at both men and toward Michael, an anxious look on her face as if she was determined to make them understand. "Rani-Sanjana's parents both died last year. I feel sorry for her. But she loves the White Palace and her husband and is so very excited to be a mother."

"I'll wager she's terrified her child will not be a son," Lieutenant Bancroft said. "The Shah has no patience for women who bear daughters. Perhaps she forgot to mention what happened to the Shah's other wives when they did not produce an heir."

Michael's heart sank. "Lieutenant—"

"It isn't true," Helen said.

"These people are heathens, my lady. I have seen men and women cast themselves in front of a heavy cart that carried an idol, hoping to be crushed and reincarnated into a better life. Did the Rani tell you why it is that neither she nor her husband have mothers? The women were *suttees*, and it is the fate that pretty little queen has to look forward to."

"Lieutenant, that is enough." Michael's voice was rough with anger.

She looked back, and he rode nearer, nosing his horse into the space between Lieutenant Bancroft and Lady Helen. He was furious that the lieutenant would tell her these things. "My lady, do not—"

"I want to know, Captain." She looked past him at Lieutenant Bancroft. "What is a suttee?"

The lieutenant rubbed his hand over the back of his neck in a nervous gesture. Apparently the man realized, albeit too late, that this topic might be upsetting to a young lady. "A suttee . . . uh . . . it means she will burn alive on her husband's funeral pyre."

Lady Helen's face turned white. "I don't believe you," she whispered. Her eyes narrowed angrily. "Why would you say such a thing? Captain Rhodes, tell him it is not true."

Michael's throat had constricted to the point that he did not know if he could breathe, let alone speak. "I am sorry, Lady Helen . . ."

"No." She looked between both men and turned her head to look at Sergeant Carter. She must have seen the apology in their faces, but it did not stop her lip from trembling. Urging her horse forward, she rode ahead alone.

Michael watched her go, a mixture of anger and sorrow making his chest tight.

"I am sorry, Captain." Lieutenant Bancroft's face was pulled in a grimace. "I did not think . . ."

"*That* is the smartest thing you have said all day," Michael spat out the words and rode ahead to see if he could repair the damage the lieutenant's careless words had done.

When Michael rode up next to Lady Helen, he saw tears on her cheeks, and the sight made his heart clench. "My lady . . ."

"Why did you not tell me all this, Captain?" Her voice shook, and he could see she was close to breaking down completely. "Why did you try to convince me that India is wonderful and beautiful? I feel like I have been deceived."

"I did not mean to deceive you. I have only ever sought to protect you."

"Protect me from the truth?"

"My lady, I—"

"I deceived myself," Helen said. "I did not see this place for what it truly is. I was distracted by bright silks and flowers and painted elephants. But all of it is artificial. A disguise to hide the horrible truth." She pulled a scrap of lace from her reticule and dabbed it against her eyes. "I feel so foolish."

"You are not foolish at all."

She rode quietly for a moment. "Is it true what the lieutenant said about the other wives? Will the Shah have Rani-Sanjana killed if she does not have a son?" She turned to him, and his first instinct was to soothe away her fears and tell her nothing of the sort would ever happen. But he could not lie to her.

"The Shah's other wives—those who have had daughters— apparently died in childbirth. Nobody can prove it, but it is believed his displeasure is the reason for their deaths." He blew out a breath.

Lady Helen made a sniffling sound. Tears dripped from her eyes, and she hurried to wipe them away. "Why would he do such a horrible thing?"

"By British law, if a local ruler fails to produce a legitimate heir, his lands are forfeit to the Crown. I imagine he feels a sense of desperation to keep his kingdom."

"Somebody should stop him. It is beyond horrible to imagine a person so cruel—and just because he wants a son. His lands *should* be forfeit to the Crown. A British ruler would never behave so cruelly."

"I can think of a British king who acted very much the same way as the Shah." Michael knew his argument was ridiculous, but he wanted her to love India. He wanted her to see that even though a few terrible customs existed, they did not define this land. Exactly the way that a few poor rulers did not define England.

Helen looked down at her hand gripping the riding crop. "But this is different."

"How?"

"I did not just spend the morning visiting with Anne Boleyn!" Helen's voice choked, and she pulled her reins to the side. "I wish to be alone with my thoughts, Captain."

For the second time in a matter of minutes, Michael watched Lady Helen ride off in tears, and he searched his mind for something he could say to return her to the naive, charmed young lady who had left Calcutta a few days earlier.

Chapter 19

FIVE DAYS LATER HELEN SAT at her dressing table, absently turning over the golden bangle Rani-Sanjana had given her when she'd left the women's quarters. Helen had removed her own coral bead necklace to give the Rani in return, and the two had parted as friends. Thinking of the moment made her throat constrict. She glanced toward the window when she heard the trill of a bird's song, but the sound didn't raise her spirits as it would have a week earlier.

The journey home from the White Palace had been somber, and Helen had felt as if a heavy cloud hung over the group. From the bits of conversation she'd overheard, the meeting with the Shah had not boosted Jim's or Captain Rhodes's confidence in the man's abilities as a leader, and the rest of the officers were still talking about the tigers and the prisonlike palace. Though they traveled the same route, Helen noticed things she'd not seen before: beggars on the side of the road, mangy dogs, the smells of animals, and a crush of humanity crowded together on the way in or out of Calcutta. Even the fruit smelled rotten and the perfume of the flowers was too heady. The painted gods in their shrines no longer looked festive but frightening. She remembered stories of sickness and thought of her mother's nearly fatal scorpion sting. Cobras hid in the tall grass; fierce predators waited in the jungle. India was a land of death and despair.

She felt foolish that she'd been so delighted with the White Palace and the Rani and her lovely jewelry and garden. Helen had tried to sound happy when she'd told her mother about the journey, but she knew Lady Patricia could see through the attempt. It was difficult to muster the excitement she'd felt before, and the memories of the fields of flowers, the people traveling on the road, and even the peacock seemed tainted and dull. Her mother had asked Helen endless times what was wrong. Had she taken ill? Helen had responded that she was simply sore and tired from traveling. It was not the truth, though it might have been a contributor. She could not put into words what had changed on the journey; she only knew that she no longer saw things in the same way. *Helen* had changed. And it saddened her to have lost the part of her that took delight in new experiences and beauty. The part of her that appreciated anything new seemed to have been extinguished.

She lifted the elephant figurine Captain Rhodes had given her and felt a wave of tears prickle her eyes. Fanny was right; Lieutenant Bancroft was right. They all were, and it was Helen who was wrong about everything. She felt so childish. Opening a drawer, she dropped the bangle and the elephant inside and left the room.

Making her way down the staircase, she heard her mother's voice in the library. Not wanting to make an excuse for sleeping late and trying to avoid this or that visit, Helen crossed the entry hall to the doorway and stepped outside to walk in the gardens. The sun shone on the pond, birds called in the trees, flowers bloomed, but Helen felt empty.

She thought back to the conversation with the Rani. When Helen had asked about her family, Prema had steered the conversation in a different direction. Helen had thought it was only to protect the Rani's feelings after the recent deaths of her parents. She had no idea it was so much worse. So much worse than she could even imagine without tears blurring her eyes and choking her throat. How had Rani-Sanjana endured such a terrible thing as seeing her mother burn alive? What kind of barbaric country was this? And why had Helen been so intent upon believing that she saw India differently than everyone else?

Everyone except for Captain Rhodes.

She walked around the pond and sat in the pavilion where she'd talked to the captain on her first day in India. She'd believed they had a special connection and that he understood her and her interest in this new place like nobody else had. She'd been a fool to believe that Captain Rhodes saw the truth while all the others did not, when in reality the situation was exactly the opposite. He was the one in the wrong and had misled her while everyone else attempted to convince her of what she should have realized herself. If only she hadn't been tricked by pretty things.

As if her thoughts conjured him, Captain Rhodes approached from a side path.

Helen did not stand to greet him nor acknowledge when he sat next to her. Merely the sight of him made her want to weep again, and she'd done enough of that over the past days.

"My lady . . ." His voice was low and carried a note of worry.

"I am sorry. I am not pleasant company today." Helen rubbed her arms and kept her eyes upon the white stone floor, hoping he would understand her words to be a dismissal.

He remained on the stone bench and leaned forward, resting his arms on his knees. "I've been hoping to find you ever since we returned."

Helen realized she'd not put on a bonnet before leaving the house and could not depend on the brim to hide her expression. She bent her head forward, and a curtain of curls fell between them, making her feel much safer to speak directly. "Are you here to tell me more falsehoods, Captain?"

"No."

"Then why have you come?"

"I want to make everything right. To make you smile again. I cannot bear to see you hurting." She saw his hand move toward her, but he must have thought better of it and balled a fist on his leg.

Helen felt a small wave of disappointment that he had not taken her hand. "You cannot make it right. Nobody can." She lifted her head, pushed her hair over her shoulder, then turned fully toward him so he could see the frustration in her face. "I am a fool to have been so charmed by silk curtains and beautiful birds that I did not see what was right in front of me."

Captain Rhodes's eyes were not as bright as usual. His gaze was earnest but sad. "You are not a fool. You are wiser than most people I have known. You look beyond the surface to understand the whole of something before you judge it. That is not foolish, my lady."

Helen considered his words for a moment. Everything about his manner indicated sincerity, but as much as she desired it, she could not make herself believe what he said. She shook her head and returned her gaze to the floor. "I fear I have looked too deeply. I cannot go back to believing as I once did, Captain. The magic is gone, and I can only see what is ugly and horrible."

He did not speak for a long moment. When he did, Helen was taken aback by the sadness in his voice. "I am so sorry, Lady Helen."

She clasped her hands together, twisting her fingers. "How can you still love India when you know such awful things?" Helen honestly wanted to know.

He leaned back and stretched his legs out. "Perhaps that is why I love her," he said slowly. "Because although awful things do exist here—the suttee ritual, disease, poisonous snakes, poverty—the people still wear beautiful clothes and dance at festivals and laugh and make music and paint elephants." Captain Rhodes crooked a finger beneath her chin and lifted her face. "Perhaps knowing there is ugliness and pain beneath makes the beauty on the surface so much more remarkable."

Helen looked into the captain's eyes and saw pleading. He wanted her to understand, to feel as he did. And his words warmed a place in her heart she hadn't felt since before the journey from the White Palace.

She wanted to believe him. She wanted to feel as she once did, but was it too late?

As she contemplated what he'd said, she realized Captain Rhodes still held her chin. He still looked into her eyes, and his face was very close. Helen parted her lips to draw in a breath, and his eyes darted to her mouth.

Quickly, Captain Rhodes jumped to his feet. "Shall we walk, my lady?"

Helen's skin was hot, her blood rushing, and she felt faint. She stood and took his arm, unsure of what had transpired between them. Captain Rhodes looked extremely uncomfortable, and he held his arm stiffly beneath her hand. She could hear his breath coming in quick bursts as they walked. "I thank you for finding me, Captain. I will think about the things you said."

"I know you will, my lady. I find it admirable how deeply you consider things before forming an opinion." He stopped near the pond and turned to her. "But, Lady Helen, in all your pondering, do not forget to feel." He tapped a finger to his chest, over his heart. "You have an intelligent mind, but never forget that some truth can only come from within."

Helen nodded, thinking about his words.

He gave a small tug on her arm, and the pair strolled through the gardens in a silence that Helen felt to be comfortable and not needing to be filled with meaningless chatter. She knew Captain Rhodes was allowing her time with her thoughts. The day grew heated, and Helen did not have a bonnet to shade her face, so they eventually began to make their way back toward the house.

When she heard her name, Helen turned to look down a pathway and saw Lieutenant Bancroft waving as he strode toward them. She waved back and glanced up at Captain Rhodes's face, noticing a muscle tense in his jaw. He must still hold the lieutenant responsible for Helen's melancholy since he had been the one to tell her about the mysterious deaths of the Shah's wives. Helen hoped the captain's anger wouldn't last. She didn't like to be the source of ill feelings.

"Lady Helen. Captain Rhodes." The lieutenant bowed his head to her and saluted the captain.

Captain Rhodes nodded a greeting.

Helen smiled widely and dipped in a slight curtsy but maintained her hold on the captain's arm. She put more exuberance into her voice than she felt in an effort to assure Captain Rhodes that there was no reason to be cross with the lieutenant. "Lieutenant Bancroft, what a lovely surprise. I do hope you have come to visit me and not my father."

"Indeed I have, my lady."

"Would you two gentlemen care to join me for tea? I find myself quite wishing for some fruitcake, and with the heat I would wager the two of you are in need of something cool to drink."

"I would indeed love that, but I am afraid I haven't the time, my lady. I only came to issue an invitation. Tomorrow night will be the last full moon before the majority of us leave for Simla. A group of officers are planning a moonlight picnic. We shall journey by horseback to a small temple a few miles away. I think it should be the ideal setting for a wonderful evening. And of course, Captain, you are invited too."

"Oh." Helen glanced to Captain Rhodes, wondering what his reaction would be.

He did not respond, only watched Lieutenant Bancroft. Finally Helen spoke up to dispel the awkward silence. "I would love to join you, Lieutenant. And, Captain Rhodes, I hope you will come as well?"

Helen had a moment of panic when she remembered the fiasco of asking the captain to attend the ball, but a picnic did not require dancing or any sort of activity that she could think of that might be difficult with his wooden leg.

When the captain still did not speak, Helen squeezed his arm, and he glanced at her.

She raised her brows and tipped her head toward Lieutenant Bancroft, reminding him that the man's offer still hung in the air between them.

"Thank you, Lieutenant. Yes, I should be glad to attend," Captain Rhodes said, although his tone did not correspond with his words.

Lieutenant Bancroft's brow ticked the smallest bit, but he maintained his cheerful countenance. "Excellent. We plan to meet at seven at the arch before the Raj Bhavan. The night should be full dark by then. My lady, I shall arrive to fetch you at half past six. And do not forget a cloak. The jungle can be chilly after dark."

The jungle?

A shiver went over Helen's skin, but she smiled brightly so the captain would not know she felt any sort of unease. Just knowing that Captain Rhodes would be there helped dispel her nervousness. "Thank you, Lieutenant. I shall expect you then."

Chapter 20

LIEUTENANT BANCROFT ARRIVED PRECISELY ON time. He assisted Helen to mount her horse, and she rode alongside him through Chowringhee toward the *maidan*. The city was unusually quiet, with only the occasional sound of a carriage or laughter from within a house. Helen found Calcutta to be quite altered without the chatter and calls of vendors and the songs of birds. The noises of the day were replaced by the buzzing and chirping of insects that sounded unnaturally loud to her ears. Helen heard an occasional dog's bark and the hoot of an owl.

The full moon was breathtaking. It seemed so much larger and brighter than it had in England. Could it possibly be the same moon? The entirety of the land was lit, but instead of warm sunlight that revealed colors, the moonlight made everything look as though it had been painted with liquid silver. Bats swooped through the sky, and glowing fireflies hung in the air. Except for the fact that the world was colored in shades of purple and gray, she could see the details around her quite clearly.

The sounds of muffled voices greeted them as they reached the lion-topped arch. Helen counted nearly twelve people, and of those, only four women. She recognized a few of the company but found that the shadows somewhat hid faces and offered the feeling of anonymity and excitement that reminded her of a masquerade ball. She saw Captain Rhodes immediately. There was no mistaking his figure astride his gray horse. She waved and smiled when she saw his face was turned toward her, and he lifted a hand in return.

Helen wondered if Captain Rhodes would ride through the group to join her, but he remained where he was.

She heard a familiar high laugh and looked around until she could make out Fanny in the shadows, sitting prettily on her horse as she spoke to Sergeant Jacks and Ensign Porter. Helen did not know whether she felt relieved that she would know another woman on the outing or frustrated that it was Fanny.

Lieutenant Bancroft halted near Sergeant Carter. It seemed the two were the organizers of the expedition, and they explained the plans to the rest. "Servants have already gone ahead to prepare the picnic," Sergeant Carter said. "We shall travel two by two in order for the dust to settle between parties. Captain, if you'd like to accompany me to lead the way, and Lieutenant Bancroft has offered to follow at the rear with Lady Helen."

Helen looked to Captain Rhodes, wondering if he would disagree. Having him closer was much more comforting than knowing he would travel at the head of the spaced column. She saw that he watched her for a moment, but as the group shuffled around, Captain Rhodes joined Sergeant Carter, and the pair led the way out of the city toward the jungle.

Helen's eyes adjusted to the darkness as they waited for each pair ahead of them to reach a suitable distance. After the last couple, Lieutenant Bancroft nudged his horse forward.

Even with the precaution of traveling at intervals, the dust made her vision unclear and filtered the moonlight. In only a matter of moments, the road became little more than a wide path overhung with trees. Though moonlight still shone through the thick branches, the way was much darker than the wide-open city streets.

They rode in silence, and Helen wondered if Lieutenant Bancroft was disappointed in her company. She could not think of any topics of conversation that might be of interest to him—excepting, of course, hunting. And she most certainly did not want to revisit the conversation they'd had on the journey from the White Palace.

"The night is lovely, Lieutenant. Thank you for inviting me."

He started as if pulled from his thoughts, and Helen cringed, wishing she had remained silent.

"A moonlight picnic is one of my favorite traditions in India. In a few weeks, it will be too hot during daylight hours to do much of anything, and nighttime activities will be quite popular. You shall particularly like a late-night cruise on the river. Quite the thing, you know. Then soon enough, of course, groups will begin to leave for Simla."

"Tell me more about Simla, Lieutenant. I have heard it is beautiful."

"The journey is quite long. Weeks aboard a flat-bottomed riverboat, and weeks longer riding, but you will think the trip quite worth it, my lady." He turned his face toward her, and the shadows deepened his dimples as he smiled. "The cool air and mountain mist almost remind me of England. You shall play croquet on lush grass, walk through beautiful gardens, and pick wildflowers. In Simla, you will find mountain paths that lead past waterfalls and patches of strawberries. The respite from jungles and heat offsets a bit of the homesickness." His soft voice sounded wistful.

"I am sorry you are homesick."

"Yes, well, a foreign post does not last forever. And some believe the war with the French to be nearing an end. With any luck, I shall not have to endure another Christmas away from my family. But, of course, you—" He glanced at her quickly then adjusted the straps of his reins in his hand.

Helen hadn't realized the lieutenant felt homesick. She was also surprised to realize she did not. But she hadn't left her family behind as the soldiers had. She thought she would feel differently if her mother and Jim were not with her. *And Captain Rhodes.* As soon as the thought entered her head, she wondered whence it had sprung. But as she considered, she realized that Captain Rhodes, with his steady manner and easy smile, did help ease any pining she might have felt for England. She wondered if the captain had already arrived at the picnic spot, and a coil of heat twisted inside her when she thought he could be at this very moment speaking with Fanny.

As they journeyed farther from the city, Helen had the impression that the jungle never slept. Monkey shrieks sounded menacing instead of merry. Yelps and grunts came from the trees, and though they did not sound close, Lieutenant Bancroft unfastened the strap that attached his musket to his saddle. Helen thought she heard a growl but did not know whether the sound was her imagination. Her heartbeat sped up, and she moved her horse closer to the lieutenant's, wishing they'd ridden in a carriage. She strained her ears for any sound of a tiger, but gratefully she heard none.

Nearly an hour after they'd set off, Helen and Lieutenant Bancroft arrived at their destination. The smell of cooking meat filled the air. He had been right—the location was splendid. The clearing surrounded a white, open-aired temple that was roughly the size of Helen's drawing room. Pillars held up a roof that stepped inward as it rose to a tall point. The entire building was carved from white stone and glowed in the moonlight.

Servants had arranged portable tables and stools, and nearly out of sight, on the other side of the temple, a fire burned and two men stood nearby turning roasting sticks.

A syce helped Helen dismount and led away the horses. Lieutenant Bancroft offered his arm, and they walked toward the tables. She searched for Captain Rhodes but saw only two remaining seats on the other table, not close to where he sat talking with the man next to him. Helen felt disappointed that she would not be able to speak to him during the meal.

She heard Fanny's laughter again, and her eyes narrowed when she saw the flirt sitting across the table from Captain Rhodes. He nodded and said something Helen could not hear but that sent Fanny into gales of laughter. Helen clenched her teeth. The sound made her furious. If only she'd arrived sooner.

Supper was served, and Helen nodded and commented while Lieutenant Bancroft and Sergeant Carter spoke. But while their conversation centered around hunting and speculations about the war in Spain, Helen's attention was constantly drawn to the other table. What was Captain Rhodes saying? Each time Fanny giggled, Helen could not help but think *she* should be the one sitting by the captain and laughing at his jokes.

"And, Lady Helen, you have heard the rumor that Lord Minto means to resign? Perhaps the general mentioned it," Sergeant Carter said.

Helen was not entirely sure what the conversation had been about, but she didn't have any information about Lord Minto resigning. "No, I am sorry. He did not mention anything to me."

"I wonder if he means to spend the rainy season in Simla *then* leave or simply depart directly from Calcutta," Lieutenant Bancroft said in a thoughtful voice.

"Why make the journey just to return a few months later and make another?" The sergeant shrugged. "Best to leave from a port city and not waste the time."

"Yes, but if his replacement does not arrive . . ."

Helen's mind strayed back to the other table, and she wondered why it bothered her to have Captain Rhodes speaking with Fanny. *Why, because he is* my *dear friend, and Fanny cannot possibly appreciate his wit nor his kindness.*

When the meal was completed, the officers and ladies wandered around the clearing while the servants packed the furniture and dishes into a cart pulled by bullocks. The cart departed well ahead of the party to ensure that the dust from its passing settled before the officers and ladies made the return trip.

Helen took the lieutenant's offered arm and walked with him to the small temple and up its stone steps. Wreaths, flowers, and wooden bowls with traces of food had been laid beside the entryway.

He pushed a bowl aside with his foot and snorted. "Gifts for their gods? Even an utter fool must realize animals and insects eat the food. Rather ridiculous, wouldn't you say?"

Helen's insides sank when she heard his mockery. The offerings had appeared so heartfelt. "It is not ridiculous to the person who left it." She did not dare to look at his face for fear she had offended him.

"I am sorry, my lady. I just find it rather absurd."

"The practice is strange to me too, Lieutenant, but to some it is sacred." They stepped farther into the temple, and Helen studied the carvings in the moonlight: elephants, armies, deities with angry faces and many arms. She thought she would like to return in the daytime to get a better look at the figures.

A noise sounded behind them, and they both turned. Helen thought Lieutenant Bancroft must be as relieved as she to have something to distract them from a subject that had become uncomfortable.

"Captain Rhodes!" Helen smiled when she saw who had climbed the steps behind them. His familiar form filled the entrance, but she could not see his face in the shadows. She glanced past him to ensure that Fanny had not accompanied him.

"Captain." Lieutenant Bancroft nodded.

"I did not mean to intrude. I beg your pardon." Captain Rhodes moved as though he would turn around, but Helen did not want him to leave. She'd not had a chance to speak with him all night. "Did you enjoy your supper, Captain?"

"Yes. Very nice."

"And this temple. Is it not beautiful?" Helen swept her hand around the open space. Detailed carvings formed by expert craftsmen covered every pillar and wall. It appeared as though the builders had not wanted one inch of the temple to be unadorned. She thought of the time required to create such a beautiful structure. "Amazing," she said.

"Truly." He turned again to leave.

Helen's spirits wilted, and her chest felt heavy. Did Captain Rhodes not wish to talk with her? Why had he approached the temple in the first place? Was he intending to see the inside and changed his mind when he saw her there?

"Lieutenant Bancroft and I have been discussing our future plans, Captain," she said in a last attempt to convince him to stay. "You are coming to Simla as well, aren't you? We would feel very disappointed without you, would we not, Lieutenant?"

"Yes, sir. Of course we would."

Captain Rhodes was silent for so long that Helen wondered if he would not answer. His face was shadowed, but she knew his gaze was upon her. "I do not know," he finally said. His voice sounded choked, and she wondered why he was unhappy.

"Captain Rhodes," Fanny's voice disrupted Helen's thoughts, "it is time to return."

He glanced over his shoulder. "If you will excuse me."

"Of course, sir," Lieutenant Bancroft said.

Helen did not respond. She didn't think she could make her voice work properly.

When it was time to depart, the group kept to the same formation. Helen and Lieutenant Bancroft were the last to leave the clearing. As they rode back along the path, Helen's heart felt like it was made of lead. She couldn't stop thinking of Captain Rhodes and the tightness in his voice. Why might he not go to Simla with the other officers? Just imagining months in a faraway place without him made her eyes burn.

Lieutenant Bancroft reached forward and pulled on the reins, stopping Helen's horse. "My lady, I have something to ask you." He lifted her hand from where it had rested on her leg

Helen looked up, and a feeling of dread settled over her. The lieutenant had never presumed such familiarity. "Yes?" She tried to keep her tone light, but her stomach was rolling over and over.

He squeezed her fingers and lifted them to his lips. Helen's heart thumped, but she felt dismay rather than elation. *Please, no.*

"Lady Helen, I would like you to marry me." He spoke the words bluntly. Not with unkindness, but the lack of emotion took her by surprise.

"Why?" The word slipped out before she even thought it.

He did not seem deterred by her question. "We are an attractive couple, and with the shortage of British women in India, I am lucky to have found one I can imagine marrying. I have no doubt we will rub along well together. You are easy to talk to and pleasant to look at." He shrugged his shoulders.

Helen didn't know what to say. She could hardly imagine a less romantic proposal. "Lieutenant—"

"My lady"—he sighed loudly—"I want to leave India. I wish to return home so badly that I ache. As a married officer, I will be given special consideration in assignments. And, of course, it does not hurt that you are the general's daughter."

"I—"

"Please accept, Lady Helen."

The horses both whinnied, and Helen's mount stepped a few paces away, pulling her hand from his. She pulled on the reins to steady the animal.

"I have not been to your father. I shall do it promptly tomorrow morning."

Helen had allowed this to go on long enough. Two weeks ago she was quite convinced she was in love with Arthur Bancroft. His dimples and curls were the very things she had hoped for in a husband. But even though he was a pleasant enough person—and very handsome—the thought of sitting across the table from him every evening while he spoke of his day, sharing a home, having his children . . . She could not bring herself to feel any cheer at the idea. The warmth that had heated her cheeks and sent her heart fluttering when she was in his presence had dissipated, and she had not even noticed it was gone.

"Lieutenant, I am sorry if I led you to believe—"

A roar pierced the night, sending the horses into a panic. Helen tried to regain control of the rearing animal.

A tiger.

The roar sounded again, this time closer, and Lieutenant Bancroft pulled his musket from his saddle. "Ride to the others!" he called and bounded away into the jungle.

Helen's mind emptied, and her muscles tensed so tightly she could not move. She gripped the reins as the horse reared, kicking and tossing its head.

Her bonnet came loose and flipped forward over her face. The terror at being blind brought a surge of energy that woke her from her paralysis. She batted the bonnet away and pulled tightly on the reins, trying to turn the animal toward the road.

For an instant, the terror rose again, threatening to take away her reason. She whipped her head back and forth, but she could not tell from which direction she had come nor which she should go. The horse continued to kick up dust, and Helen coughed until she finally loosed the reins and allowed the animal to bolt. She clung to the saddle, praying the horse had chosen the right direction.

Chapter 21

A ROAR THUNDERED THROUGH THE jungle, and Michael froze. *Lady Helen!* He whipped Ei-Zarka around and spurred the horse in a gallop, not caring that he churned up dust as he passed the other pairs on the road. His only thought was to reach her. A tiger's roar could carry for miles, and he had no idea how close the animal was or what it was roaring at. His imagination conjured images that only made him more frantic.

He left behind group after group, ignoring their questions and protests about the dust as he kept riding. Another roar sounded. This one was definitely closer. Sparing no thought for his horse, he urged the animal faster, leaning forward and digging his heels into its flanks.

An object in the road caught his eye, and he jerked on the reins, pulling Ei-Zarka up short. He peered down, and his heart flew into his throat. Helen's bonnet. What had happened? His mouth went dry, and his breathing sped up. He didn't think he had ever been so frightened. He turned Ei-Zarka in a circle, darting his eyes around the road and into the trees, but he could see no signs that anything had taken place. Where had she and Lieutenant Bancroft gone?

For a moment he debated whether to ride into the jungle, but he would never find her if that's where she had gone. He did not even know on which side of the road to begin a search. He urged Ei-Zarka forward again, continuing toward the temple and praying that she had stayed on the road.

Michael burst into the clearing and took in the scene before him. Lady Helen was unsteadily seated on her saddle as her horse shuffled its feet, pulling its head from side to side as she struggled to keep it calm. A low snarl came from the tree line behind the temple. Michael saw three leopards slinking toward them. They must have smelled the meat and waited for the large group to leave, but the predators would have no problem taking down one young lady on a horse.

The horse rolled its eyes and snorted, backing up and sporadically jerking to the side. Lady Helen somehow managed to hang on as it rose up onto its hind legs. It was only a matter of time before the horse shook her from its back or bolted through the trees. When the animal slammed down, jarring her forward, Michael made his move.

He drove Ei-Zarka forward, coming up as closely as possible to her horse, and leaning to the side, he snatched Lady Helen around the waist, sliding her off her saddle and onto his own.

The leopards chose that moment to leap forward, and her horse darted into the trees. Michael pulled the revolver from his jacket. "Hold on." Digging his heels into Ei-Zarka's sides, he twisted around, firing a shot as the horse bolted. Michael steered toward the road and glanced back once before they dashed from the clearing. Holding tightly to Lady Helen, he did not slow until they had covered at least a mile; then he allowed Ei-Zarka to slip to an easy walk. Turning his head from side to side, he scanned the tree-lined road and strained his ears for any other predators.

Finally, he concluded they were safe and turned his attention to the young lady in front of him. She sat across the saddle, her face buried against his chest. He shifted around, hoping to make her more comfortable, but she just clung tighter. Now that his terror had somewhat lessened, he saw she was sobbing.

"You are safe." He spoke in a soft voice, rubbing his arm up and down her back. He tightened his arms around her and lowered his face to murmur against her hair. "I have you now, *larla*." The endearment fell from his lips before he had realized, but Lady Helen seemed too distressed to have noticed.

He held her as they rode, and little by little she relaxed into him. His fingers combed through the ends of her loose curls, which were every bit as soft as silk. The moment seemed perfect until his mind reminded him of the circumstances that had led to it.

Easing back, he twisted slightly to see her face, discerning in the shine of the moon light that it was damp. He deliberately tightened his grip on the reins to keep from brushing away her tears. "Can you tell me what happened? Where is Lieutenant Bancroft?"

Helen raised her eyes to his face, and he saw her lip tremble. "He went after the tiger."

Of course he did. He should have known the man would not be responsible when it came to Lady Helen. He had proven himself utterly incapable of seeing to her safety. And now . . . Michael nearly groaned aloud in frustration. The lieutenant had not made it a secret that he planned to propose tonight. When Lady Helen had spoken of their plans for the future, Michael knew it was a surety. The ache that was always present when he thought of Lady Helen grew into a piercing pain. She loved the lieutenant. He knew it all along, and her bright smile when she'd seen him in the gardens yesterday reminded Michael again of the fact. Now it was done. And no heartache in his life had even come close to what he felt at that knowledge.

Helen settled back against him, fitting perfectly into the circle of his arms. Her hair was loose and flowed over her shoulders, smelling like lavender. "I knew you would come for me, Captain Rhodes."

"My lady?"

"You always do."

It was true. He knew with a surety that his concern for her would never lessen. He would think of her every day, rush at the drop of a hat to her side whenever she needed. Which was precisely why he needed to leave Calcutta. Lady Helen was not his to save.

Chapter 22

Helen awoke when she heard Azān. For a moment, she lay quietly and listened, then remembered her fright the night before and her stomach turned over. The entire episode took on a surreal quality in her mind. It had happened so fast, and yet she remembered each second as if it had drawn on endlessly. She had never felt such raw terror, and the mere memory made her shake even now, in the safety of her bedchamber. She clutched a pillow to her stomach, clinging to it while she breathed in and out to calm herself.

It had been well past midnight when Captain Rhodes had delivered her to her house, insisting that a servant be sent to wake Jim. He'd refused to leave Helen alone when she'd been so distraught. Jim and her mother had both arrived in the drawing room in their nightclothes, wide-eyed and worried. They'd asked questions, listening to the retelling of events until Helen's shaking returned. Exhaustion and recounting the story had started another bout of weeping. She felt foolish, falling to pieces in front of her family and the captain, but she could not stop. Finally, her mother had sent for Sita and prepared an herbal draught to help Helen sleep.

Helen sat up, pushed herself back against the headboard, and pulled her knees to her chest, wrapping her arms around her legs.

From the very instant she heard the tiger's roar, her thought had been Captain Rhodes. Her mind had held on to thoughts of him as the horse had panicked and she'd prayed the animal would take her in the right direction. He would be waiting at the end of the road and would drive away the fears. When she'd reached the temple and realized she'd taken the wrong direction, despair threatened to crush her, but a small light of hope glowed deep within—hope that he would find her. And Helen had clung to it with every bit of her will.

The relief when Captain Rhodes burst into the clearing had felt like sunlight breaking through the clouds on a cold, rainy day. Even now, just thinking of it sent ripples of warmth from her chest all the way to her toes.

She let out a soft sigh as she remembered the feeling of being held in his arms. *Captain Rhodes.* When she thought of him, her cheeks heated, her heart swelled, and she had the most indescribable urge to grin.

She wrapped the feeling around her, allowing it to push away the fear. She rested her cheek on her knee and sighed again. She was very fortunate to have a friend like Captain Rhodes.

Still contemplating the events of the night, another emotion wriggled its way inside her, bringing with it a sour taste. *Anger.* Why had Lieutenant Bancroft deserted her in the middle of a dark jungle? And equally disturbing was his marriage proposal.

A few weeks earlier, Helen had thought herself quite in love with the lieutenant. He was handsome and charming, an elegant dancer, and everything else she had thought she wanted in a husband. But now her feelings could not be more the reverse. She considered their interactions in the short time she'd known him and did not quite remember exactly when she'd stopped feeling her heartbeat quicken and her cheeks heat in his presence. His touch on her hand the night before had not sent wild butterflies loose in her stomach. And it had been some time ago that his dimpled smile had stopped making her giddy. When had her feelings changed? Perhaps it was when she'd grown to know the shallow man behind the handsome exterior.

Helen rose and moved to open the screens and watch the sunrise. Birds sang in the trees, and the smell of flowers wafted on the already warm air. On the road below, she saw women talking together as they carried large pots on their heads, bringing water for the day. Children laughed as they played around the women's feet. It was difficult to believe this was the same land that produced such horror as she'd experienced the night before. She remembered what Captain Rhodes had said about India. Perhaps he was right. Perhaps the land was all the more remarkable because of the harshness beneath the surface.

Happiness returned as she thought about the captain and how he seemed to know exactly what to say.

Helen glanced up as the door opened.

Sita entered with a pitcher of warm water and bowed. "Miss-Sahib, you are well?"

"Yes. I feel much better, and I would like to wear my yellow dress today. Thank you."

Helen stood and allowed Sita to assist her as she washed and dressed. Her thoughts returned to Captain Rhodes, how he'd snatched her from her panicked horse, fired his weapon at the leopards, then spoken softly to calm her. Liquid heat filled her heart as she remembered his low voice and gentle words while he'd held her.

She looked into the mirror above her dressing table as the ayah arranged her hair. "Sita, what is *larla*?"

Sita met her eye in the mirror and looked back down as she continued pinning curls. "In my language, we say *larla* to a baby, a person we love. In English, it is meaning . . . 'dearest.'"

Dearest. The warmth inside her grew until she thought she might burst. Captain Rhodes had called her dearest.

Perhaps her mind was sluggish from the sleeping draught or maybe she was still coming fully awake, but the realization hit Helen so suddenly that she gasped. She felt the blood drain from her cheeks and then return in a rush of fire.

She was in love with Captain Rhodes.

But how was it possible? His touch did not send her stomach tumbling nor make her unable to form a coherent sentence. She did not blush and lose every thought in her head when he smiled. With Captain Rhodes, she felt at ease, happy. He cared for her, listened to her, made her feel important.

Her mother's words came into her mind. *I trust Jim with my heart and know without a doubt he would never hurt it. I am safe to say anything or be anything with him and he will not think less of me. That is what love is, my dear.*"

How had she not seen it? She had been so certain love meant being swept away in a whirlwind of volatile sensations that she'd not realized real love was not uncomfortable at all; it was exactly the opposite—the ability to simply feel at ease in another's presence.

Happiness, safety, surety that he would always come for her. That's how she felt with him.

When her mother was ill, her first thought had been to find Captain Rhodes. When she'd been afraid, when she'd been overjoyed by the pianoforte, upset by what she'd learned at the White Palace—each time, there had been only one person she'd wanted. Only one person she'd been able to speak to without feeling as though she said exactly the wrong thing. Only one who knew just how to cheer or comfort her.

And she could not imagine what her life would be like without him.

Helen jumped to her feet—apologizing to Sita when she nearly sent the woman toppling backward—and hurried from her bedchamber and down the staircase.

Suddenly, seeing Captain Rhodes was the thing she wanted more than anything. She felt a pull to be near him and did not think she would be able to concentrate on anything else until she saw him now, knowing what her true feelings were. And hoping she would see those feelings reflected back in his gaze.

Would he call on her today?

The soldiers drilled early, before the heat made marching too difficult. Helen figured he would not call before ten at the very earliest. She did not think she could wait.

Remembering that Lieutenant Bancroft had promised to call on Jim this morning threw a bit of gloom over her delight. She certainly needed to speak to the lieutenant before he spoke to Jim. Helen just hoped the man would realize his proposal of marriage was a matter that should be discussed at the general's home and not this morning at the fort.

When she entered the dining room, her mother and Jim both stood and hurried toward the doorway.

Lady Patricia slipped an arm around Helen's waist and led her to the table. "Helen, dear, are you well enough to be out of your bed?"

"Yes, Mamá. I feel much better this morning." She sat at the table next to her mother, unable to stop the smile that pulled at her cheeks.

Her mother's face relaxed.

"Brave girl." Jim nodded. "Rallying after the night you had."

Helen grinned at his praise. She took a sip of the watermelon juice a servant placed before her. "And did you see Captain Rhodes this morning?" She hoped her expression did not betray her to be anything more than casual. "I imagine he was quite tired, having to rise early for drills after such a late night."

"Seemed well enough." Jim cut into a piece of sausage. "He's asked to speak with me today. I expect him in a few hours."

"Oh." Helen's hand shook as she returned the glass to the table. "Ah, that is . . . good." She took a bite of toast to keep herself from saying anything else idiotic. Captain Rhodes could be meeting with Jim for any number of matters, and Helen had no reason to think the purpose of his visit had anything to do with her. *But what if* . . . Her heart started to flutter, and try as she might she could not swallow the bit of toast that had turned to sand in her mouth. What if he'd felt the same as she when he held her in his arms? How could he not? How could he have spoken such gentle words, called her *larla*, if he was not in love with her?

Glancing up, she saw Jim and her mother exchange a glance.

"Are you sure you are recovered, Helen?" her mother asked. "Perhaps you should rest after breakfast."

Helen took another sip of juice. "Yes. I am quite well. I hoped to practice in the drawing room this morning if you do not have need of me."

"Fine idea," Lady Patricia said. "And we shall not be at home to callers today, to give you a chance to rest."

After breakfast, Helen asked the butler to direct Lieutenant Bancroft to her when he arrived to speak to the general; then she sat to play the pianoforte.

Less than an hour passed before the lieutenant was shown in.

He strode toward her, lifting her hand and kissing it. "Good morning, my darling. I am glad to see you returned home safely last night. I had a bit of a chase, but unfortunately that blasted cat escaped. However, now that I have an idea of his hunting territory—"

Helen did not wait to hear the remainder of his story. "Lieutenant, I wanted to speak with you." She clasped her hands behind her back.

He blinked, obviously surprised at being interrupted. "Oh. Of course."

"Why did you leave me?" Helen burst out.

"I do not . . ." He squinted his eyes and tilted his head, looking genuinely confused by her question.

Helen balled her hands at her sides, frustrated that he didn't even have the slightest idea why she was upset. "You left me alone in a dark jungle, sir. I was very frightened."

"But the other group was merely a hundred meters ahead on the road. And you know how I wanted to bag a tiger. Surely you must understand the opportunity does not arise often."

"Sir, I do *not* understand. It was inexcusable."

"But, Helen."

"And do not call me by my Christian name. I do not wish for so familiar a relationship."

"But—"

"I cannot marry you, Lieutenant."

"Because of the tiger?"

"No." Helen blew out an exasperated breath and relaxed her clenched muscles. She'd had enough of being angry. The lieutenant hadn't meant to cause her any distress. He had simply been so focused on his own objective that he hadn't taken into account how upset his actions had made her. "It is not because of the tiger. I love someone else."

He leaned his head back, his mouth forming an O as understanding dawned on him. "I don't know why I did not see it before."

"And, I should tell you, I do not ever wish to display hunting trophies in my house."

His eyes flew wide, and he took a step back. "Lady Helen, I . . . cannot . . ."

"It is true. I am afraid we are ill suited, sir."

"I suppose we are." His shoulders slumped the slightest bit, and Helen could not help but feel sorry for him.

"Lieutenant, Miss Cavendish does seem very interested in seeing Lord Minto's trophy collection. I do believe she mentioned it."

The corners of his mouth drew down, and his brows raised as he nodded. "Does she really?"

"And I know she does not like India in the least and cannot wait to return to England."

"Promising . . ." He offered his arm, and Helen took it and walked with him. "It seems as though I have no reason to speak with the general after all."

"I am sorry indeed that we are such an abysmal match," she said.

He patted her hand then lifted it, turning toward her in the drawing room doorway. "Think nothing of it. It was very nice to be nearly engaged to you for a few hours, Lady Helen."

He kissed her hand again, but she did not feel unnerved this time. It seemed to be a friendly gesture instead of something more intimate.

She curtsied and smiled. "And it was nice to be nearly engaged to you too, sir."

He pressed her hand against his chest and pulled her closer, whispering into her ear. "I wish you the best of luck with your endeavor."

"And you with yours," Helen whispered back.

Hearing footsteps in the entry hall, she and Lieutenant Bancroft drew apart. He stepped back, and she saw that Captain Rhodes had been admitted into the house without their notice.

Helen's heart tripped. "Captain. How nice to see you." She could feel a blush rising on her cheeks as she smiled.

He did not return her smile, nor did he pause but continued walking toward the general's library. He nodded his head sharply. "My lady. Lieutenant." His lips pressed together tightly, and his jaw was clenched.

"Captain?"

But he did not glance backward as he stepped into the library and closed the door behind him.

Chapter 23

MICHAEL STOOD BEFORE THE GENERAL'S desk, watching his commander's brows draw together and his frown deepen as he read the paper Michael had given him. The sound of Helen's playing started, and he had to forcibly restrict his thoughts to the matter at hand. Such distraction was making it difficult to focus.

Finally, the general lowered the paper and raised his gaze. "A transfer?"

"Yes, sir."

He squinted his eye as he turned his scrutinizing gaze on Michael. "May I ask why?"

"I am ready for a change, sir." Michael recited the answer he'd prepared. He remembered the intimate moment he'd stumbled on moments earlier between Lady Helen and Lieutenant Bancroft. Her blush at being discovered had only strengthened his resolve to go through with his request.

General Stackhouse's expression didn't change, and Michael got the distinct feeling that he saw more than Michael intended.

"Any particular request regarding a station?"

"No, sir. Nowhere in particular."

Jim let the paper drop onto his desk and rubbed his forehead above his patch. "Captain, it is completely within your rights to request such a thing, though I can't say I'm happy about it. You're a fine leader, and you'll be missed. Finding a replacement with your knowledge of the language and customs will be blasted near impossible. And I know my wife, and especially Helen, will take it hard."

A swell of emotions rose inside him. Michael swallowed forcefully over the obstruction in his throat as he fought to keep any reaction from his countenance that would betray him to General Stackhouse.

Jim's brow ticked the slightest bit. He opened his mouth and then closed it, his lips pressed tightly together in a look of resignation. "Very well, Captain. I do not know how long it will take to reassign you, but I will start the transfer process immediately."

"Thank you, sir." It was done.

General Stackhouse cleared his throat while Michael remained at attention, awaiting a dismissal.

"I wish to thank you again, Captain, for bringing Helen home safely."

Hearing her name so soon after seeing her with Lieutenant Bancroft stung his heart. Michael breathed deeply to ensure that his voice would not betray the emotion inside him. "Of course, sir."

"I am considering disciplinary action against the lieutenant. What was the man thinking, leaving her alone like that?"

Disciplinary action sounded nearly too tempting for Michael to pass up. He'd not mind teaching the man a lesson himself. But he thought of how it would hurt Lady Helen for the man she loved to be punished, and he could not endure the idea of her tears again. "The lieutenant went after the tiger in order to protect her. He could not have known Lady Helen's horse would turn around and lead her from safety."

The general's brow raised, along with his chin, as he considered Michael and his explanation for the lieutenant's actions. He focused his gaze, and Michael felt his collar growing tight. Not for the first time, he got the impression that General Stackhouse saw more than Michael wished to reveal.

A knock sounded on the door, and at Jim's bidding, a servant entered, handing him an envelope. Jim glanced down at it. "Very well. You are dismissed, Captain."

Michael saluted and turned on his heel, leaving the library. The meeting left him feeling wrung out, as though he'd been examined a bit too thoroughly. He walked toward the entryway, wishing he did not have to pass the drawing room but at the same time feeling drawn to the woman creating the beautiful music within it. He shook his head and quickened his step, feeling as if his heart and mind were at war. He'd allowed his heart to win the major battles thus far, and all it had brought was pain. Time for his head to take over. And beginning the transfer process was the first step.

He stepped through the entry hall quietly and nodded to the butler as he walked through the door. He'd hoped giving his request to General Stackhouse would provide some measure of relief, but he felt even more anxious than he had when he'd arrived—anxious and sick with jealousy. Lieutenant Bancroft did not even begin to deserve Lady Helen.

Thanking the syce, he took Ei-Zarka's reins, but before he could mount, he heard his name. Michael turned to see a servant hurrying toward him. The man bowed his head and asked him to please return to the library at the request of General Stackhouse.

Michael handed the reins back to the syce and hastened back inside.

The general sat in his chair with one elbow on his desk, massaging his temples. He looked up when Michael entered. "Close the door and take a seat, Captain. We have a situation."

Michael moved to the chair in front of the desk.

General Stackhouse's brows were furrowed, and the lines around his eyes and mouth had somehow become deeper in the past three minutes. The man's expression, which at the best of times could be considered stern, was downright furious. "From our intelligence in the Shah's kingdom." He held a folded paper toward Michael. "The Shah's daughter was born yesterday."

Michael sucked in a breath through his teeth as he looked over the missive.

"The Rani claims it is our fault that her child was born female, that Helen somehow put a curse on her with a beaded necklace in order to prevent an heir."

Michael nodded once, maintaining an impartial expression. The Shah's accusation was preposterous, but knowing the beliefs of these people and the Shah's fear about losing his kingdom, it was not a surprise that witchcraft had been blamed and that the British had been accused. He did not like Lady Helen being singled out in the least but understood why the Rani had done it.

"That is the most ridiculous—" The general stood and started pacing.

"Wise woman," Michael said. "The story probably saved her life."

The general turned toward him, and his scowl deepened. "You did read the part about the Shah claiming my daughter is a blue-eyed witch?"

Michael nodded. "The Indian people are very superstitious. And although the accusation is insulting—"

"It's a relief that the man no longer seems to have designs on Helen."

"My thoughts exactly."

The men's eyes met briefly, and Michael saw more than anger at the Shah or concern for the tactics required to prevent a war. Though the general tried to maintain a professional facade, fear for his daughter, his family, showed in the tension around his eyes.

Michael felt an equal apprehension, though worry was woven through with envy. He had no family to protect, and he had to remind himself that the general and Lieutenant Bancroft were the ones who should rightfully safeguard Helen.

General Stackhouse sank into the chair next to Michael. "Funny how a thing like family makes a declaration of war seem less of a concern than an unfit man pursuing my daughter." He smiled wryly. "It appears my priorities have turned entirely around, wouldn't you say?"

Michael understood. They were talking about the potential of lives lost and countryside ravaged, and they had been incensed by the Shah's insulting words toward Lady Helen. He cleared his throat and turned his mind toward military matters even though Lady Helen was his gravest concern at the moment as well.

After a moment, Jim spoke again. "He's planning to attack the smaller stations outside of Calcutta. We should send word immediately to Barrackapore, prepare to defend the stations, and march the remainder of the regiment, hopefully taking the battle as far from Calcutta as possible."

"Yes, sir. How much time do we have?" Michael asked.

"Hours. He could even now be approaching the borders, though I don't imagine his entire army will arrive for days. I want the brigade ready to march tomorrow at the latest."

"I will send word immediately, sir."

"Captain, I shall need you to remain here, assume command of Calcutta."

Michael's stomach sank. He knew the general paid him a compliment by giving him such a responsibility, but he hated the reminder that his leg made him a better candidate for a supervisory position than for battle. "Yes, sir."

They both stood, and Michael saluted.

"I know you will understand why I must delay your transfer request." General Stackhouse squinted his eye. "I'd not leave this city, or my family, with anyone else." His voice had taken on a low tone.

"I understand, sir."

Chapter 24

HELEN SAT AT THE PIANOFORTE, her fingers drifting idly over the keys. The regiments of Jim's brigade had left Calcutta the afternoon before, save for the company that remained to defend the city and the fort.

Though the time was near to ten, her mother had still not risen from bed, an action quite unusual for Lady Patricia, who normally tended to her herb garden before the day grew too hot. Helen knew the sight of Jim cleaning the barrel of his weapon and applying grease to the firing mechanism had upset her mother more than Lady Patricia had let on. She'd kept her head high and smiled and waved until Jim's horse had turned at the end of the street; then once he was out of sight, her shoulders had drooped, and Helen saw tears flow from her mother's eyes. A sight she did not think she had ever seen before—even at her own father's funeral.

Lady Patricia had attributed her emotions to her delicate state, but Helen knew her mother was afraid.

The notes Helen played took on a sad tone as she realized how worried Mamá was for Jim—and how worried she herself was. Soldiers marching to battle had never been a part of their world until Lady Patricia had married a military man, and suddenly the names and uniforms belonged to people they cared about.

Helen listened to the rustling of the *tatties*—curtains woven from dried grass that the servants kept wet in hopes of cooling the room with a breeze—and the creak of the punkah as it swayed back and forth. She thought of the sound made by the gourd-shaped pungi, the mournful notes weaving over and around each other much like snakes in a basket. She absentmindedly followed the tune with the keys, trying to recreate the hypnotizing feel of the music.

She remembered the day at the bazaar: the jingling of ankle jewelry, the chattering of monkeys, the lilting sound of people speaking rapidly together in a foreign language. She thought of Captain Rhodes, and her fingers faltered. What had changed since he'd brought her home from the moonlight picnic? He'd hardly spoken to her. Had she been mistaken to assume he loved her? Could she attribute his neglect to the worries over the regiment going to battle?

The memory of that night, of feeling safe and warm in the captain's arms, made her stomach leap and flutter. She tried to capture the sensation with the notes she played and found her tune taking on a quicker, higher tone.

The love she knew Captain Rhodes felt for India blended together with her own fascination with the country. The sound of Azān filled her mind, and she incorporated it into her song. Helen allowed the music deep into her soul, opening her heart and letting the contents spill into the tune. The fear and later bravery of leaving her home, the love of her parents, the delight of the painted elephant, exotic birdcalls, a peacock that danced to foretell rain, the antics of a pet monkey, the silver moonlit jungle, the anticipation of a new baby, Captain Rhodes's voice as he called her *larla*.

Low chords joined the song as she remembered the worry of seeing her mother ill, the soldiers marching to battle, terror at being lost in a dark jungle, the tigers. The two sounds joined together into a tune that spoke so much emotion that Helen found tears dripping from her cheeks onto the keys. She continued to play until the sound of the music mirrored the deepest emotions of her soul.

Helen dropped her hands into her lap and bowed her head, feeling fatigue take her energy. She wiped her fingers over her cheeks and decided she wouldn't play anymore today. She wanted to hold the memory of her song in her heart and not allow any other music to disturb it while her sentiments were so raw. She didn't know how long she remained, letting the song absorb into her mind, but a soft knock on the doorway of the drawing room roused her from her contemplations, and she looked up.

The butler entered, placing his palms together and bowing his colorfully turbaned head. "Miss-Sahib, I am sorry to disturb you. The child who delivered this note said it is urgent."

Helen thanked him and took the paper from him. She saw only her name on the outside and did not recognize the handwriting. A small object fell out when she unfolded the paper, and it made a sound like a marble when it hit the floor. Helen knelt down, reached beneath a chair, and picked it up. A coral bead?

She looked from the bead to the letter. Only one line was written on the paper. *Meet me at the banyan tree near the garden wall.*

The Rani.

Helen stood and slipped the paper into a pocket of her skirt as she hurried outside. As she walked toward the large tree, questions tumbled through her mind. Had Rani-Sanjana left the palace? Was she in danger? Why had she sent for Helen? Was she hiding?

A woman wearing a blue sari stood near the tree. Her sari was wrapped around her hair and face so that only her eyes showed.

When Helen was near, the woman moved the covering from her face enough that Helen glimpsed who she was. *Prema*, the Rani's ayah.

Helen opened her mouth, but Prema held up her hand. "Do not say my name." She spoke in a low voice, her eyes darting around. "I must speak to you." She led Helen deeper into the hanging roots of the tree.

"Has something happened to the Rani?" Helen asked in a whisper.

Prema shook her head. "My mistress sent me to warn you. The army is moving into a trap."

Helen's heart began to pound. "I do not understand."

"Explosives. When the soldiers march through the gorge, they will be crushed."

Captain Rhodes would know what to do. "Come with me to the fort, you must tell—"

"No. I leave now before I am seen." Prema's eyes were wide with fear.

"Why did you come to me?" Helen asked. "Why did she send you?"

"The Rani likes you, Lady Helen. She does not have many friends, and"—Prema leaned closer, her whisper barely audible—"the Shah is wicked."

"It was dangerous for you to come," Helen said, realizing now why Prema's eyes were wide and her voice a whisper.

"Yes. I cannot return."

"Where will you go?"

"It will be safer for both of us if I do not tell."

Helen gestured toward her house. "You can stay here. The army will protect you."

Prema shook her head. "No. I will obey my mistress and not put you in danger." Her eyes softened, and Helen realized she was sad. This woman had given up her position, left her home behind, and put her life in danger to deliver her message.

"Will you wait here for just a moment?" Helen said. "Please do not leave before I return." She didn't wait for an answer before running inside and up the stairs to her bedchamber. She poured the contents of her reticule onto the bed, grabbing her pin money and stuffing it into the pouch with the Shah's jewel, then she ran back outside, praying that Prema was waiting.

She stood in the same spot beneath the banyan tree.

Helen put the pouch into her hands. "Take this. And please, if you need anything, send word. I will—"

"No, you will not see me again." Prema clasped her hands.

"Thank you." Helen blinked at the tears that had pooled in her eyes. She waited for a moment, watching as the woman hurried from the garden and down the street, but Prema did not turn before disappearing into the crowded Calcutta street.

Helen did not allow herself to contemplate. Any time lost could make the woman's sacrifice in vain. She rushed to the stables and asked a syce to saddle a horse—her own had not returned from the jungle—then rode as quickly as she could from Chowringhee, through the maidan, toward Fort William.

When she reached the main gates, a soldier stepped from the guardhouse.

"I am looking for Captain Rhodes. Is he here?" Helen said.

"Left near half hour ago, my lady." The soldier shaded his eyes as he looked up at her. "'Spect he'll return after tiffin."

Helen thanked him and turned the horse toward Captain Rhodes's house, hoping he was at home.

When she approached the bungalow, she saw the captain and his two servants sitting in the shade of the porch. The three men jumped to their feet.

"My lady." Captain Rhodes caught the reins and assisted her from the horse. "What is wrong?"

"A trap, Captain. The army is in danger. Jim—" Her voice caught, and she shook her head from side to side, frustrated that she would allow her sentiments to prevent her from delivering the message.

Captain Rhodes lifted her hand gently, and his gray eyes held hers. "Tell me."

She cleared her throat as his steadiness calmed her. "A messenger came to me from the Rani. From her ayah. There are explosives, and the pass is a trap. When the soldiers march inside, the Shah means to explode the rocks and crush them." Now that she no longer felt desperation to deliver the message, the realization of what the Shah intended to do crashed down on her, tightening her insides and filling her with fear.

"And you are sure this messenger tells the truth?"

Helen had not even considered that Prema would have told a falsehood. "I . . . I think so. She seemed truthful, and she risked her life to bring the message. She appeared frightened."

He studied her face for a moment then spoke quickly to his servants. He turned back toward Helen. "I must warn them."

The thought of Captain Rhodes rushing toward an exploding mountain made her knees feel like jelly. She clutched his arm.

Naveen stepped out of the house with a pack, a musket, and a sword.

Helen clutched Captain Rhodes's arm tighter as her fear became a reality. "Captain, surely you can send someone else."

Basu Ram led the captain's gray horse toward them.

"There is no one else, my lady. I know the route."

Basu Ram fastened the musket to the saddle, and Captain Rhodes pulled his arm free to attach his sword around his waist. He scribbled a note on a paper, asking Naveen to deliver it to the fort, and Helen watched helplessly as he mounted his horse.

This might be the last time she saw Captain Rhodes alive. Her head felt light. "Before you go—"

"I will make sure he is safe, Lady Helen."

"Who?"

"Your fiancé. Do not fear."

Helen stared at the captain. What could he possibly mean? "Captain . . ."

"I dare not waste another moment. I will do all in my power to keep the man you love safe." He lifted his hand in a farewell and spurred his horse, riding away from her in a cloud of dust.

"But, that man is *you*," she said in a small voice that was swallowed by the pounding of hooves. Helen's heart ached, and she thought her legs would give way. Not caring that his servants glanced at one another with uncertain expressions, she sank down onto the porch steps and covered her mouth with her hands.

Something pushed at her arm, and Helen looked down to see Badmash sitting on the step next to her. His dark face was turned up toward her, and he laid his hand on her elbow. Helen stroked her hand down his furry back, and he snuggled against her leg. She glanced toward her horse and saw it drinking from a bucket of water. One of the servants must have tied it to a tree branch near the bungalow.

She turned around when she heard footsteps behind her.

Basu Ram stepped around the side of the bungalow. He kept his head bowed as he approached Helen and handed her a large banana leaf with chunks of mango and watermelon. Naveen must have left to deliver the captain's message.

Helen took the fruit and placed it on her lap, feeling suddenly self-conscious. The poor man must not know what to do with a weeping woman on his master's front porch.

Badmash snatched a piece of fruit and took small bites, dripping juice onto her skirt. Helen returned to stroking the monkey's back. The small animal's presence was soothing.

"Thank you. I am sorry to be a bother, Basu Ram. I will not linger."

"You are welcome to remain as long as you wish." He crouched down on the ground in the porch shade and gazed at the road Captain Rhodes had taken. "I have no children. Since he was a small boy, Rhodes-Sahib is like my son."

"I care about him too," Helen said, surprised with herself for speaking the words aloud for the first time and even more surprised at the person she'd chosen to confide in.

"Yes, I know, Miss-Sahib."

Helen studied his face. Basu Ram's beard and curled mustache were nearly white. His hands were gnarled, the dark skin around his eyes wrinkled. At first glance, he was not pleasant to look at, but he carried an air of serenity that calmed Helen's frantic nerves. Though it was strange and decidedly improper, she found herself wanting to remain on Captain Rhodes's front porch, eating fruit, conversing with his servant, and petting his monkey. Perhaps because it was a way to feel close to him.

But it was only a matter of time before her mother would wonder what had become of her. She lifted Badmash from where he rested on her leg and set the banana leaf on the step.

"Thank you, Basu Ram." She walked toward the horse, looking around for a way to mount.

Basu Ram turned over an empty bucket and motioned for her to use it like a mounting block. Once she was atop the animal, he handed her the reins, much like he had done with Captain Rhodes only a half hour earlier. "Do not fear, Miss-Sahib. He will be well."

Helen could only nod as she turned toward home. Though it was not yet noon, the emotional whirlwind of her day left her feeling weary, and when she arrived at the general's mansion, she made her way straight to her bedchamber.

Sita helped her to undress, raising her brows at the juice and monkey fur stuck to the skirts, but Helen's red eyes must have been the reason she remained silent.

Helen lay on her bed, staring up through the mosquito netting as Sita wetted the tatties at the window. Helen's limbs felt heavy, and her chest ached. If only she had told him before he'd left. If only Captain Rhodes knew he'd taken her heart with him.

Chapter 25

FOR THE REMAINDER OF THE day and through the night, Michael rode Ei-Zarka hard, stopping only to rest and water the horse. He was two days behind the marching regiments, but a lone horseman should be able to overtake a slow-moving army. His only hope was that he would reach them before they entered the pass.

As he galloped through the green hills, he tried not to allow memories of traveling this same path with Lady Helen to distract him. But his body ached, and his mind was tired. Try as he might, he couldn't push the thoughts away. Finally, he allowed himself to feel the full force of the emotions he'd fought against since the moment he'd met Lady Helen on the docks of the Hooghly.

How had his life changed so completely in a matter of weeks? He felt raw. His heart had been pulled in so many directions, yet he'd continued to allow it to happen—allowed himself to feel so deeply for a woman he'd known all along would never feel the same toward him. And now he suffered the consequences, watching her fall in love with someone else. The ache inside his chest grew, and he pushed Ei-Zarka harder, wishing he could outrun his own feelings.

He'd promised Lady Helen to return Lieutenant Bancroft home safely, and that oath kept him moving forward, focused on his goal. He could not bear to return to her with the news that he'd not been fast enough.

He splashed through the river, and his mind turned to the messenger from the Rani. Had it been a trick? The Shah had found servants who had served in British households, no doubt as a way to expand his understanding of the English, perhaps even to tailor them as spies. Michael would not put much past that man. He tried to think through the various schemes that the Shah might be planning and could come up with no reason the man would send a message to Lady Helen warning her of a trap.

If he intended to reroute the army through the hills, he would have the disadvantage as the British would be able to maintain their cavalry lines and infantry columns that made its army the most deadly force in the world. The pass was the part of the journey the general had hoped to avoid, hoping, perhaps, that the Shah's army would meet them in the clearing before they had to travel through the narrow canyon, where the army would be stretched thin and left vulnerable.

Why would the Shah want to give up the one advantage he had?

Michael turned these thoughts over in his mind and wondered again about the messenger. He didn't like the fact that the Rani's servant had managed to reach Lady Helen so easily, and in the note to the lieutenants in his company, he'd requested special guards to be stationed around the general's house. The Shah had singled out Lady Helen as the source of his troubles, and Michael was frustrated that he'd not thought of setting a watch over her earlier.

***

When he finally arrived in the clearing before the pass, he saw the army had halted. His eyes traveled around the space until he found General Stackhouse beneath a canopy on a small rise, in conference with the colonels of the different regiments. He saluted the rear guard as he passed and galloped straight toward the officers.

The all looked up when he approached.

General Stackhouse's face turned ghost white when he saw Michael. "Captain, what has happened?"

"A trap, sir. Lady Helen received a message from the Rani. The pass is set to explode."

The men looked toward the opening to the pass.

"All in Calcutta are safe, sir," Michael added, realizing that the general must have worried he'd ridden all night to deliver news about Lady Patricia or Lady Helen.

"Blasted Shah," General Stackhouse said. "Wondered what they were waiting for. Well done, Captain. Looks like our path will take us over the mountains instead of through."

He turned toward the other officers. "Colonel Kimball, you already sent ahead scouts?"

"Yes, sir." Colonel Kimball darted a worried look at the dark opening to the pass. "Yes, sir. An advance party of fifty on horseback. Lieutenant Bancroft is leading them."

Michael did not wait to hear anymore. He spurred Ei-Zarka toward the pass.

He entered the dark shade between the cliffs and spurred the horse faster. The eerie feeling of being watched in the claustrophobic space returned as he dodged around boulders and piles of smaller rocks that had slid from above.

He'd ridden more than a mile, when, seeing the red coats ahead of him, he yelled for them to halt. The men at the rear of the party turned.

"Retreat!" he called. "Get out of the canyon!" He hurried past to warn the others, glancing up at the tops of the cliffs, where he heard shouts and saw men running. If they discharged the explosives now . . . Michael continued forward, calling to the soldiers to turn around.

Lieutenant Bancroft and Sergeant Carter rode at the head of the party, and the pair twisted in their saddles when they heard Michael's shout.

"A trap," he yelled. "Retreat!"

Both men's eyes rose to the cliffs, where the enemy was no longer making any attempt to remain hidden. Understanding dawned in both of their expressions, and they turned their horses.

Michael waited for both men to pass him and then followed, leaning forward in the saddle as the group of fifty galloped through the canyon.

Ahead, Lieutenant Bancroft's horse stumbled and fell forward. He sprung from the saddle, holding on to the reins and pressing his head to the horse's neck, speaking softly to calm the animal.

Michael dismounted next to him. The horse tossed its head and rolled its eyes back, refusing to set down his hoof. The leg was injured if not broken.

"Take my horse, Lieutenant."

"Of course I will not, sir."

A loud explosion sounded, and the ground shook.

Michael looked behind them and saw a cloud of dust. "It is an order. You have a fiancée. I will not allow you to die." He put Ei-Zarka's reins into Lieutenant Bancroft's hand.

Another explosion sent rocks falling down into the canyon.

"Lady Helen? She would not have me, Captain." He thrust the reins back. "She loves someone else, and it's fairly obvious who." He looked pointedly at Michael, and turned back to his horse, urging it forward. The horse moved slowly, stepping gingerly on its injured foot.

Michael stood frozen. Lady Helen had rejected the lieutenant? But—no. Could it possibly be because she loved *him*?

Another blast shook the canyon, and Lieutenant Bancroft swung into the saddle, still speaking in a low voice to the limping horse. The panic at hearing the explosions must have outweighed the pain in the animal's foot because it started to gallop unsteadily forward.

Michael followed. The urgency he had felt before was eclipsed by a frantic need to get out of this canyon. To return to Calcutta, to Lady Helen.

The dust from the explosions enveloped them as more blasts shook the canyon. Boulders crashed around them, the noise deafening. He pushed Ei-Zarka as hard as he dared. The horses screamed in fear. He heard men atop the cliffs and before him yelling.

A crash sounded right above him, and Michael was thrown from the saddle. He hit the ground hard on his shoulder and rolled, hoping to protect his head from the rocks showering down on him. A sharp pain pierced his side, and shadows clouded his vision. He fought against the darkness that spread through his mind, knowing that if he allowed it to pull him under, he'd never wake. Desperation was not enough, and the thick shadows pulled at him. *Lady Helen.* He'd never told her . . .

Michael sank into blackness.

Chapter 26

HELEN LOOKED UP WHEN HER mother entered the drawing room. She smiled, but the smile dropped from her face when she saw her mother's expression. Lady Patricia's brows were pulled together, and one hand was pressed against the skin beneath her neck. Helen's insides turned to ice. *Jim.* She jumped up and rushed to her mother. She reached for her hand and found a note crumpled in it. "Mamá, what is it?" Helen pulled her toward the sofa. "You must sit down. Has something happened to Jim?"

Lady Patricia sat next to Helen, turning her knees toward her daughter. "No. Jim is well. Oh, my dear, I am so sorry. It is Captain Rhodes."

Helen felt like she'd been struck. She tried to draw a breath, but it wouldn't come. The room closed in on her, darkening her vision as her heart raced. "No. It can't be."

"Jim sent word that the captain has been injured." Lady Patricia pulled Helen into her arms, but Helen did not allow herself to relax. Her mind was reeling. "I fear it is very serious, my dear," Lady Patricia said. "I sent instructions that the captain should be brought here instead of the hospital."

Helen could only nod. It seemed that her mind could not manage to grab on to any thought. "When?" she said.

"Within the hour." Lady Patricia pulled back and looked at Helen's face. She took a handkerchief from her pocket and offered it to Helen, then sat up straighter, still holding Helen's hand. "I have already sent for Lal Singh. He will be here soon, and then we will know what we are facing." Her mother was much better at implementing a plan than dealing with emotional matters. Her face softened again as she took the handkerchief and dabbed Helen's cheek. "But, Helen, his condition does not look good."

Helen sat on the drawing room couch, her mind blank and her pulse sounding so loudly in her ears that she thought she would go deaf. Her stomach tumbled, and she shook. What could she do? She glanced up and realized her mother must have excused herself. She paced before the sofa, straining her ears, and finally heard the sound she wished for and dreaded. Horses drawing a cart.

She hurried into the front hallway but caught only a glimpse of the captain as her mother directed the soldiers to carry him on a stretcher to an upstairs bedchamber. His head and face were bloodied, his clothes and hair covered in red dust, and he was so still. The image of his limp hand dangling as he was conveyed up the stairs brought a fresh wave of tears to her eyes. She followed them, wishing she knew what to do.

Helen was instructed by Lady Patricia to wait outside, while she, the hakim, and the ayahs tended to him. She sank into the same chair Captain Rhodes had sat in while Lal Singh had cared for her mother. She remembered shaking his shoulder and his blinking, sleepy eyes when he'd awoken, looking at her as if he was not sure whether he was awake or not. His eyes that were the perfect shade of gray. At this moment, there was nothing she wanted more than to see them again.

***

An hour passed before her mother called her into the room.

Captain Rhodes lay unmoving, his face pale with dark bruises showing on his forehead and shoulders.

"Is he going to be all right?" Helen whispered. She noticed that her mother's hair had fallen from its pins and her face looked tired.

"His arm and collarbone are broken, but Lal Singh set the bones in place." Her mother pulled down the blanket, showing bandages wrapped around his arm and chest. "His head injuries worry us more than anything. A procedure such as adjusting bones should have been extremely painful, but he did not awake at all."

"But he will . . ." Helen looked from her mother to Lal Singh. "He will awake. He is just sleeping now." Her throat was tight.

"That is our hope, my dear," Lady Patricia said.

Helen moved closer to the bed, touching Captain Rhodes's hand. It felt cold beneath her fingers. He looked as if he were simply sleeping. Surely he would wake soon.

Lady Patricia and Lal Singh spoke with the ayah, discussing the herbs the hakim wanted to administer.

Helen stood on unsteady legs and willed her mind to think. How could she help Captain Rhodes? What would he want? The memory of his story—waking in the army hospital alone and plunging into despair woke her to action.

Her mother had done precisely the right thing. She'd not allow a doctor to hack at Captain Rhodes or draw away his blood when Lal Singh knew much gentler methods to heal him. He'd not wake in a cold, lonely hospital. Helen shivered, and her stomach knotted into a tight ball, but she pushed her thoughts aside. He *would* wake.

"Mamá, you must rest. I am going to fetch Captain Rhodes's servants. And his pet."

Lady Patricia opened her mouth and closed it again; she glanced to Captain Rhodes then back to Helen. "We have plenty of servants to care for him. And, a monkey? Do you really think this will be helpful?"

"I do. Basu Ram, Naveen, and Badmash are his family. He will want them near when he wakes."

Once she was certain her mother would rest, Helen took the carriage, and for the third time in a few weeks she approached Captain Rhodes's bungalow. But today she neared knowing she would not find him there; realizing that she must inform his friends of his condition made her feel heavy as she walked up the steps to the door.

Basu Ram answered her knock. He did not speak, but when he saw her face, he closed his eyes and lowered his head. "Rhodes-Sahib?" he said in a soft voice. "He is dead?"

"No!" Helen said. "Do not say such a thing. He is at my house and hurt very badly." Her eyes filled with tears. "He will be all right." A sob clogged her throat, and she clapped her hand over her mouth, surprised by the rush of emotion. Her shoulders shook as she wept, but she did not care if Basu Ram saw it. He'd seen her weep before, and he knew why. A moment later, she swallowed hard, shaking her head and calming herself enough to speak. "Please come with me. He needs you. You and Naveen and Badmash."

"We will come."

The servants sat uneasily on the plush carriage bench, and Helen sat across from them, holding Badmash on her lap. The animal seemed to sense that something was wrong and held on to Helen's hand with both of his.

"I do not know if he will wake," Helen whispered without looking at the men.

Basu Ram spoke in a soft voice to Naveen, who answered back.

She turned toward them then lowered her eyes, nervous to say what was in her heart. "Will you pray for him?" She hoped her request would not be inappropriate. She was not certain how Hindi and Mohammedan prayers worked, but she knew these two men prayed faithfully.

"Yes, Miss-Sahib," Basu Ram said.

She looked at him, and her lip began to tremble again. She squeezed her eyes shut, took a shaky breath, then let it out slowly. "Thank you. I did not know . . ."

"Miss-Sahib, whether He is called Allah or Brahma or God, we all pray to the same Supreme Being." He raised his eyes upward. "You must trust Him."

Helen could not find the words to express how grateful she was. Her throat tightened, and she could only nod.

The carriage stopped at the front of the mansion, and Helen carried Badmash into the house. She led the servants to the upstairs bedchamber, finding Captain Rhodes exactly as she had left him. The monkey screeched and leapt from her arms, climbing up onto the bed before anyone could stop him. He pushed the captain's head from side to side, making chattering noises. Naveen lifted him up, but he scrambled back down, crawling into the space next to the Captain's arm and shooting a look of defiance at anyone who would move him.

"Leave him." Helen held her hands up in front of her. "Captain Rhodes would want him near."

The servants nodded their agreement, and Badmash maintained his post.

Lal Singh spoke at length with Basu Ram and Naveen, and feeling helpless, Helen collapsed into a chair next to the bed.

In the following hours, she joined with her mother and the native men and women as they took turns wiping Captain Rhodes's face with a damp cloth and spooning tea into his mouth.

The realization came with a jolt. *This* was the beauty of India. *This* is what Captain Rhodes was talking about. In this very room were men and women, old and young, of different religions and cultures, all focused on one task. All concerned for one man. Helen was surprised to feel an overwhelming surge of love for the people of this country. For a servant who risked her life to save enemy soldiers, a queen who defied her evil husband, men who prayed for their master, a doctor who administered gentle remedies. For an entire country that made their world beautiful and celebrated life amidst the horrors around them. The feeling warmed her, and she wished more than anything she could tell him about her epiphany.

"Come, Helen. You must sleep now."

Helen looked up when her mother spoke, realizing she had dozed off. The evening had grown dark. The ayahs were lighting candles, and the men had left for the night. Captain Rhodes had not moved.

"I do not want to leave him, Mamá."

"I know, my dear." Lady Patricia tugged on Helen's arm, lifting her to her feet. "He will be watched over through the night." She turned to Sita and her ayah. "If he wakes, send for Helen immediately."

The women bowed their heads, and Sita took Helen to her bedchamber, assisted her into her nightclothes, and left her to return to Captain Rhodes.

Helen lay on her bed, wishing again that there was something she could do. She thought of what Basu Ram had said in the carriage. *You must trust Him.*

The words brought peace to her, and Helen slept.

***

The next morning, Helen did not wait for her ayah but hurried into her clothes and rushed down the hall. She knocked softly and pushed the door open, but her heart sank when she saw that the captain had not moved. Sita sat on a chair in the corner and bowed when Helen stepped inside, but she shook her head at Helen's questioning look. He had not woken.

"I will fetch your breakfast, Miss-Sahib." Sita spoke in a soft voice as she left the room.

Helen walked closer to the bed. Badmash was curled in a ball next to Captain Rhodes's bandaged arm. She smoothed the blankets over the captain, careful not to disturb the monkey, then perched on the very edge of the bed.

The bruises on his forehead were a darker purple this morning. Helen did not know whether that was a good sign or not.

"Captain, please wake up." She hadn't meant to say the words aloud and startled as they rang through the quiet room. "Please. I have so much to tell you. You must wake." She scooted closer, feeling a need to speak to him in hopes that somewhere deep inside he could hear. "I know what you meant about India. I know now why you love it here. Because you cannot truly love something if you only see the beauty on the surface: you must see all of it, even its faults."

Badmash opened his eyes, watching her, but did not protest.

Helen ran her hand over the fold in the blanket. "I found my song, Captain. It is strange, and the melody is inconsistent. There are sounds of India and of fear; parts of it do not seem to fit at all, but there are also strong chords for when I felt brave and light notes of when I was happy." Now that she was warmed up, the words poured out. "Maybe nobody else will like it, but I do not care because it is my very own. And it comes from my soul."

She lifted his hand, taking it in both of hers. "And something else has happened. I have fallen in love. I love *you*, Captain Rhodes, and I am sorry I did not tell you earlier. I did not realize it myself until I was alone and frightened in the jungle. The only person I wanted to see was you. I knew you would find me. I—" She pressed his hand to her cheek as her throat clogged with tears. "Please wake up, Captain. I cannot bear to lose you."

Beneath her fingers she felt movement. Captain Rhodes's hand tightened on hers.

Helen gasped, praying that she had not imagined it. "Captain?"

His eyelids fluttered, and he squinted at her, letting out a low moan.

She leaned closer. "Captain, it is me, Helen. You are at my house." She knew the words sounded foolish as soon as they left her mouth, but it seemed important for him to know he was not in a hospital.

He released her hand and brushed his fingers over her cheek. "I'd have thought this was heaven if I didn't hurt so blasted much." His voice was raspy.

"You need water. I will find Lal Singh or my mother. They will know what to give you for pain." Helen moved to rise.

"No. Do not leave."

She settled back, scooting closer to his side and grasping his hand again. "I won't leave." His eyes grew clearer as he blinked and gazed at her. "Were you listening to me all this time, Captain?"

"I thought you were talking to me. Was I mistaken?" The corner of his lips quirked. "Or, I may have been in the middle of the best dream of my life. Perhaps I shouldn't have woken."

He shifted and grunted, the corners of his eyes crinkling and his mouth pulling in a grimace.

"You mustn't move." Helen glanced toward his bindings. "And do not even joke about it. If you did not wake . . ."

"If I did not wake, what would have happened, *larla*?" His voice was soft, nearly a whisper.

"My heart would have broken."

He moved his hand to cup her cheek. "In that case, I am glad I did. Your heart is far too dear to me."

Helen leaned against his hand, closing her eyes. "Captain?"

"Michael."

She opened her eyes and smiled. "Michael. Did you hear what I said?"

"Yes, although I am afraid I may have imagined it."

"You did not imagine it. I love you, Cap—Michael."

He slipped his fingers beneath her ear, cupping the back of her neck, and pulled her toward him. "My lady . . ."

"Helen."

His lips quirked again, and his eyes softened into a look that made her stomach turn over in a slow roll. "Helen. I have loved you since the very instant I first saw you."

She rested her arms carefully against his chest and leaned forward until her face was mere inches from his. "I am sorry it took me so long to realize it." She felt his heartbeat beneath her hands, matching the rhythm of her own. The rolling in her stomach was replaced by a fluttering as he pulled her to him.

Michael pressed his lips against hers, and colors exploded behind Helen's eyelids. Every worry, sorrow, or fear was replaced by reassurance and comfort. With him, she did not have to worry about saying the wrong thing or pretend to be any other than she was. He knew her heart, the good and bad she kept hidden from everyone else, and he loved her for it.

Helen melted into the kiss, sliding her hands to his scratchy cheeks, surprised by how soft his lips were and the way they moved against hers; she thought she could continue kissing Michael forever.

At the sound of a man clearing his throat, Helen jumped up. Heat shot up her neck as she looked to the doorway and saw Jim and her mother. "Oh, yes. I . . . Captain Rhodes is awake, and I was just . . ." Helen looked around the room, not able to meet their eyes as she tried to think of something to explain why she was kissing the injured officer in their guest chamber.

"It's about blasted time," Jim said.

"Sir?" Helen's gaze snapped toward him, and she stared. What was he talking about?

He strode into the room. "Glad to see you are awake, Captain. And that the two of you have come to your senses and realized what the rest of us have known for weeks."

Helen glanced at Michael and saw a grin spread across his face.

"You do know I'll insist upon you marrying my daughter now." Jim scowled.

"Of course, sir. I would not have it any other way."

Helen looked at the doorway and saw that her mother was smiling and dabbing at tears.

Jim clasped his hands behind his back and rocked on his heels, maintaining his angry glower, but Helen saw a twinkle in his eye. "And I am denying any transfers for you, Captain. Although I do think your bravery in rescuing half a company deserves commendation. I plan to recommend you for an advancement." He tapped his finger on his chin. "Major Rhodes. It has somewhat of a ring to it, wouldn't you say?"

Michael moved as if he would rise but winced and relaxed back into the pillow. "Thank you, sir."

Helen embraced her mother and was surprised when Jim wrapped his arms around them both. "You know, I would not agree to part with you for anyone less." He pulled back and kissed her forehead then cleared his throat. "Very well, I am going to have my breakfast." Jim turned toward the door, and Helen could have sworn he brushed away a tear. He motioned between the two of them. "As you were. Carry on, then."

"Yes, sir." Michael said.

When the door closed behind her parents, Helen and Michael found obeying the general's order to be no trouble at all.

Epilogue

HELEN TIED THE RIBBONS OF her wide-brimmed hat, giving one last glance around her bedchamber to ensure she'd not forgotten anything. Michael had left her for an hour to change out of her wedding gown and see to any final packing. He would come to fetch her any moment to begin the journey to Simla.

Michael, *her husband*. Helen's grin had not left her face all day, and it was beginning to hurt her cheeks. The wedding had been beautiful. Lady Patricia had fretted, worried that Helen might miss her sisters, but truly she'd not cared one bit. Only one person had mattered, and he'd looked resplendent in his red regimental jacket and polished boots. Helen had hardly heard a word of the ceremony. Her eyes had continually wandered to Michael's face, and each time, he'd been watching her with soft eyes and a smile nearly as large as her own.

Lord Minto and the new Governor-General, the Marquess of Hastings, both congratulated them as they'd walked down the aisle of Thomas Middleton's church, holding hands as man and wife and thanking the other members of the Raj for coming to the ceremony.

When she arrived home, Helen had slipped the Rani's gold bangle onto her wrist and wrapped a red silk shawl around her shoulders to greet guests at the wedding breakfast. Sita had presented the shawl to her as a wedding gift, insisting that a bride should wear red. White is the color of mourning in India, she'd said. The soft fabric and bright color made Helen feel beautiful and festive—as a bride should, she thought.

Michael had run his fingers over the delicate gold embroidery on her shoulder. "You look like a princess," he'd whispered.

A soft knock sounded at the door, and Helen turned as her mother entered. "Your husband has sent your trunks ahead. He is waiting for you in the entry hall."

"Thank you." Helen embraced her mother, feeling her expanding stomach between them. "Do hurry to Simla, Mamá."

"We shall be only a few days behind you." Lady Patricia straightened the red shawl. "You were the loveliest bride I could imagine, Helen. Jim and I could not be happier."

She embraced her mother then hurried down the stairs.

Michael stood inside the doorway, and Helen's heart tripped when she saw him. Would it always do so?

She skipped down the last few steps and flew into his arms.

He sucked in a breath between his teeth, and she stepped back, studying his face to make sure she had not squeezed his tender ribs too tightly.

"I shall hope for such a greeting every time I see my beautiful wife." He lifted her chin and pressed a kiss to her lips.

Helen wrapped her arms around his neck and sighed. "I shall hope for this greeting every time I see my handsome husband," she said and kissed him again.

"I'd hoped once you were married I wouldn't have to keep walking in on such displays." Jim rolled his eyes with an expression of long-suffering as he came down the steps with Lady Patricia. "Don't the two of you have a bridal tour to be getting on with?"

Helen and Michael exchanged a smile, and she embraced her parents. "Travel safely, Mamá. Jim. I shall see you in a few weeks in Simla."

The butler opened the door, and Helen took her husband's arm as they stepped through.

She stopped with her foot in midair as she saw what awaited her. A massive elephant stood at the bottom of the steps. Basu Ram held on to a rope around its neck. The animal's gray skin was painted in colorful flowers and swirls. It wore silks, and a golden headpiece rested between its eyes. On its back was a canopied box with a seat that looked like a small sofa.

Helen pressed her fingers to her mouth. "Oh." She felt like a little girl and wanted to jump up and down giggling, but somehow she managed to remember that she was a major's wife.

Basu Ram made a noise, tapping the elephant's leg with a stick, and it knelt down before them.

"Shall we, larla?" Michael led her toward the animal, and the men helped her climb up into the *howdah*, then her husband joined her.

She clung to his arm as the conveyance leaned from side to side while the animal stood. They were so high off the ground.

A chattering sounded, and Badmash climbed over the seat, settling between them.

Helen laughed as Michael scooped him up and deposited him on the floor. "I worried we might have company."

She waved to her parents as the elephant took them away from her home and toward her new life with the man she loved. The man who knew a painted elephant on her wedding day would mean more to her than any gift he could give.

"Thank you, Michael," she whispered, settling back against him. "I cannot imagine anything more perfect."

Happiness welled up inside her, and music filled her soul. She looked ahead at the Grand Trunk Road that would take them to the Ganges River and realized it did not matter whether she was in London or Calcutta or Simla or somewhere in between. With Michael, wherever she was would be home.

About the Author

JENNIFER MOORE IS A PASSIONATE reader and writer of all things romance due to the need to balance the rest of her world, which includes a perpetually traveling husband and four active sons, who create heaps of laundry that are anything but romantic. Jennifer has a BA in linguistics from the University of Utah and is a Guitar Hero champion. She lives in northern Utah with her family. You can learn more about her at authorjmoore.com.